D1191065

St. George
and the
Godfather

Also by Norman Mailer

Advertisements for Myself
Ancient Evenings
Armies of the Night
Barbary Shore
Cannibals and Christians
The Deer Park
The Executioner's Song
Existential Errands
The Flight
Marilyn
The Naked and the Dead
Norman Mailer: Pieces
Norman Mailer: Pontifications
Of a Fire on the Moon
Of a Small and Modest Malignancy Wicked
and Bristling with Dots
Of Women and Their Elegance
Pieces and Pontifications
Some Honorable Men: Political Conventions,
1960–1972
A Transit to Narcissus
Why Are We in Vietnam?

St. George
and the
Godfather

---

by Norman Mailer

ARBOR HOUSE
LIBRARY OF
CONTEMPORARY
AMERICANA

ARBOR HOUSE   NEW YORK

To dad
(alias Isaac Barnett Mailer)

Introduction

Almost everybody who has written about American politics since World War II has tried to describe Richard Nixon, that sinister jack-in-the-box who popped out of our television set, semaphoring with his broken arms: "Surprise! Guess what Daddy brought home from the office? A secret bombing of Cambodia!"

Mailer has had to describe Nixon hundreds of times. You'd think he'd weary of it. Instead, he just gets better. Here are two passages from *St. George and the Godfather*, his account of the 1972 Democratic and Republican conventions. First, Nixon as mind/body dualism:

> It is as if he is wearing two breastplates and yet you can still get peeks of his midriff. He walks like a puppet more curious than most human beings, for all the strings are pulled by a hand within his own head, an inquiring hand which never pulls the same string in quite the same way as the previous time—it is always trying something out—and so the movements of his arms and legs while superficially conventional, even highly restrained, are all impregnated with attempts, still timid—after all these years!—to express attitudes and emotions with his body. But he handles his body like an adolescent suffering excruciations of self-consciousness with every move. After all these years! It is as if his incredible facility of brain which manages to capture every contradiction in every question put to him, and never fails to reply with the maximum of advantage for himself in a language which is resolutely without experiment, is, facile and incredible brain, off on a journey of inquiry into the stubborn refusal of the body to obey it.

And now Nixon as synthetic personality:

> . . . a bland drone of oscillating ideological dots. In its impact as it comes over the tube, his personality is close to the nature of the tube itself, closer than anyone else in political life. (Which may be a way of

saying that while Nixon is speaking, if the set should regress down from color TV with a clear image to nothing but the bare and vibrating gray screen offering no more than the drone and the glare of the dots, shock and shift of mood would be felt less with Nixon on that screen than with anyone else!) . . . a politician of the center does well to look for a personality which will cohere to the spirit of centrality of the television tube and so be part of the cure which is found in the reducing drone of the TV atmosphere.

"Part of the cure" for what? Why, for a "dread" that is, of course, "existential." *St. George and the Godfather* wouldn't be a book by Norman Mailer if it didn't mention existential dread. Mailer is in favor of dread; it encourages us to name God. Television, he says elsewhere, is aspirin for dread. The politicians of the tube would drone away, flatten out, dissipate all magic, black and white, all discrepancy, all heroism. Nixon, managing his own coronation in Miami, "tickling every straw in the broom," is "the Eisenstein of the mediocre and the inert," the perfect putty-faced flower of what Mailer, contemptuously, calls "the Wad." The Wad is most of us, the dread-denying lumpenpublic.

The Wad is not entirely Republican. Another of its drones was George Wallace of Alabama, at least until he was shot; knowledge of death, Mailer suggests, improved the governor's dreadfulness. And Mailer—or "Aquarius"—has his doubts about "the liberal mind" that opposes itself to the Wad. He finds George McGovern decent if unexciting; he is reminded of an astronaut, as well as Gary Cooper. He quotes the senator from South Dakota approvingly: "Money made by money should be taxed at the same rate as money made by men." And, of course, Aquarius always votes Democratic except when he is running for mayor of New York on his own ticket. Nevertheless:

The best of the liberal mind and the worst were [McGovern's] troops, all the warriors for a reasonable ecology and a world where privilege could no longer paralyze were in his army as well as all the social whips for a new state of collective mind opposed to any idea of mystery in any organism social or human—a spirit of science concentrated into pills to push behavior.

This is the Mailer who has never reconciled himself to the Enlightenment, the march of reasonable men toward self-perfection, humorless progressivism. He belongs in the company of Vico and the German romantics, even, perhaps, with de

Maistre, that counterrevolutionary, "against the current" of social engineering. Like Henry Adams, with whom he is so often compared as a political reporter on American warts, he prefers the mystery of the Virgin to the machinations of the Dynamo. This may explain his insistence here—and the silliest pages in *St. George and the Godfather* are devoted to Mailer's charmless incomprehension of feminism—on what he calls "the apocalyptic fuck."

Besides, there are some Republic faces distinctly un-Wadlike:

> Nor did he think that order was to be debased before the virtues of the slovenly. He had had enough of the slovenly forever, including its swamp-like effusions in his own mind. And indeed he had regard for many a Republican face. There were distinguished faces on that floor. He saw faces that were models of discipline, or of elegance, or orderly style, faces which spoke of fire and pride and the idea that character was the only ceramic to hold human fire and pride; there were dry Republican faces which proved models of crystallized wit, and kindly urbane gentlemen whose minds were rich with concept when they thought of the commonweal. One could even say that if there was a drop of common but immortal belief in every Republican, it might be over that drop of American blood. It was where they would have their sacrament.

He is reaching here for something important to him, a religious sense of transcendence from the Wad:

> In America the country was the religion. And all the religions of the land were fed from that first religion which was the country itself, and if the other religions were now full of mutation and staggering across deserts of faith, it was because the country had been false and ill and corrupt for years, corrupt not in the age-old human proportions of failure and evil, but corrupt to the point of terminal disease, like a great religion foundering.

I would submit that civil decency has as much to fear from religion as it does from such rationalized systems of social order as the Gulag and the death camp, but I'm not here to talk about Mailer's well-known Manicheanism. A sense of evil is good for a reporter. He is, anyway, being metaphorical. When it comes to the metaphorical and the analogical, he is no Virgin, all Dynamo. Cynthia Buchanan has said he combs metaphors over the bald spots in his theory. She is right (although one prefers the metaphors to the theory): swamps, yeast, pills, gyroscopes, cancer, prize fights.

No wonder he wishes Eugene McCarthy, rather than George

McGovern, had been the Democratic nominee in 1972, and this is before the Eagleton fiasco. Mailer says to McCarthy, "I like McGovern, but I just wish he spoke with a little metaphor from time to time." McCarthy replies: "Methodists are not much on metaphor." And "left conservatives" like Mailer and McCarthy are rather too easily disposed to disdain. If I remember correctly, the Jacobins were rich in metaphor, their best one being the guillotine. Let's turn the Wad into chewing gum.

But if we allow Yeats his faeries and Druids and rough-beast slouchings, and Ezra Pound his funny money, and Saul Bellow his anthroposophy, why not Mailer his Wad? It is a source of energy; it dazzles him into sentience. Awake, he notices smells, looks, body-language, failures of character.

On Hubert Humphrey at the convention: "He had the old wounded bitter-mule look of a nag whose teeth have been counted too often." (However: "Later in the afternoon a feeling of tenderness for Humphrey came back into the heart. It was analagous to the tenderness one used to feel for Boris Karloff in *Frankenstein*. How the dead in Vietnam still groan in the American bed.") Boston's Mayor Kevin White "was the size of a mayor," not a president. John V. Lindsay, having just switched parties, violates "the oldest law of politics. You don't join a fraternity and offer to become its president in the same week." And Wilbur Mills, before anybody could imagine a Tidal Basin:

His head was pear-shaped. It was as if there had been a yeast set loose in his flesh, and most of it had settled around his jaw rather than his brow. So even his ears were big on the bottom and pointed on the top. The lower part of his face was full, even bulbous, a beanbag—his features got skinnier as your eyes went up, his forehead was narrow and his straight hair plastered on top of his flat little head must have been half a millimeter thick. If he had even run for President, *Mad* magazine would have flown themselves to the moon on the whoomph of such unexpected gas.

In fact, in most of Mailer's books fiction or journalism, we know exactly what his people look like and smell like and how they move around. Is this true of the people in other contemporary fictions about politics and dread? The visceral is where he lives, even as he struggles to find a place to station his sweaty point of view. If, after too much Aquarius in *Armies of the Night*, in *Miami and the Siege of Chicago*, in *Of a Fire on the Moon*, you would rather Mailer talked for himself in *St. George and the Godfather*, maybe he would rather have, too. He would go on to abolish the writer entirely in *The Executioner's Song*, and then end up in the head of an Egyptian pharaoh in *Ancient Evenings*, as if dread needed a whole new set of metaphors: no more movies, no more science, just your basic sex and death.

Still: the visceral and the magical. As a novelist and political reporter, he follows what Wilfrid Sheed calls the "Chestertonian principle of exploring the psychosis proper to the group, the identifying madness, and letting it enter him, like an exorcist opening himself to the devil." In Mailer's schema, angels and devils are all about us. Where, on this soulscape of enamelized, transistorized artifacts, might they be lurking? He sniffs them out, choosing between butchered farm fowl and the hunted stag, bicycles and bathyspheres, aluminum and leather. He assigns value and blame, names unknowables, ascribes and signifies: Under that bush, the terrible angel of Rilke; inside that Tupperware, a demon that giggles. He loots nomenclatures for a blessing and the curse. He invokes the "loyalties of the dead."

And it therefore doesn't matter whether, in 1972, he underestimated Ronald Reagan, who would, according to Aquarius, "never beef up to a political heavyweight," and that Henry Kissinger thumbed him like a harp; and that to this day he thinks that he can pat a liberated woman on her pretty little head. This book is written in blood on brain bandages: *This* is the way these conventions in Maimi felt to a wonderful American writer whose personal dread is also his magnifying lens: stunt man, Quixote, paranoid, exorcist, gyroscope, an alchemist who tortures himself instead of the metals. He mainlines on contradictions. He will not congratulate the winner, knowing what all of us are about to lose. Contemplating Nixon, he observes: "Even in politics, some hands are not yours to shake."

Finally, the dead in Southeast Asia groan in his bed too, and they are not at all what he meant by an apocalyptic fuck. We bombed for practice, out of compulsion. It had become

> an activity as rational as the act of a man who walks across his own home town to defecate each night on the lawn of a stranger—it is the same stranger each night—such a man would not last long even if he had the most powerful body in town. "Stop," he would scream as they dragged him away, "I need to shit on that lawn. It's the only way to keep my body in shape, you fools. A bat has bitten me!"

This is brilliant metaphor; it was also bitter prophecy.
—John Leonard

Contents

PART ONE

Portraits and Powers

1

PART TWO

Politicians and Princes

91

PART THREE

Program

123

PART ONE

Portraits and Powers

1

Greetings to Charles Dickens across vales of Karma: it was the best and worst of conventions. The hope that democracy would yet be virtuous lived in the broth and marrow of the mood. Nonetheless, our convention was so dismaying in its absence of theater that the sourest law of the police reporter was also confirmed—deaths are more interesting than births. The Democratic gathering of 1968 had been martial, dramatic, bloody, vainglorious, riotous, noble, tragic, corrupt, vicious, vomitous, appalling, cataclysmic; the old Democratic party foundered with a stroke, even if the patient got up from bed, staggered around America through September and October and only gave out on Election Day to that somber undertaker's assistant Richard Milhous Nixon. In contrast, history might yet decide that the Convention of '72, no matter how tedious, boring, protean, and near to formless, came out a rare and blithe watershed in the civil affairs of men. (Plus the expanding affairs of Ms.) So Norman Mailer, who looked to rule himself by Voltaire's catch-all precept, "Once a philosopher, twice a pervert" and preferred therefore never to repeat a technique, was still obliged to call himself Aquarius again for he had not been in Miami two days before he knew he would not write objectively about the Convention of '72. There were too many questions, and (given the probability of a McGovern steamroller) not enough drama to supply answers. He would be obliged to drift through events, and use the reactions of his brain for evidence. A slow brain, a muddy river, and therefore no name better suited to himself again than the modest and half-invisible Aquarius. Enough of Ego Liberation.

2

There were ghosts on the convention. And the sense of having grown old enough to be passing through life a second time. Flying to San Francisco in 1964 to write up the convention which nominated Barry Goldwater, he had met an Australian journalist who asked why Americans made the interior of their airplanes look like nurseries, and he had answered, in effect, that dread was loose in American life. Was it still loose, that sense of oncoming catastrophe going to fall on the nation like the first bolt from God? Such dread had taken many a turn—from fear of Communism to fear of walking the streets at night, which was a greater fear if one thought about it (since the streets were nearer). It was a fear when all was said which suggested that the nation, in whatever collection of its consciousness, was like a person who wakes up often in the middle of the night with the intolerable conviction that something is loose in the system, and the body is on a long slide from which there will be no remission unless a solution is found: the body does not even know where the disease is at. Nor will the doctors, is what the body also knows in the dark.

Now, eight years later, on a plane to Miami, comfortable middle-aged Aquarius finds himself in another conversation about the convention to come, and the old dread is still loose. Only now it is buzzing about McGovern and the thousand dollars a year George would give to every living American. The man in the Whisperjet seat next to him is a distinguished Senior Citizen, one vigorous and far from elderly Jewish gentleman named Bernhard whose son it soon develops is Berl Bernhard, main gear of the campaign staff for Ed Muskie. The father, a retired banker, has the sun-tanned freckled hands and face and white hair of a man who not only has retired to live in the sun, but still plays respectable sports in the sun, golf one would guess, and some tennis. Mr. Bernhard talks with all the force and authority, the barking opinionated good manners, of a Jewish banker who has spent his life living with other men of boldness and restraint. He is cockaloo with wrath about McGovern. Bernhard hates Nixon, but he is still not going to vote in November just so deep is his rage at McGovern.

They get into a discussion of McGovern's economics, and it is quickly evident that the numbers cannot be calculated—McGovern's friends and enemies have been putting the problem into computers whose answers sink deeper into the bottoms of the bottomless. It is possible that the unsounded mysteries of economics will burble up and alter everything if you give a thousand dollars a year to every living American. But there is not even a chance to talk to Bernhard about the feasibility of paying for the idea through taxes. Bernhard is an intelligent tough-minded man and must certainly be cynical enough by now to know that even if McGovern were wholly sincere in his scheme, he would never find a Congress to match him, but it is as if something else is loose, something formerly nailed down in the banker's scheme of things, for Bernhard's wrath shifts next to McGovern on questions concerning Israel. Much discussion of many bills and how McGovern voted quickly ensues.

Aquarius let the argument go. He was not certain himself how he felt about McGovern, and by now he had an absolute disbelief in political argument. Just as there used to be mating customs in Southern colleges which required boys and girls to talk about fraternities and sororities for a couple of hours in the back seat of cars before they explored their first kiss, so he had been bemused many a time by the peculiar protocol of political argument over issues and records. It was as if each side in such a debate was trying to lay down bricks fast enough to build a wall which would be higher than the other's even if the wall when built would obscure the view. Politics was a game in which points were scored and one tried to obscure the depth and gravity of the process. Yet the ways in which people governed one another were ultimately as intimate as carnal relations. One had only to think of the death penalty to recognize this. One had only to think of a solution to the death penalty he had once offered—which is that all States not ready to banish capital punishment ought then to provide a professional executioner who would be obliged to kill each condemned man with his bare hands by open gladitorial combat in a stadium (like the Astrodome?) before the citizenry. This idea naturally met with much success.

No, at the least, it seemed to him that the concern people took with their vote was certainly much out of proportion to its effect—even the average hour or two-hour wait on line Election Day was a sizable demand upon the collective selfishness of the citizenry—or was, unless people voted out of deeper motives than they recognized. Was it altogether impossible that the average man might be engaged in some inarticulate transaction with eternity? —a cosmic whale of a thought for a man like Mailer who usually did not get around to vote. Of course, Mailer was nowhere near so good at answers as he was at posing questions, but he had the instinct to know when his question was good. This question was swell. It was, on consideration, incredible how people could keep studying the minutiae of a convention on a television set for hours when the greatest part of those details had to be incomprehensible to them, or at best next to void of connotation, low in entertainment value, and usually boring—the TV men were first to yawn. What mysterious human ceremony was in process?

Nor did the sense of having passed through similar events diminish once he was in Miami Beach. Collins Avenue, however, hot as ever in July, seemed tolerable, as if he had grown forgiving to heat. Having written with more detestation about Miami Beach than any author he knew—"the sensation of breathing, then living [in that city] was not unlike being obliged to make love to a 300-pound woman who has decided to get on top," it was as if he had written out his hatred, and the good citizens of this incredible city were cordial to him. They did not seem to mind what he wrote. It was, he concluded, the only place left on earth which still looked on bad publicity as

good publicity. But he was irritated. He could not grasp
why his own mood was so different until he recognized
that Miami Beach was the true surrealist froth on the wave
of Populism, not a 300-pound woman, but a deep red-
orange female Senior Citizen, sexy as hell, her age
balanced by her baubles, her infirmities as goofy and
vulgar and overloaded as Wolfe's and Pumpernik's, or her
Moulin Rouge Motel with a sign outside: Have Your Next
Affair Here! and so if the Republican convention of '68
had been as much of a mismatch as bluegrass sown in
the swamps of the Everglades, this convention was perfect.
Miami Beach was as crazy as any group of Democrats,
and the pride of the city was to show that life would still
be good even if you were getting along on one leg and
one breast—there was sunlight, makeup, plastic and pros-
thetics, mutual interest at all ages, and tolerance for every
kookery of the middle class. If the older residents had
been fearful at first of the arrival of the Yippies, their
meeting would yet provide a ceremony—the "marriage
of the generations"—and indeed the first news Aquarius
picked up on his arrival was the description of a march
the week before from Convention Hall to a golf course
named Par Three. It was the first street action for the
Yippies, but what a long throw from the darkening
shadows of every police-congested block in Chicago. Here
the Yippies came out with flags painted on their faces,
and a blond girl dressed as Martha Mitchell was led by
Jerry Rubin up to the Press where it was announced that
the Republicans should free her by convention time. A very
fat girl was gotten up as Rocky Pomerance, the police
chief, and another girl dressed as a Vietnamese. Every
few blocks she would fall to the street and scream and
the surrounding Yippies would make guerrilla theater of
kicking and beating her. In front of Convention Center
the march was joined by Mayor Hall who led the Yippies
until they began a chant to end the fornicating war. So the
Mayor turned around and put a finger to his lips. When
they chanted louder, he left. It was cool. The Yippies
were welcome to be obscene, but not even a Miami Beach
politician could afford to hang around. Still, there was no
sweat on either side, and people watching applauded
from time to time. Some even joined the march for a block

or two. There was probably more spectators' applause than one would get marching through any other city in America. That night the Yippies gathered at the tube and glued themselves in to watch TV news they had made.

What a town! A police chief who permits himself to be parodied by a fat girl, and a mayor who can put a set of permissions together.

3

But good Mayor Hall—if the reader can take the shock of this truly American shift-transmission—is out at Miami International Airport, Blast Site One, to give his city's greetings when George C. Wallace comes in. Tall, with silver-white hair, and the look of a man who has lived agreeably in the tropics, he has the quiet almost too agreeable confidence of a movie star of medium rank who has begun to enjoy his white hair and his retirement. Actually, Hall is a millionaire, and by repute could play lead hound of the Baskervilles if the spoor was publicity.

He was obviously too intelligent to expect any himself this day—there was something self-effacing in the way he bent over to whisper a few words to Wallace, but indeed who in America would dispute the throne of publicity when Wallace was near? The Governor's arrival in Miami was a form of Instant Déjà Vu, spooky to the recurring sense of a dream, for the Press had watched him on TV just two hours before when he landed at Montgomery long enough to give a speech and shake the hand of Acting Governor Jere Beasley in order to reassume (by the laws of Alabama) his power to be governor. Aquarius and others of the Press had studied the TV set like primitives looking at reflections in a pond of water—what omens for the tribe were here to be gathered? Indeed attention was high enough to read significance into every rollover of the color from red to green to gray, or from any flipover of image or burst of dots. Yet, it was just TV, and all the television colors were keyed to the baby-blue sky above the Governor's gray-silver suit, with peaches and pinks and creamy tans in the background: perhaps a new genre was being created—Soap Opera Sublime—and they played "The

Star-Spangled Banner" after his plane came in, huge Air
Force Military Airlift of a plane Richard Nixon had been
careful to turn over to Wallace for the Governor's private
use, complete with a ramp which flew out in sections like
an animated giant pterodactyl's tongue in a King Kong
film, and lo! the strains of the music came up as they
wheeled the Governor down the ramp with an awe which
pushed through every electronic valve in every TV trans-
mitter and actually socked into the room where they were
watching—it was obvious that the thin body in the wheelchair being rolled down one ramp and up another to give
his speech had become an object of veneration (in Montgomery, Alabama, at least) which was equal to any relic
of any major saint's bone that could be certified as a
thousand years dead. And the band played "The Star-
Spangled Banner" as slowly as a hymn to the martyred
spirits beyond. When the speech was over, and the Governor in his new voice, the measured dignified voice (almost beautiful in its modulation away from the old
gut-bucket banjo-string twang of the mean folksy natural
voice), had come to his conclusion by saying, "And my
campaign should make it clear that the average citizens
are now the kings and queens of American politics. And
we are going to be responsible for your desires," the
process was reversed, and the wheelchair drawn back up
the ramp, the long tongue pulled into the plane again.
With the banshee scream of the jet's motors shrilling over
the set, there was discussion in the watching Miami Press
over how *he* had looked, as if the set would *reveal*, when
they all knew that a little too much green and the Governor would look like fare for the scavenger fish, a little
too much red and he would impress as ready to run
again, yet they would all insist on interpreting every clue,
Aquarius as much as the others, perhaps as part of an
obsession with some force or desire he could not name,
not yet, but it was the political mystery to him, and as
close to disclosure as the filling of a tooth which promises
it will soon fall out. He felt that with this convention he
might finally discover something about politics which had
eluded him until now, some mystery, yes, would be at
last discovered, and had the opportunity to brood upon
this near to pleasant sensation after the rush from the TV
set to the Miami Airport, Blast Site One, where the Press,

after being inched up and testified to, vouched on and sworn for by man or credential and sometimes both, were squeezed through a Secret Service gate one by one and disgorged into the Democratic National Convention area, a small enclosure of white gravel on one of the fringes of the airport where, surrounded by high wire fence, they could stand to the side of a space extending thirty feet across from one camera stand with a red-and-white-striped peppermint awning over to an identical stand with a podium for the speaker. Banks and batteries of light glared in the bright sunlight high up on light trees made of pipe and painted silver, and in the near distance like a military unit on the march which had stopped to bivouac for an afternoon there were ambulances and white trailers parked about, olive-drab trucks and orange TV trucks, wires, cables, tools, even the Miami populace, a couple hundred of them, stuck out on one side of the wire fence to yell hello to Wallace.

It had been a rush to get there and then a long wait. While they waited, reporters entertained themselves by talking to Endicott Peabody, campaigning for an open convention to pick the Vice-President, ideally himself, Chub Peabody, last Harvard man to make All-American, and he looked and talked like George Plimpton might have if George had made the Detroit Lions and stayed in pro ball long enough to get his face broken a couple of times through the face mask. Peabody kept telling the reporters that he was pleased Senator Mike Gravel had also announced for Vice-President. "We're happy to have some opposition," said Peabody. "Makes it more reportable."

There was a bead of ketchup on the corner of his mouth. He was finishing a hamburger one of his daughters had handed him, and the wrapper showed where it had been bought.

"Governor Peabody, a tough political question—what do you think of MacDonald's hamburgers?" (Were 11,-000,000 votes shivering on his reply?)

"Well," said Peabody, listening to the mills of his digestion, "they keep you going."

To tell the truth and lose nothing—there was a little applause from the Press.

Now Wilbur Mills's plane came in, a private jet with seats perhaps for a dozen corporation executives, and the

Press tried to ask him questions, but helicopters overhead were patrolling the asphalt fields around Blast Site One and the noise of their motors scourged the mood. The Press could not hear Mills and the candidate could not hear the Press—Wilbur Mills, Chairman of what was invariably called the *prestigious* Ways and Means Committee. He was probably the most powerful representative in Congress, but it was unsettling to wonder which defect in his judgment had permitted all the compliments he was forever receiving to blow lesions into the stretched balloon of his judgment. For Mills was a man whose face and build said clearly, "Stop in the House of Representatives!" His head was pear-shaped. It was as if there had been a yeast set loose in his flesh, and most of it had settled around his jaw rather than his brow. So even his ears were big on the bottom and pointed on top. The lower part of his face was full, even bulbous, a beanbag—his features got skinnier as your eyes went up, his forehead was narrow and his straight hair plastered on top of his flat little head must have been half a millimeter thick. If he had ever run for President, *Mad* magazine would have flown themselves to the moon on the whoomph of such unexpected gas.

Mills was gruff. He had nowhere near enough delegates to interest anybody, and besides he was not a man to divulge information—he had gotten where he was by keeping his counsel. So in response to the question "Who will win the nomination?" Mills replied, "We'll know next week." The Press groaned. He was the living embodiment of investiture, of muscle, money, and all the constipations of power. That thin head and those broad jaws! How many bulldogs from the corporations, unions, Mafia and Pentagon had given dead news conferences over all the years of the old politics. Now, it was as if Media didn't have to listen to him anymore. Since no political purpose would be served, Mills didn't have to talk to them either. The conference ended as it began, with one's ears in the shredder of the helicopter noise—it gave intimation of what the blade of grass might hear when the lawn mower goes over.

Wallace came in at last. Off the airplane, all motions repeated, like the film run again, he was promenaded past the Press in his wheelchair and up the ramp to the podium. As he progressed he moved his left hand (the limb most visible to the Media) through a set of small and artful

movements. His hand was cupped as if in salute, the
gesture was military—he could have been an honored
general, as honored indeed as MacArthur, returning in that
salute all recognition of the legitimate homage due him,
and yet the gesture was not without pathos, for he was
also reminiscent of a boy who has military dreams, and
practices saluting the trees as he walks on a road. Wallace
was so small in the chair! And so dignified! It was the
quality he had never possessed. Aquarius had heard him
speak once at a private dinner in New York and expected
to like him more than he cared to. Instead, he had liked
him less. There had been a dull bullying streak in his
remarks, and one did not have to know a great deal about
New York politics to understand how unpleasant was the
majority of his audience—they had monomaniacal faces,
mean, pinched and recidivist to the root of that worst of
Christian essences which is Christian venom, faces to
suggest that their only problem with sanity was to keep
in line all remarks about wiping out certain unnamed
hordes of the Asiatic, the Near Eastern and the African.
But they were Wallace's people in New York. If not
typical of *folks* in the South and Midwest, still Wallace
was their leader that night, and worked them up on a set
of verbal combinations which went through the problems
of New York from innuendo to snarl, and was reminiscent
of some of the worst of the Southern mess sergeants
Aquarius had worked under in the Army, the kind who
lost patience watching Filipino kids salvage edibles to take
home from the garbage cans. Sooner or later such mess
sergeants would always mutter, "Them gooks better get
out of my way."

Wallace in Miami Beach today was another man, however. If, by more than one account, he had moved from
Left to Right over the early years of his career, every
evidence in recent months spoke of how he was now
moving back to the center. For a time at least. The mail-
order hate-you-fancy-pants clothes which once he wore had
been replaced by tailored weeds. The influence of a new
and beautiful wife, niece of Big Jim Folsom, was evidence
no one could ignore, never ignore a deep brunette with
eyes like black diamonds who had gone to Rollins College
to become a movie star, had worked as a professional
water skier, and in the Florida primaries drove the pace car

to start the Daytona 500 (invitation delivered by the president of the race track, who was chairman of the pro-Wallace Florida delegation). No, Wallace was no longer the small-town demagogue with the gas to go as far as that could get him. He seemed interested in inching away from political positions too hopelessly penned off to the side of a national consensus—he had even in Florida suggested to audiences that if they didn't agree with his stand, they should vote for Shirley Chisholm for she at least "tells the truth unlike all those pointy-headed liberals." Shrewd politics which would draw votes from his nearest competitors Jackson and Humphrey, but it was certainly not a speech to issue from the Curtis LeMay Wallace of 1968.

Then in the wake of the assassination attempt had come pilgrimages: the Kennedys, McGovern, Muskie, Humphrey, Larry O'Brien, visits and gifts from Nixon, recognition from the Pope. If never respectable before, now respectable: grand opening of the tightest psychic sphincter of them all—small-town Southern pride. He was indisputably a national figure. With all "the grabs" of an abdominal pain. The tree falling in the forest knocks down another tree and one thinks of the Ronald Reagan part in *King's Row*. "Where's the rest of me?" was his scream in the middle of the night at the maniacal injustice of infirmity. Even as they wheel him up to the podium at Blast Site One, his hands and arms betray involuntary fear, and indeed as the wheelchair stops, he starts to topple forward—his body ends at his navel and he is like a top-heavy toy. So he grabs the podium like a boy learning to swim will grab the dock. Yet his face is handsome now in the instant of fear. The hint of hog-jowl complacency is gone, all gone, smelted out by pain and by meditations conceivably of retribution for acts of the past, perhaps he looks now the way he was meant to look, an ex-bantamweight boxer with all the lean dignity little boxers have when they retire and keep from gaining weight. And a band supplied by the Democratic National Committee, with straw boaters, black pants, bow ties and red-and-white-striped shirts, a bit of political brass with electric guitar, drums, two trumpets, a trombone with a hank of Confederate flag attached to the end of its slide and a whistling eel of a clarinet all finish saluting him. Hello Dolly alias

Hello Lyndon alias Hello George is done and played and Wallace speaks in the new voice of the national hero, legions of the dead from every American war in the shadowy Taps of his voice, telling the crowd that he is "a national Democrat in a national Democratic convention" and the ear hears him again on TV, "I'm going to insist that they adopt a platform that tells the average citizen we are responsive to his needs and conscious of his desires." A fine sentence.

If every politician is an actor, only a few are consummately talented. Wallace is talented. The new modest measured voice creates another man. If one did not know of his history, he could be a slim and small Southern general of impeccable dignity with a warming touch left of the common folk, all this as he speaks at the airport now, but the stories which follow the flight of the plane and will soon see print speak of the uncontrollability of his internal plumbing and his fears before speaking which are so terrifying that his wife must assure him she will, if necessary, go on in his place. He is the first note of the real that Aquarius has encountered at this convention, and his presence, a work of art, remains in the back of the mind, for Wallace brings with him the clank of chains down in the dungeons of the moon-reaching blood-pumped crazy American desire. Now he finishes by thanking "Gawd for having spared my life" and is given a rich and lingering farewell by Wilbur Mills, who, trademark face, never makes a move without significance to those who can read the blockbuster body language of the old politics. And all the sadness of the South, and the rage of Southerners that they know about a life which others don't, and it is going to perish (it has been perishing for a hundred and ten years and more), is in the muggy air of Blast Site One.

4

Hubert Horatio Humphrey, having arrived in the hollow hour after the Governor from Alabama was gone from the airport scene, stated when asked whether he expected to win, "You bet I do. I didn't come down for a vacation. I came for the nomination." His flair in the campaign had been to talk to Black audiences. With Jewish Senior Citizens he was as always super-sensational—when the moment came, he would lean in toward his wife and say, "Muriel and I can hardly wait until we pay a visit to Israel again and charge up our batteries in that lovely land," but such talk was analogous to strip-mining the emotions of the aged. Coming on with Blacks had been his unique ability among all these white candidates—for years!—he had a rhythm when he spoke. He laid down every favor he had ever done for Blacks, did it in cadence, you could hear the repetitive roll of the soul drummer hearkening to a Black *duende* at these rhythmic calls on history, and when Hubert was done with his deeds, he would bark up in a little electronic voice-box of a voice—his larynx grown rough enough to scrub floors—"Yes, now, and now my friends, I need a favor from you," and his audience, Black respectables and Black Mafia, would go roaring down the oratorical river with him.

But this morning, day after his arrival, giving a press conference in the Carillon Hotel, he had nothing like the same happiness. The room had a very low ceiling and was overlit; the effect was to crush the Press in upon him, exaggerate all scrutiny and he had the old wounded bitter-mule look of a nag whose teeth had been counted too often —the Press, part of his first love affair with politics (for they had adored him once), now were next to openly con-

temptuous. And he was wary with them. He knew their
need for a villain. A story flies best when it has a hero
for one wing and a villain for the other. And Hubert was
drawn toward villainy like the moth who rushes toward
that far-off star which summons it into the flame. A villain
in '68, he had California in '72, and after the greetings
this morning were done, "I haven't had an audience of the
Press this large in months," he said for commencement,
drily, all the backed-up surly sad dignity of a man who
knows he is regarded as a clown, knows he has even
acted as a clown for that is the style by which he may
swim, but now is trapped as a clown for that is the world's
fixed estimate of him. "I open myself to your questions,"
he said. All the concentrations of fatigue from months of
campaigning had been reduced and concealed under coat-
ings of TV makeup thick as barnacles until there was only
the hint of two small discolorations under his cheek bones,
but like the worst sort of bruise they gave hint of tendrils
in the injury ready to travel far. Standing in front of a
shiny blue-finished cotton backdrop, he wore a blue suit
with a broad light-blue silk tie, and these fabrics gleamed
as he spoke of party, mission, and the needs of people. His
eyes were tiny, his forehead was large as a rising orange
harvest moon, and there was an old man's sadness in his
downturned upper lip, the curve of a bowl turned upside
down, his lower lip pinched determinedly upon it. "I
believe we'll now have a free and open convention," he
said, and next to him, Muriel wore a royal-blue tailored
suit with a white blouse, her colors well installed between
the hues of his suit and his tie. Next to them, harbinger
of danger and sudden mortality, stood a sad Secret Service
man in a dark green suit and dull-colored shirt, a dark
somber maroon-striped tie. The Secret Service man had a
great pallor as if for years he had been guarding artifacts
beneath fluorescent lights.

Quickly someone asked about California. Humphrey's
answer was unctuous, cynical, sincere and wicked all at
once, as if the separate parts of his face were no longer
flesh so much as jointed shells. He was alternately pious
and full of candor, quick to insist that McGovern was
inconsistent if he called for winner-take-all with the California votes when such a principle went directly against the
guidelines McGovern had drawn himself, yet as quick to

admit that if he had won in California and McGovern lost, he would be as concerned as George that his delegates were being taken away. "I'm sure I would have been fighting for every single delegate just like Mr. McGovern, and I don't think we ought to get uptight about it." Politics, what the hell, was politics. Uptight was the mix of morality and gamesmanship. Besides, Humphrey suggesed, didn't he have the most votes in all the primaries—didn't that suggest, he left it unsaid, that any means was reasonable to stop McGovern? Of course, grumbled the Press, there were arguments as to who had the greatest number of popular votes in the primaries, face-offs as opposed to running unopposed. Humphrey went on. He was confident they would stop McGovern.

"How loyal will Muskie be in a floor fight?"

"I think," said Hubert full of twinkling clownsmanship, "that his credentials will be as solid as a Maine rock."

He drew laughter. It gave him life. He worked now for more laughter. To his claim that he had 700 solid delegate votes, "delegates with a strong preference or legal commitment to vote for Humphrey" (said Humphrey), there came the query, "If you don't get the 700 votes, won't that open a credibility gap?"

"Not a bit," he replied quickly with an old politician's tart distaste for a reporter so gauche as to prod into an obvious insincerity, a functional insincerity. That response drew a very large laugh. The mood was growing jovial. He would, said Humphrey, ask for a pledge "prior to Monday night from all candidates for loyalty to the party."

Would McGovern go along?

"He may. We talked recently on the phone—just a good friendly talk."

What did you talk about?

The sly look came back to Humphrey's makeup-battered face. "We," said Hubert, "talked politics."

The meeting ended in a jovial buzz. Only in the echo of this small event, only in the distance, did the sound of the wound linger, long-gone sound of some psychic explosion on the way to the campaign of '68. Time had glued him together with less than her usual address. Humphrey looked like a man whose features had been repaired after an accident; if the collar slipped, the welts would show. It was the horror of his career that as he came to the end of it,

his constituency was real (if antipathetic to one another
—what did his Blacks, old and middle-aged Jews, and trade
unions have to do with one another?) but he was not real,
not nearly so real as the constituency, more like some
shattered, glued, and jolly work of art, a Renaissance priest
of the Vatican who could not even cross a marble floor
without pieties issuing from his skirt. Father Hubert. He
had the look of a man who knew where the best wine
was kept, but old age would have to conquer his desire to
lisp when dogma was invoked.

5

As if he has formed a taste for greeting politicians, Aquarius is out again Saturday to see if he can catch the arrival of John Lindsay who is due just before McGovern comes in at Blast Site One. Lindsay is arriving without a ceremony to greet him. Lucky even to be a delegate (since the New York group in a forthright sweep of the McGovern broom has passed this year over Averill Harriman, James A. Farley, Robert F. Wagner, Meade H. Esposito and Patrick J. Cunningham among others) the Mayor of New York has been picked by Democratic State Chairman Joseph F. Crangle as a delegate-at-large. All advance word is that Lindsay is by now so unpopular with some factions of the New York caucus that he will keep a "low profile" at the convention.

He arrives in a commercial airliner with other delegates. It happens that his plane comes in by the last gate, at the end of a long passenger corridor, and there are only a few Miamians waiting to greet visitors or family. Plus one TV unit. They interview Lindsay. Out of the race, plastered with humiliating defeats in Florida and Wisconsin (where his share of the vote was as low as 7 percent), he carries his loss well at this moment—his features have the eloquence of fine-carved bone. Those features suggest he will yet have the last laugh on his enemies, for he will grow more handsome as he gets older. Even the hint of pain in his expression gives an agreeable distinction to that movie star face which has aroused so much animosity in New York.

"Do you think you have a chance at this convention?" asks the TV interviewer.

"Oh, nobody is burning down the aisles to get to me," says Lindsay.

He is altogether cut off. Having left the Republican party to join the Democratic, he had two choices in the spring—to work for the new party but run for no national office until new credits had been established, or to enter the primaries and prove so powerful a vote-getter that his candidacy would emerge. Since he had no out-of-state cadres, nor real time for preparation, his best hope was as a television candidate. In Wisconsin he ran into all the force of McGovern's years of work at building an organization. "If Lindsay will admit he knows nothing about the grass roots, I'll agree I don't know my way around 21" said McGovern. And Meade Esposito, Brooklyn boss, and Lindsay's familiar enemy, sent a telegram: "Come back, little Sheba."

Of course, Lindsay violated the oldest law of politics. You don't join a fraternity and offer to become its president in the same week. The question was whether he was obsessed with the squandered virtues of the position he had not chosen. It was obvious Humphrey, Jackson or Muskie were all unable to unify the party, but Lindsay, if only he had remained out of the primaries, would now be the only Democrat who could lead a coalition against McGovern, and prove acceptable to some McGovern delegates. At the least, he would have been the most glamorous Democrat in Miami, and everyone's candidate for Vice-President. But Aquarius does not ask the question, for the answer is obvious. No politician as young as Lindsay is able to choose the prudent course when there is no final obstacle between the splendors of his personality and the presidency—just the need to get the votes. He has to assume he will get the votes. Men are not in politics because they hold a low view of their charm.

But by the schedule, our leading man is due to be in. Quickly, the few reporters decamp from Lindsay and rush to get to Blast Site One. McGovern's arrival, however, is dramatically delayed by a tropical storm which keeps the plane circling in the air almost an hour (as if to speak of oncoming dark hours of the Republic) and then is still near to anticlimactic. The crowd, although larger than Wallace's, is not a patch on the crowd which greeted

McCarthy in Chicago in '68 and that crowd, Aquarius
recollected, had been too tame for him. Nor is McGovern
his kind of candidate. He respects him for his political positions, admires his hard work; he more than admires his
political victories (since Aquarius by his own feeble record
knows what it is to get votes) but there is a flatness of
affect in McGovern which depresses and the muted singsong of his conversational voice might lead one to divine he
grew up in a rectory, if indeed one did not know it already.
There is a poverty of spirit in the air. While it is certainly
not a poverty of moral principle (for even arriving at the
Blast Site with a rich suntan and a superbly tailored light-
blue suit of a luminous silver sheen, McGovern is an embodiment of principles strong as steel) it is perhaps a
paucity of pomp and pleasure which those very moral
principles forbid—McGovern, every story tells you, doesn't
even have a trusted flunky to pack his bag each morning
but does it himself (shades of Henry Wallace and Abe
Lincoln). It is not that he does not have a nice personality
—if he is even half so decent as he seems, he is probably
the most decent presidential candidate to come along in
anyone's life, and if he is not half as decent as he looks,
then he is certainly a consummate actor. Still, it is all unexciting. He has come from back of the Democratic field and
out of 5 percent of the polls to succeed in building a campaign organization without parallel in the grass roots, has
done it all over two years of work and with the finely tuned
foresight to forge a new set of principles for selecting delegates which has worked almost entirely for him, all those
women, those young, those minorities giving him parts of
the vote in states he could barely have entered before, he
has brought the catboat of his small political fortunes into
exactly the place where the winds of history were blowing
for him, has put some of the air into those political breezes
himself, has pulled off a feat of political appropriation which
speaks of greatness—in the history of American presidential primaries, the McGovern campaign of '72 must be a
modest equivalent to the Long March of Mao Tse-tung.
Yet there is no excitement. It is as if a fine and upstanding
minister has moved into the empty house up the street:
isn't it nice to have Reverend and the lovely Mrs. McGovern for neighbors? For certain, if McGovern's politics were
more conservative, one would speak of him as the Demo-

cratic Nixon. For both men project that same void of
charisma which can prove more powerful than charisma
itself, although vastly less agreeable (as if one is alone in a
room with a television set).

Aquarius could hardly dare to explain why he thinks it
is important for a candidate to have charisma (he is much
more mystical about the presidency than fashion permits:
he thinks, when all is said, it is a primitive office and in-
spires the tribes of America to pick up the modes and manners of their chief). While nobody he ever met seemed to
be in love with the Republican President, history might yet
decide Nixon was the man who forged the peace with
Communism in the Twentieth Century. Yet could one
measure the damage to temperament, bravado and wit
which the emotional austerities of Nixon had laid on the
nation? It was even possible Nixon had prepared the very
toned-down climate in which a mild and quiet voice like
McGovern could flourish. If that were so, and McGovern
was yet to win, then what would happen to people who
believed that Nixon was a chip off old Nick? Was McGovern
then the second chip? All this was obvious nonsense for
people who took their politics straight, and were happiest
at three in the morning with a lukewarm beer and six hard
issues to be discussed, but assassination was not the worst
fertilizer for theories of demonology or Satanist perspec-
tives on the seizure of history. Aquarius could travel far
along these lines, but then he was forever ready to look
for the devil in many a plain case: the nature of the un-
dramatic Satan, true evil one, was to conceal himself, after
all.

At any rate, cleaving to the good American principle
that no successful man is ever to be completely trusted,
Aquarius clung to every instant of study he could obtain
of McGovern in action. Appearing the day after his arrival at the La Ronde Room of the Fontainebleau, he responded to the question "Do you think the winner-take-all
principle is fair?"

"I don't. I was opposed to it. And in 1976, California
will come under the same guidelines as the other states.
But winner-take-all was the rule California chose for itself
for '72, and while we were opposed to that rule, we played
by it and we won. I submit that if you want to change the
rules after a game, that is certainly permissible, but you

cannot change the score of a game which is already played."
It was the agreeable logic of the playing fields of Mitchell,
South Dakota. "Are your agents," asked a reporter, "mak-
ing any headway on the California question with Senator
Muskie's people?" With a smile McGovern said, "Not to
my knowledge."

"Have you had any conversations with Senator Muskie?"
"I talked to him about this matter."
"What did you say?"
Very drily. "I asked him to meditate upon it."

He did not suffuse himself in that fog of imprecision by
which other politicians would bury, trap, suffocate, or slip
a question, he had hardly the air of a politician, indeed he
was more like a teacher dealing with a matter common to
him and his students. Yet it was still not easy to know
what one thought of him. If the force of his psyche was
with you in the room like a fine silver blade, strong as steel,
yet there was also that damnable gentle singsong prairie
voice, that tight voice of a thousand restraints which sings
of not a thing but its singsong resentment against the fact
of its restraint—one had heard such voices on Midwestern
bankers, and on athletes and bureaucrats and YMCA secretaries, on ministers, and kids selling subscriptions, and on
the baby-faced killer who had always been the nice boy
next door, it was the mild self-negating ripple of a life devoted to causes external to oneself and to the show of acts
of Christian love. No, it was not a voice to find easily
agreeable, for it spoke of Methodist beds of Procrustes
where good souls and bad were bent equally into the rigor
and rectitude of a bare, arduous, and programmed life.
Small wonder that in his boyhood sneaking out to see a
movie was mentioned by him as an example of forbidden
fruit, yes, his voice gave small pleasure because it revealed
so little of the man. And yet McGovern also seemed somehow reminiscent of an astronaut. It was in that sense he
gave off of Christian endeavor, of total commitment of
strength, of loneliness and endless stamina, of the tireless
ability to bear interruption of his mood, and all of that
same   astronaut   impersonality,   professional   gentleness,
vaults of reserve, that subtle charisma so unlike the live
hearth of conventional glamour, rather an incorruptible
filament of charisma, which could be a halo if talking of a
saint, but was invisible in McGovern until one became

aware of it. For this charisma was not of personality but of purpose. It spoke of a bravery next to weightless—of course! That sense of a fine blade, stern and silver, was exactly what one felt when meeting certain astronauts. There too was the same sense of a psyche which had traveled already to a space beyond. "It would be nice, I suppose, to have a few more exciting personal qualities," McGovern had once said—it was a remark in the syntax of Neil Armstrong.

It gave focus, then, to think of McGovern this way. Indeed the image grew more comfortable as one wore it along, for McGovern had been a good pilot with a Distinguished Flying Cross for thirty-five bombing missions over Europe, and had, according to his biographer, Robert Sam Anson, the reputation of coming back to base "with more gas in his tank than 99 percent of the other pilots," which would be characteristic of spacemen who were noted for their passion to conserve fuel.

Seeing John Glenn at a party, his first reaction to the observation was "George? I don't think of him as an astronaut." Then Glenn hesitated. "I suppose the one quality in an astronaut more powerful than any other is curiosity. They have to get some place nobody's ever been before." So the question remained alive. "Yes," said Glenn. "It's possible George has that kind of curiosity."

6

There were parties in plenty. If the image of McGovern as a lonely astronaut piloting the ship of state through new moral galaxies of democracy was one million-footed mile of metaphor, the ten thousand feet of the delegates had by now come to town, all 5,114 of them with their alternates and their fractions (some 22 Rhode Island delegates would have 15/22 of a vote—an excruciating dismemberment to make 22 bodies count for 15), the working total for all to come to 3,016 votes or 1,509 for a majority, and the delegates were, of course, a bona fide new species, 80 percent never at a convention before, 14 percent Blacks, Latins and Indians at 6 percent, women at a full 38 percent. The young (under twenty-five) were 13 percent of the whole and another 20 percent were under thrity-five; professionals, teachers and housewives made up close to half the count, and 95 percent of the delegates had a year or more of college. It was a mass of hard-working citizenry, more honest, uncompromised, innocent and sober than delegate legions of the past, and the work overflowed into so many caucuses of category (Black, Latino, Women and Youth) and such immersion in state caucus that the convention became as complex as a field of tunnels and burrows, the nights of the convention set records for working hours, some delegates busy from early in the morning until early in the morning, from 8 A.M. for example to 6 A.M., and if they could hardly be a majority, the drinking parties, such as they were, had ceased by Sunday night. Yet, over the weekend, there was material to brood a little on the nature of McGovern's candidacy and the glum conclusion that his revolution was a clerical revolution, an uprising of the suburban, the well-educated, the modest, the reasonable, and all the unacknowledged genetic engineers of the future. The best of the liberal mind and the worst were his troops, all the warriors for a reasonable ecology and a world where privilege could no longer paralyze were in his army as well as all the social whips for a new state of collective mind opposed to any idea of mystery in any organism social or human—a spirit of science concentrated into pills to push behavior. If as a good Democratic voter, Aquarius thought it would be time to worry over such foes when McGovern was in, yet he noticed over the weekend celebrations that most of the fun was to be found in the polar ends of the party, in the Wallace delegates whooping it up to the music of Ferlin Husky and in the warmth and faction of the Black Caucus on Monday morning; whereas the Mc-Govern youth at the Doral, while certainly nice, had the subtly wan look (beneath Florida tan) of kids who get their kicks by replaying on tape recorders conversations they have just lived through.

The Wallace party for delegates had been a hog bath for heavy perspirers, with hard liquor, lots of gravy on the spareribs, and a sense of animal warmth coming off all those red country faces, meanness, spite, spice, loyalty and betrayal, carnal equalities all over the place like a cross between a horse auction and a roadhouse on Saturday night. Delegates with Jackson, Mills, and Humphrey buttons were there, in for a good time, and McGovern delegates also having a good time, there to show party solidarity with Wallace, all but the Blacks were there. And in the midst of all this white soul food and sexual savory there was the elucidation of a fine plot, with a Mills campaign official to drop it quietly in the ear. It seemed the Stop-McGovern forces were not without a plan—their plan was Teddy Kennedy.

"But how could he take it after McGovern is stopped? None of the kids would work for him."

"Oh, McGovern would have to call him personally and ask him to run."

"Why would McGovern do that?"

"Where else," the man said wisely, "can McGovern go? With a third party, he's dead."

"Does Teddy Kennedy know about this?"

Silence. The moment is weighed. The confession is contemplated. "He will disown us if a single word is printed," says the Mills man, baring all.

Of course, he is not talking about a plot but a scenario. This momentous secret cabal is hardly to be offered to Aquarius for the sake of his art, no, it is merely a move to create interest in Mills. And a ploy to pick up the credit later if Kennedy is ever nominated. Yet, as a scenario, it offers virtues. For if McGovern were actually stopped, only Teddy Kennedy could put the party together, and indeed could do it only if McGovern requested it of him, which was indeed a scenario to carry in one's mind so long as the issue was in doubt. At least it gave promise that this dull and quiet convention could yet burn a hole in all the plots and dramas of men.

Was it therefore with thoughts of Elizabethan tragedy and apocalyptic shift that he studied the face of Cornelia Wallace when the Governor came down in his wheelchair and from the short podium addressed the delegates in welcome, and gave his blond daughter Lee, age eleven, to the microphone that she might give her little speech, bright and sassy was the child's speech for the folks, and practiced in oratory like her father? There were enough people in front of him to render the Governor and his daughter invisible, and Wallace's speech was benign, the king of a small castle welcoming his guests to the groaning board. But Cornelia Wallace's eyes were stellar while he spoke and, as she looked at the crowd, her rich face was animated with theatrical vitality—she could, for example, have passed convincingly as the most beautiful opera singer in the land —she was certainly the most beautiful woman he had seen in politics since Jackie Kennedy, and if Cornelia Wallace was nowhere as grand, she was certainly more vivid as she clapped her hands to the beat of Ferlin Husky. What a dramatic couple would the Governor and Cornelia Wallace yet become.

So that was a good party, the best he sensed glumly the Democrats might offer for the rest of the week, and steeped himself in parties as much as he could; it was a way, given his habits, of apprehending some modes of reality, and was bored later that evening at the Democratic Telethon— there was too much money in the back of the room, and the money was wan—comparisons might not be fair considering the compressed energy of the squeezed Wallace horde. Again that sense of being on the edge of some political revelation teased him. For twenty-four years, going back to the Henry Wallace days of 1948, he had been watching actors raise money for progressive politicians—there was an affinity between the two like red meat and red wine, or was it hot dogs and sauerkraut? Something in progressive politics believed in the forced feeding of message to the mass, and where was the professional actor who did not subscribe to the art of manipulated instruction? But this was hardly the revelation whose edge he might inhabit. With an alternating sense of melancholy and elation he felt as if he were coming close to some simple understanding of politics, clear as the simple step across a profound philosophical divide, even as once, how many years back, he had thought to himself, "The world's more coherent if God exists. And twice coherent if He exists like us." And had come to live as well with ideas of a Devil whose powers might be equal or sometimes prevail as in the bullets of assassins which found the mark (although his philosophical canon was to make no final assumption on the origins of any deadly message). Deep thoughts for a telethon—were they in reaction against the bright optimism of actors whose new ideas were twenty-four years old for him? He was in a foul mood at his inability to fit the five thousand and more souls of this convention into some idea of one living creation in one bower of history.

His spirits improved with the Yippies the next night. Their role in this convention was small if McGovern were nominated; once he was stopped, they would be catalytic agents to thousands of furious young sympathizers for McGovern. But the mood in Flamingo Park was balmy on Sunday night. A feast was being provided for the old and the young—the Yippies never engaged in an action without a theory and the beauty of the new theory was that it was designed for Miami Beach since it had declared there was no real war between the young and the old. The villains were the middle-class generation between, those sons and daughters of the grandparents who were also the mothers and fathers of the Yippies; that was the middle generation which had collapsed into conformity and fear of Communism, but the old had radical memories of the Depression and the pains of forging the unions. Since

this was the first time any of the young had made an over-
ture to the old, and since the Yippies were easier to get
along with than anyone had thought, some of the old citizens of Miami Beach felt ready to fraternize, and a few
even came to the free feast in Flamingo Park where the face
of Richard Nixon had been drawn on a field by laying out
hundreds of quarters of watermelon in the pattern of his
face. The thought was that the old would dive in to eat and
massacre his image before the cameras of the Media;
they had certainly gorged on watermelon in an earlier
feast' for the generations. Indeed, one Yippie cutting a
watermelon had almost cut off an old man's hand because
those senile fingers had plunged into the meat so fast, but
this Sunday night the old were not numerous, and it was
the kids who gorged on the watermelon and ate the free
health food served up to hundreds, the lettuce and onion
rings, the lentil salad and unpeeled carrots with the skin
washed and sliced. Unpeeled cucumbers were also served,
hard-boiled eggs, organic bread, plus the huge quarters of
watermelon which had just lain on the field. The Yippies
were dressed in every rag and feather of color, in belts and
pieces of leather, in dungarees and cut dungarees, and their
chests were brown from living in the sun, their hair and
beards had gleams of gold, their tents were colorful in the
evening. The encampment in Flamingo Park was somewhere between a love-in and an army bivouac, with pup
tents scattered irregularly in the grass, and squad tents to
the corners, field-size latrine trailers, and CBS trucks near
the trailers, but there were also colored balloons in the
trees and a hand-painted sign: YIPPIE—TEN DAYS TO
CHANGE THE WORLD.

Jerry Rubin and Abbie Hoffman appear. Since they are
writing books, they have Media passes, and Rubin's de-
clares he is working for *Mad* magazine; Hoffman has
written Popular Mechanix on his. With his rug of dark
hair, his big beaming nose, and his ferociously happy smile
(as if he has just worked loose a rusted nut with his
teeth), Hoffman has the skip of a man who has spent his
life lying on his back looking up into the oil pans of a
thousand jalopies, and eyes to suggest that "nobody knows
the chimneys I've swept." And, yes, he is a mechanic of
sorts, he and Jerry Rubin, both mad mechanics, tinkering
with the Rube Goldberg traps of all the mad social ma-

chinery which fails to run the nation, and now laughing
together at the Media passes, watching middle-aged people
come into the park to look, Miami Beach residents suddenly confronting themselves as tourists, smelling the pot
which dissipates as slowly as the odor of honeysuckle, feeling the peculiar peace of this bivouac (even though ten or
fifteen of the children have eyes spaced out into the next
county and Zippies with a pirate flag on their shirts stalk
about—they have become the unmanageable Left to the
Yippies' new center of establishment—"I'm having an
identity crisis," said Rubin with his broad smile which
welcomes all human phenomena including upheavals in
himself), yes, across all of this peaceful Miami Beach
evening, hot and placid as the streets of Flatbush in
Brooklyn on a very hot July evening, the schizophrenia of
the Republic is murmuring at the edges of the horizon—for
this peace will not last. In August, the Republicans will be
here, and the honor of the young is bound to protest the
war; riots in the street will not necessarily prove a disaster
for the Republicans. If legend has it that Allen Ginsberg
once told a college audience he drew the line at nothing
but incest, and the audience told him, "Draw the line at
nothing," now Nixon was coming to draw the line.

Were the armies of the final Armageddon forming in
the seed of men not yet born, or would even this calm
summer end in blood?

7

But then in this hour of the night before that convention would begin which was to bring McGovern his nomination, there was doubtless a drop of blood already on the streets. For even as the feast was proceeding in Flamingo Park, a group of SDS were blocking the driveway to the Playboy Club where a party for the big sponsors of the Democratic party was commencing, and before they were removed, a fire engine had been called to deal with a blaze outside the Bunnies' dressing room, alleged to have been started by a commando of Women's Liberation who would remind the Bunnies that they were degrading their sex even as they were being exploited. The police in full squadron, led by Pomerance, cleared out the demonstrators. But not before a number of sponsors had difficulty entering the party. The purpose of the raid may even have succeeded, for the party was spoiled. The old mood of Chicago lay over the guests, and the hours of confrontation and nightmare when the party had divided within itself returned, bringing the memory of how more than one good drinking Democrat, complacent for years with his bourbon, his special reserve of broads, and his warm appreciation of his own attention to the interests of the workingman, had exploded in rage against a thousand upstarts in the ranks of the delegates, and had come to realize in Chicago, in the ham heats of his clenched fists, that there were Democrats he would like to kill before he even tapped the nose of a Republican. Those powers of the Democratic party which resided in the trade unions and the Mafia recoiled from Chicago and the loss of the election to Nixon with such numb

stunned horror that the newest recruits to the party
regarded them separately and together (how often together
were the unions and the Mafia now lumped!) as the
villains of the party, the corrupt and grease-impacted
bottlenecks in all the arteries of Democratic progress.
What made it worse was that their rage for being cast
in such a position was able to burn on a true core of guilt.
The union men were guilty of much. They had fattened
themselves and their unions with the profits of the Cold
War, had supported the scandals of Vietnam out past
the time when men could turn against that war and still
be called honest, and they knew they had adulterated the
quality of work, and blown nonproductive air into the
processes of production, they were part of the engines
of pollution which squeezed the waste into the gears and
skins of the products they made. They had delivered a
living wage to the American workingman, but at the cost
of an immersion in unneeded armaments which debauched
the American economy, and had to listen to the accusations
that they had left brothers on the factory line to marry
the corporation. If true, it was a miserable materialistic
marriage with endless bickering over what share of the
benefits belonged to whom—but the corporation and the
labor union chief were married to each other through
every hatred. And now the labor unions had lost the
party. These new delegates had come out of caucuses.
They were people who had been willing to sit through
weary long parliamentary evenings in order to prevail. Some
would call it political intensity, but the union leader,
veteran himself of a hundred negotiations in which he
had worn out the softer executives who confronted him
across a table, had now in his turn been ground out
by the boredom of facing implacable students and teachers
and hippies and clerks. By McGovern kids. Whe were
even worse than McCarthy kids, for some of the new
ones had been fourteen years old in 1968, and had one
characteristic which was calculated to drive the union
leader into fever—these kids had been raised by mothers
who loved them, and taught them the world was theirs
to shape—so they had a complacent innocence altogether
near to arrogance. The trade unionist reared more often
than not by a mother who laid the frequent back of her

hand on every idiot potato and onion and lemon head of a kid in her brood, could now have the immense anger of seeing his leonine powers lifted by a horde of suburban ants who had never been stepped on, and now could hardly be. Since these kids knew nothing of transcendence, he hated them. The unions had once been built by the unstated belief of organizers that they could transcend the given, the old leaders had come from the ranks, and the past was filled with legends of labor chiefs who had taken six shots from a .45 and chased their assailant as their life was pouring into their shoes; now the spiritual descendants of these men, installed here at a Thousand-Dollar-a-Plate dinner (ticket free), had to put up with women who set fires in Bunnies' dressing rooms and boys with beards who lay down on the road in front of their Cadillacs. The rage rose. Thinking of McGovern, the deposed labor leaders felt the natural hostility of sinners toward ministers. And before the evening was over, Hubert Humphrey came to the party, walking slow, naturally tired, his voice even more fatigued than his feet. The decision to pick the California delegation by majority of those eligible to vote had probably ended his chances.

8

Out of the deliberations of Larry O'Brien had the decision been made.

What a secret domain in the midst of open convention! Moving around a ring made of a strip of paper, one finds oneself first on the outside, then on the inside. Since one has not quit one's plane, it must be a twisted ring. History has moved from a narrative line to a topological warp.

McGovern had come into the last week of the California primary with his polls showing a 20 percent lead; enough for his aide, Frank Mankiewicz, to remark, "It won't be a convention, but a coronation." Somehow, nobody understanding how, McGovern on June 6 beat Humphrey by only 5 percent. Suddenly, the political air was full of lag—a sail was about to jibe. Humphrey, for whom four years have passed with one heart-pricking thought each morning—What *I* could have done with the presidency!—must have been like a young Chicano who lolls on a summer street and sees an elegant model go by. What *I* could do with her! All of that knowledge going to waste! Is there any motive more powerful? Since McGovern had had four times as much money to spend in California, it was not hard for Humphrey to find a moral victory in those close results. So he urged the Credentials Committee to overthrow the California primary: the principle of winner-take-all had denied the new guidelines. Of course, the Credentials Committee was filled with politicians kin to Humphrey, and they threw out more than half of McGovern's California delegates, giving them by proportion of their vote to Humphrey, Jackson, Muskie, Wallace and Chisholm. A Stop-McGovern coalition was thus formed. McGovern had been so close to a majority that the loss (151 of 271) was critical. The center of decision shifted from the depths of political life to the fourth dimension of the courts. A Federal District judge upheld the Credentials Committee, then the United States Appeals Court ruled against his decision. McGovern had the delegates back. And lost them as quickly to a stay of judgment ordered by the Supreme Court upon the Appeals Court ruling. "The convention itself," said the Court, "is the proper forum for determining intra-party disputes as to which delegates shall be seated." So the party chairman, Larry O'Brien, was put into the position of offering the decision which would make George McGovern the candidate of the Democratic party, or, most probably, stop him. In a party whose incompatibilities had been equaled only by its paradoxes, the result of the most open selection of delegates in the conventions of this century had now come down to the word of the nearest man Democrats still had for a boss, Larry O'Brien, who worked as campaign manager for Jack Kennedy, Lyndon Johnson, Bobby Kennedy, and Hubert Humphrey. Not unnaturally, he spoke of "awesome" burden.

O'Brien declared it would prove "an absolutely impossible situation if there was the remotest idea of a suggestion that O'Brien was pro or anti anyone." But what an occasion for distrust. O'Brien's first assistants were James O'Hara, a labor congressman from Michigan, and Joseph Califano who had worked for Lyndon Johnson in the White House. What a park for paranoia! Could Hubert Humphrey have planned a better terminus for the game than to have his chances judged by a party man? Of course, the McGovern strategy offered the return of an old nightmare: Chicago might be repeated. "I don't think," McGovern said, "people have fully assessed how the party could destroy itself if the reform process is denied after all that has happened in American politics these past few years."

The first and crucial decision for O'Brien was to determine how many votes were needed to establish victory. Should McGovern be required to amass 1,509 votes, an absolute majority of the convention, in order to win his challenge against the Credentials Committee, or should the 151 contested delegates be removed from the total of 3,016, and a majority of 1,433 thereby prove sufficient?

McGovern could almost certainly command this latter figure. "We went over and over it," O'Brien said. "The stakes were never as high. It took us three days and nights before the light came on." They were talented lawyers with years of exploring complicated situations but it took them three days to reason that if the absolute sum of 1,509 was decided upon, then the moot 151 delegates would in effect be voting upon their own challenge. For while they would not be allowed to vote, McGovern would still have to get as many votes to win as if all 151 had been there to vote against him. So O'Brien reduced the number to 1,433. It was equivalent to giving the nomination to McGovern. The old pol had decided for the new politics.

What consternation in the coalition! Wallace's campaign manager Charles Snider asked if this was what they got after their candidate "almost died in the service of the party." Jackson's representative promised that Jackson was "triple-pissed." Humphrey's man called it a "hostile act," and Muskie's aide Sherwin Markham said he might make a move to force adjournment of the convention. There was laughter. "Don't laugh," Markham told them.

Will it be easier to understand the decision if we assume O'Brien might have preferred to give the advantage to the Stop-McGovern coalition, but was compelled to accept McGovern's arguments against his inclination? (It must of course be supposed that the argument was never decided on logical merits—when the stakes are high, logic is obscene to a politician.) More natural is it to expect that O'Brien was looking for the survival of the party. A decision against McGovern was equivalent to creating a third party which could come close to getting as many votes in this next election as the Democrats themselves—probably that could kill the old party forever. Whereas if McGovern won the nomination, he might never be able to make peace with the old pols and the trade unions, nor find any real money, but at worst he would lose the election, and if he lost badly it might be easier for the old party to rebuild in '76 with old hands restored, and some of the McGovern cadres conceivably chastened. The wisdom of Solomon was O'Brien's. Such things happen to the Irish. Of course in the three days it took for the light to come on, there might have been more than one phone call to a compound near Hyannis.

9

Next morning Ed Muskie called a press conference where he read a statement. He stood there in his light-blue suit and he was knob-eared, knob-jawed, blue-eyed, knob-nosed, still gangling in his sixties, homespun (as if actually pondering whether he might have karmic ties to Lincoln), and with it all, was stately. Indeed, he looked like a gentleman of the frontier out of the Nineteenth Century—he had the dignity of simple manner, of a man who has absorbed his share of pain without brooding on the cost to his features.

Of course, such pain had come lately. Politics is not an art of principles but of timing. The principles are few and soft enough to curve to political winds. The fundamental action of politics is to gain the most one can from a favorable situation and pay off as little as possible whenever necessity forces an unpopular line. In every political profit, there is a loss somewhere—in every loss, a profit if one knows how to find it. That is all there is to politics if one considers principle. But when it comes to timing, politics is an art which makes the moves of athletes look heavy. Timing becomes as vertiginous as genius. Timing, and the power to contain huge ambitions and never lose one's temper. Since politicians make few remarks people have not heard often tested before, they are given little credit for their best remarks, and are never forgiven for their mistakes. They are not supposed to make mistakes. So they dare not lose their temper.

Muskie had made every mistake in the last few months. He had run a primary campaign with the slogan "Trust Muskie," in a year when nobody was trusted. Probably, he trusted himself. He had a slow honest bottom-of-the-barrel integrity on tough issues. He was ready to scrape the barrel of his own insides on difficult issues, searching within until he felt the authenticity of a bona fide answer. It was a good way for a politician to work so long as he was successful—people began to believe in the depth of his comprehension. Once he began to lose primaries, however, it turned inside-out. He could not recover his timing —suddenly he seemed always too strong or too weak. When his temper made him emotional at unpleasant slights to his wife in New Hampshire, the Press turned. They began to look for his nuts and bolts after Florida and Wisconsin—since they had once predicted his victory, now, unforgiving, they looked to take him apart. By now it would not have mattered if he began to do something right—they had him fixed as a man who was now always wrong. So as he read his statement, an unwilling pathos came off him, like a sound issuing through gritted teeth. He was a man of pride, he wanted no pity, but it was a torture to him that he had been thought of and looked at as the next President for two years and more, and now he was without position or honor or respect in his party, the butt of jokes from the staffs of other candidates, even stories of his own staff making remarks to the effect that he needed a transplant for his vertebrae. His only crime was that he had tried to run for President in his own way, his own way had failed utterly, and nobody forgave him. Nobody forgives a favorite who loses by seven lengths.

So now he looked to regain respect. To be the statesman who bound the wounds of his party. With dignity his words issued; he was taking pleasure in the weight of his courtly rhetoric:

> We have witnessed over the last several weeks a growing polarization of our party. . . . The credentials disputes have become weapons in a battle for votes among presidential candidates. This has spawned litigation, accusations, resentments, and antagonisms. . . .
>
> Moreover, what we have had to say about each other has become increasingly strident, intemperate and accusatory. Foul has been claimed in circum-

stances where foul may not have been intended or
administered. We have heard impugned men and
women who have labored long, diligently and well
in an effort to ensure the openness and fairness of
our convention.

In short, we have seen this convention being turned
into two armed camps. . . .

Therefore, I have sent the following message,
together with a copy of this statement, to each candidate for President:

> I earnestly ask that you meet with me, the other
> candidates for our party's presidential nomination,
> and Chairman O'Brien at his office or a place pro-
> vided by him at 1:00 P.M. today for the purpose of
> arriving at joint recommendations for presenta-
> tion to the convention which would resolve the
> major disputes over credentials and procedure
> which now threaten to embroil us all in protracted
> and damaging controversy. At that time I will be
> prepared to present specific recommendations
> designed to resolve these disputes in a manner
> which does not finally determine the nomination.

> While I have not discussed this invitation with any
> of the other candidates, it is my earnest hope that it
> will be accepted by all of them.

But once again his timing was to prove atrocious.
O'Brien had decided California. So nothing was left to
compromise. McGovern did not need others. Indeed only
the other candidates met on Monday afternoon with
O'Brien. They had to look foolish. McGovern would
hardly enter a meeting where his vote would be one
against five. So the Press turned again on Muskie. He was
derided as pitiful and incompetent. If he had grave sins,
and hell was awaiting him, he must certainly have paid a
tithe in purgatory. How raw must the inside of his
stomach feel.

10

O'Brien had never been chairman of a convention before
—by the time he was done, many were asking if they had
ever seen a convention chaired as well. It was as if he had
studied the style of every man he had ever seen with a
gavel, and appropriated the best of what he could use from
each. Since he was a man of parts and a good deal of wit,
he appeared to the thousands of delegates who were young,
new, and reluctantly innocent of conventional ways, as an
arbiter of manners, wise, senatorial, urbane, firm, good-
humored and never pious. Since he was a representative of
the old politics who had proved sympathetic to the new
politics, he also possessed the essence of political sex appeal for new delegates—nobody is more attractive in politics than a formidable adversary who is now your friend,
indeed, nothing gives more fortification than the powerful
manners of an enemy joining the court. For witness to this
principle, we need only contemplate the illimitable charisma
of William F. Buckley if he ever became a liberal Democrat.

So, from O'Brien's opening speech—"The first challenge
we face this week is to decide whether party reform will in
fact make the Democratic party better able to deal with our
real problems, or whether party reform turns out to be an
exercise in self destruction"—O'Brien had attached the
interest of the delegates to himself and to his own doubt,
and to their ability to convince him. He was saying, in
effect, "I am here, like yourselves, a man of contradiction
and confusion who wishes to discover if his love of party is
justified." Since he did this with a sense of tradition—in
appearance he looked like a benign version of Joseph
Kennedy when the founding father was still young—the
readiness of this young convention to maintain decorum

found its perfect focus. "Getting here," said O'Brien, "was only half the job. Now we must go to work. The hours will be long. The job will be tough. But we must prove to the American people that the Democratic party should again be entrusted with America's future. I think it comes down to this: do we have the guts to level with the American people? Only *you* can answer this question."

They gave him the ovation he deserved. He was a work of art. Had there been any dirty deal in the Democratic party, over the last twenty years, he did not know about? He seemed born with the ability to walk through a barnyard on his way to the cotillion and never have to wipe his pumps. So he gave dignity to the notion that a man could be a political animal and still acquire class. Since they were all thinking of a life in politics, they admired him for it. Perhaps the measure of the best art is that it does not excite envy.

Of course, O'Brien would have need of his newly acquired status. The wars of nomination were on. It was the next irony of this convention (whose drama like some masterwork of the absurd was never so much in its proportions as in its disproportions) that the climactic event of the entire week occurred on the first vote over the first challenge (which was not even California but South Carolina) and proved to be a drama of obfuscation since the result seemed to suggest McGovern's forces were in trouble whereas in fact they now controlled the convention. To magnify such irony, the South Carolina challenge also brought McGovern's herculean labors of the last two years down to a fine point of parliamentary procedure which resided within the other fine point of O'Brien's decision to make 1,433 votes enough to win the California challenge. Because it was the essence of parliamentary nuance that a chairman's ruling could not be challenged on its own direct application (or else what was a ruling worth?) but only on a parallel situation, so South Carolina was chosen by the Humphrey coalition for a test inasmuch as it had been selected by lot as the first vote on the night. The California challenge being not yet decided, all of the 151 Stop-McGovern delegates could still vote. Now, in the new situation, nine of South Carolina's seats being contested, a vote of 1,504, by O'Brien's ruling, would be enough to win. Of course, if the final vote fell between 1,504 and 1,509, then the chairman's decision would have made a critical difference in the result, and there would be legitimate ground for "controversy." Then the entire convention would be obliged to vote on the wisdom of his decision. Still retaining their 151 contested delegates, the Humphrey coalition could easily prevail on such a point. Having won, they would then be able to pass a new ruling requiring McGovern's challenge on California once again to obtain 1,509 votes, equivalent to stopping him. What a broil of maneuvers ensued! The Humphrey coalition had to win the South Carolina challenge in such a way that their final total fell into what they called—all shades of television—the "twilight zone" between 1,504 and 1,509. McGovern had to win by more than 1,509 or lose by less than 1,504. Since he had also promised the Women's Caucus that his forces would support the South Carolina challenge (which demanded, by way of the guidelines, that nine seats now held by men be delivered to women) McGovern's aides soon had to face the dilemma of taking a dangerous chance with the nomination or betraying his promise. To pose such a choice is to name the result. McGovern had hardly selected Ribicoff, Fred Harris, Gaylord Nelson, Frank Church, Phil Burton of California, Stewart Udall, Governor Lucey of Wisconsin, Gary Hart, Frank Mankiewicz, and Lt. Governor William Dougherty of South Dakota as floor leaders in order to be outmaneuvered in the pulling of votes on a parliamentary point. Halfway through, by the best estimate of Rick Stearns, the Rhodes scholar who was directing the strategy on this roll call, there was no certainty McGovern's forces could avoid the twilight zone (which they termed "the window") if they tried to go over 1,509 on South Carolina. It was going to be too close. The women would have to be dumped. Hart telephoned the Doral Hotel to give a clue. "All right," said McGovern, "I'm going to take a nap. Call me back so I can watch California." The nap would at least give him the right to say he had not intimately directed the strategy for choosing to lose on South Carolina.

"I got busy up and down the aisles," said Hart. In the California delegation, all 120 McGovern votes had gone to the women, plus 14 other delegates. The co-chairman of the delegation, Willie Brown, took 14 votes from his own pocket. California voted 120, not 134, for the minority report. It was a way of suggesting the McGovern vote was solid while Chisholm delegates were more attached to stopping McGovern than voting for the women. It was a trick which would be exposed by the next day, but Brown was working on the premise that the California challenge coming next would be over long before word would get around.

In their turn, the Humphrey coalition was trying to reduce the majority they were being given. The chairman of the Ohio delegation, Frank King, a man with the honest dogged face and silver-rimmed glasses of a bank examiner, was thrust into the massive embarrassment of looking incompetent on television for he had to pass the Ohio delegation four times. His eyes were almost crossed with the misery of seeming unable to do simple arithmetic before half of America. But one can imagine his conversations on the phone with Humhprey Headquarters. "Frank, can you up your total six? No, wait a moment, can you bring it down by nine." Groans. "Hold tight. We're not sure yet." To complicate matters, he had to deal with four Ohio counters representing other candidates, and of course nobody trusted anyone.

Through this scramble of phone circuits, the floor leaders for McGovern, better organized, kept switching votes back and forth in the Wisconsin, Nebraska and Oregon delegations until the speed of their calculations drove and dazzled the Humphrey coalition into confusion, indeed such confusion that they finally lowered their heads, bulled into a charge, and decided to win by a big margin as if this might convince the convention that McGovern could be stopped. It convinced some of the television commentators that McGovern might be in trouble, and brought suspense to the California challenge which followed, but in effect the total had landed well outside the twilight zone, 1,555.75 against 1,429.05, and the nomination was safeguarded.

Soon after, the California delegates were restored to McGovern by a vote of 1,618.28 to 1,238.22, a solid and overriding victory (which would have been a defeat if not for O'Brien's ruling), but it possessed no excitement commensurate to the results, and probably offered its most explosive moment when black Willie Brown got some of the convention to its feet by shouting "Give me back my delegation" in the debate which preceded the vote. Since Willie Brown was small and slight there was a pathos of the streets in his cry as if he were a newsboy whose papers had been stolen, but since he was also as lithe as super-cat, and young, and super-cool as a dream of Black supremacy in his creamy stay-cool-forever clothes, he was also engaging in the highest kind of Camp as though really there to say, "Listen to the Black man cause he is the wounded and the wise warrior, and he will show you how to wipe the warts." A huge camp ground. "Give me back my delegation!" The crowd roared. And roared again when the vote was counted. The first demonstration of the convention took place.

So, California was over. It had been won and lost in June, and won and lost and won again in July, but the damage it had done would offer no easy repair, for any period McGovern might have spent in preparing for the campaign, mending the party, studying his choices for Vice-President, and presenting an air of unity to attract the money had also been lost; the first price California would exact had already been paid in the challenge for South Carolina —more than a few of the women were storing resentment. The second was immediately on its way, and showed itself in the failure of the McGovern aides to find a compromise in Illinois which would seat both the Daley delegation and the Singer delegation which had ousted it. Singer's delegates were pro-McGovern, but hardly welcome to McGovern who needed Daley if he was to win Illinois. Still, McGovern could hardly repudiate Singer without enraging all too many delegates who had not forgiven Daley for Chicago in '68. So McGovern was ready for compromise. Singer, after a pull or two on his arm, was also ready for compromise. But Daley wasn't. He hadn't built from the first story to the second story all the way to the top story of all that larcenous Chicago politics in order to have an election *half*-stolen from him at the end of his career. He was not available for compromise. He did not answer calls from the McGovern staff nor did he accept visitors who were ready to mediate. "He," said a Daley man, referring to McGovern, "needs us more than we need him." There would be reverberations in other big-city machines. If McGovern were to finally lose the election by the margin of Illinois and one or other urban states, Daley might own the honor of having been the instrument of defeat for two presidential candidates in a row.

11

On Tuesday morning, after the McGovern forces had won California on Monday night, Humphrey called a press conference, and standing with Muriel next to him, speaking in the slow and even voice one tries to maintain at a funeral when half the love of one's life now lies in the box, he read the following words:

> I have a very brief statement, and just a statement. I shall read it and there shall be, if you will indulge me, no questions.
>
> After consultation with some of my closest friends and supporters I have determined that I will not permit my name to be entered in nomination at this convention. I am therefore releasing my delegates to vote as they wish. But my withdrawal from the presidential race is a withdrawal of candidacy only. It is not a withdrawal of spirit or determination to continue the battle that I've waged all of my life for equal opportunity for all of our people, for social justice for this nation.
>
> On behalf of Mrs. Humphrey and me I wish to thank those who have worked so hard, who have given so much, who had been so steadfast in their friendship and loyalty for these many years, and particularly for these past six months. . . .

When he was done, his eyes shining with the high light that tears will take when one does not permit them to fall, he patted his wife awkwardly on the side of the cheek, as if this was something he should certainly do, and he and his wife left the room slowly. The Press followed along the hall down the red carpet and past the aquamarine chairs with their brass arms. Outside on the street, the sign at the Carillon which read "Welcome Future President Humphrey" has already been taken down and the marquee bills "American Scene Review featuring Main Street Singers." In America, titles bounce off one another like molecules in solution.

Later in the afternoon a feeling of tenderness for Humphrey came back into the heart. It was analogous to the tenderness one used to feel for Boris Karloff in *Frankenstein*. How the dead in Vietnam still groan in the American bed.

12

Humphrey's withdrawal spurs him to interview Gene McCarthy. For once, there is no Secret Service about. In fact, there is no office, just a suite of three or four rooms, and in one of them a few people are gathered. They have faces which, if studied, might give insight into the nature of the loyal—it is as if they are the last handful of the millions who once were followers of McCarthy, decent faces with an inbite of the appetite as if they can put up with political penury for years. But McCarthy is looking splendid. He has never appeared more handsome, more distinguished, and more a philosopher prince—he is probably the most impressive-looking Democrat in Miami Beach. And he takes pleasure in teasing one of his total of four delegates who is a good young woman from Chicago but aware to a fault of her own lacks. "Oh, my God," she says, "I'm just the wife of a butcher. I can't put you in nomination." "Well, you may have to," he says with as much pleasure as if he were President of Notre Dame and had just told an All-American he will have to read the works of Immanuel Kant before trying to go on to the priesthood. "Yes, we're talking of nominating me," he says with a smile. "It seems as if that's the only way we can keep our floor passes and gallery seats," and the petty details of being completely out of fashion seem to interest him as much as the details of power.

Interviewing him alone, his wit flows so naturally through each topic that it is like trying to keep track of the light on water—it is easy to see one reason the Press never adored him is that he is not easy to quote. His phrases engage in extended relations with one another across long interesting sentences full of suspension: part of what they used to call his arrogance is his love of the English language—it is possible he has come to dislike politics because its tendency is to debase language, and its necessity all too often is to amputate the limbs of a thought. There is his famous remark about liberal criticism of his indifference to carrying on the fight, "They want me not only to bare my breast but go in for indecent exposure," and he recalls how McGovern accused him in the Wisconsin primary of giving up in the summer of '68. "But that isn't true," McCarthy says. "It was just," and his voice is very quiet with the memory of the frustration, "that we couldn't get anywhere. All the sources of power we needed were closed, the trade unions"—he is about to mention the Kennedy forces who gave him nothing after Bobby's assassination—"it's all very well to talk of carrying on the fight, but that didn't give us anything to fight with." And there is a hint of sadness when he speaks of how he came to run again, "I suppose I believed the loyalty I could arouse would be greater."

A hint of the elegiac arises as Aquarius confesses his wish that it was McCarthy who would be nominated tonight. "I like McGovern," Aquarius says, "but I just wish he spoke with a little metaphor from time to time."

"Methodists are not much on metaphor," says McCarthy.

13

By Tuesday night, McGovern's nomination assured, he had still a set of delicate maneuvers to perform: poli- tics was always delicate when one's next action was obliged to break a promise. If part of the drive of his campaign had come from women who believed McGovern would support their platform demands for abortion, from homosexuals who assumed he would go down the line with them for repeal of sexually restrictive laws and from the National Welfare Rights Organization workers who had a plan for a $6,500 minimum income for a family of four, the difficulty was that too few of his supporters understood how the dance of flirtation is always followed by the politics of withdrawal. In the mind of a political leader it is no betrayal to move away from people to whom you have made promises, provided your aim remains intact to fulfill the promise (or some part of it) when elected. The dance in between has been an employment of one another; during the period of closest attachment, stature has been given, after all, to unpopular demands. Now one might expect it would be obvious that McGovern was not going to capture the heart of America on a platform of abortion, legally free homosexuality and larger grants of welfare, not when thus hairy and wet a platform would be exposed to Nixon's oratorical gang for comment. If McGovern had been sympathetic to such causes in the first phases of his campaign, it was probably the reflection of an earlier attitude that he would not win the nomination but could at least come to Miami with a solid block of delegates to deal for position. Having far surpassed such early expectations, the time had now come to separate

himself with the minimum of damage, a *delicate* political
act made more difficult by the high passions of factions
so new to politics they could not understand that the basic
shift of emphasis going from a primary to a presidential
campaign was in getting ready to plunge into the muck
of public opinion, that same public opinion which was the
direct intellectual victim of fifty years of polluted reporting
and vested editorial writing. Public opinion had by now
a power of inertia which pulled every candidate (who
wanted to win) directly toward the center of the cess as
powerfully as the momentum of a spinning gyroscope will
maintain the axis at vertical.

Still, McGovern's blow fell with decency and dispatch.
It was an open convention. (Which by the language of
politics meant it was not utterly closed.) Brutality was
never employed. The gloom of late hours was successfully
invoked and the more embarrassing of the platform
debates took place near to dawn. At 5 A.M. delegates
paraded about the floor with signs saying "Free Walter
Cronkite," a show of good humor. Indeed, not too many
delegates were coerced. Most McGovern supporters were
simply told to vote their conscience. It was obvious that
nearly all of the Wallace, Humphrey, Mills and Jackson
delegates were going to be against anything like "ass, grass,
amnesty and abortion," so just a fraction of the McGovern
votes were needed to put down the planks. They were
employed. Down went the planks, and could be forgotten
if the questions they raised were not among the more interesting of the convention: the shape of political ideas to
come was conceivably in their content.

The homosexual plank proved the measure of lag
between sex and politics. To declare that there should be
no legal restriction on sex between consenting adults was
certainly a defensible idea of human conduct—one could
even believe, if religious, that homosexuality was a mortal
sin and yet see no reason for society to punish it, not
when the soul would have its full impost of karma to pay.
There was of course the conservative argument that legal
acceptance would tend to create an atmosphere of per-
missiveness, but, reversed, the argument was just as conservative: legalization was more likely to reduce anything
gay or exotic down to the size of marriage. Nonetheless,

a plank supporting the rights of homosexuals was political suicide. For it had the power to mobilize votes against you. Out in America, far beyond Miami, lived a damp dull *wad* of the electorate. They often did not vote. It took no ordinary issue to fire their seat. But the right to condemn homosexuality (and abortion! and welfare!) was a piece of their cherished rights: woe to the politician who would deprive them of rights. Homosexuality had to go.

And welfare as well. Was there an issue which put more poison into the liver of the Wad? It is bad to find oneself at the age of forty or fifty with monotonous work, meaningless family relations, and the cowardly fears of childhood alive again at the thought of walking the streets, but it is worse to recognize that there are healthy and insolent bodies prowling around out there who command the streets and they are living on the welfare one's taxes provide! Is there a cheap politician in America who has failed to invest this argument with all the wrath of his own fear that he doesn't have enough intelligence to be running for office?

It was not that thoughts of welfare could offer any happiness to a serious politician. One could hardly build moral equity in a society where some were paid for working and some were paid not to work—that was as basic to fouling good will as sweating the day shift in a factory to support a wife who is shacking up with boy friends in the afternoon. Every afternoon. When it comes to welfare, murderous emotions are quick. Yet who has the moral right to speak out against it? When Aquarius ran for mayor, he talked to women in some of the New York welfare organizations. They were not pitiable. They were proud. They told him, "People are always saying we're not entitled to welfare, we got illegitimate children, we got boys out there on drugs. Fuck em. We're the ones who got to raise the children. We're the ones whose apartments get robbed. Our welfare checks get stolen by the same junkies they're complaining about. Fuck em if they don't like my TV set or my rug. I'm as entitled to that as they are. I don't have too much money given me, I have too little. I want more. I'll tell you what I want, candidate for mayor, I want my share of the waste."

An incontrovertible argument. "I want my share of the

waste." So long as there were wars which had no meaning and smog whose smell was equal to the excessive profits which had been derived from creating excessive desires, so long as there was massive excessive irrational earth-destroying waste as empty as the fields of Vietnam after a hundred American bombers had passed over, then anyone on welfare was entitled to their share of the waste, indeed, had title whether they would work or not, for in a society which was abstractly and ubiquitously criminal, it might be a mark of merit for a man to choose a life of crime and swindle. Certainly, it demanded more initiative and risk.

But when he had talks at this convention with workers for welfare rights, he discovered they were serious about the subject in ways he was not, and the argument that people on welfare wanted their share of the waste aroused small interest. "The problem," said a welfare organizer named David Ipshin, "is that people on welfare have only the shit jobs to go to. So where is the incentive to work? The real question is whether society will ever be able to take people off shit jobs." Dark-haired, intent, his arguments moved with the force a good lineman might use in clearing a hole. "When we ask for that $6,500, we're trying to advance the idea that it's not the fault of poor people that they're poor. We're trying to get them out of that self-defeating bag where they look down on themselves because they have no money. We're looking to get them to respect themselves. And they need a little security for that. What the hell, they're just as much entitled to a chance for new consciousness as anyone else." Later, on the convention floor, on the night of the nominating speeches, he also talked to George Wiley who was head of the National Welfare Rights Organization, a tall pale Black with a full body and a Dashiki shirt. On Tuesday night the plan for the $6,500 minimum income for a family of four had been defeated 1,852.86 to 999.75.

"You didn't really think you were going to win, did you?"

"Not this year." Wiley gave a smile. "At least we made the floor and got voted on, and ran up a thousand votes." But it is the trap of the poor that they never get full measure. 999.75 votes!

Wiley had the polite and yielding manner of a man who hears the same arguments every working day, but is not prepared to yield anything other than his polite voice, since it is possible he has thought longer about the problem than anyone else. "The real perspective on welfare," Wiley said, "is exactly who will do the unpleasant work? *Shit* jobs are what it's all about. How do you solve that problem?"

"Well, how do you?"

"Maybe by letting people be paid in proportion to the disagreeability of a task." He said this softly as if not wishing to throw it away.

"A sort of existential wage? An existential economy— where money is a measure of the degree that work has invaded your existence?"

"Of course," said Wiley. "Exactly."

Was this the first new economic war-call since *Das Kapital?* It was better than "From each according to his ability, to each according to his needs," for it stayed closer to greed, ego, stamina, and desire. Aquarius' mind was racing to the convention of 1992.

14

On Monday at the Carillon, there had been a Women's Caucus, and behind the speaker's podium a large hand-lettered banner declaring WOMEN POWER was attached to the curtain. Viewed from his angle off to the side, he first read it as OMEN POWER, a tribute to witchcraft in the new political cosmos.

When McGovern addressed OMEN POWER, an incident occurred. The speaker who introduced him said that one reason they were able to attend the convention in large numbers was because of McGovern's efforts to open the party to women.

McGovern rose, and said with modest humor, "The credit for that must go to Adam."

He was booed. "Should I have said Adam and Eve?" asked McGovern. But the laughter was tight-lipped. A humorless friction was in the air. Hisses continued. This cold reception was due warning. Not since militant Blacks arrived on the American scene, had a political group appeared who were as threatening. But there had been a legitimacy to the ugliest Black demands, obviously still was —every injustice against a black man poisoned the root of America's existence. Whereas every injustice against a lady in Women's Liberation gave every promise of poisoning her husband's existence. But just this was the intolerable disproportion of Women's Liberation—they pretended to a suffering as profound as the Blacks, when their anguish came out of nothing more intolerable than the intolerable pointlessness of middle-class life. (Which of course was as intolerable for the men.) So Women's Liberation might be a totalitarian movement, yes, more totalitarian than not was its style. It appeared to speak for a volcano of legitimate furies but its rage was more likely to derive from boundless seas of monotony, and so a species of schizophrenia resided in some of the chillier demands. Ms., for example, spoke of the totalitarian passion for spoiling the language. Mr. at least stood for Mister. But how did one pronounce Ms.? Was it Miz or 'ims? Wherever it could create a mood, language gave life to the human condition; mood was a bed of rest for the nerves. Totalitarian was the need to inject non-words into the language, slivers of verbal plastic to smash the mood. If Aquarius had a simple idea, it was that language had been a creation of the female, first forged from the sounds of communication between herself and her young. But it was a natural mark of the Twentieth Century (perverse to the core of its historical knots) to use the representative of each human promise to defeat that promise. So any dependence of ecology upon the resonance of mood would now be shattered most quickly by women.

No surprise, then, if they booed McGovern for giving the credit to Eve. She was a comic book creation of the male chauvinist pig Jehovah; Eve was acquiescent nature with tits to pop for *Playboy,* and a sea-smelling cunt. Whereas the pride of Women's Liberation was that cunts had the right to smell as bad as any man's half-dead cigar. There was the total Twentieth-Century proposition! Of course, Aquarius' real opinion was that at the bottom of Women's Liberation was all the explosive of alienated will, a will now so detached from any of the old female functions, and hence so autocratic that insanity, cancer, or suicidal collapse might have to be the penalty if the will did not acquire huge social power. Totalitarian power. What a fund of scientific jargon was their ideology. They spoke of the nonexistence of the vaginal orgasm (which was a way of certifying that they had never had one) since it was indeed most likely that the vaginal orgasm involved some temporary surrender of the will to something else, whether man, god, nature or some portion of the cosmos termed "It," but the vaginal orgasm was surrender just so much as the full orgasm of the man was the giving over of his will to something other in himself or in his woman or in the split vision of his fuck. So the best operative definition of a female in Women's Liberation might be that she had so little notion of vaginal orgasm she was convinced it did not exist and thereby was fortified in her contention that the clitoris was the last station on the line. But the liberator was wrong. Suicide was the terminal station. For people of outrageous and buried will, the failure to attain power is suicide. The liberator is first a woman of murderous will, but then many a suicide is an absolute murderer who is finally reduced to the absolute humiliation of killing himself.

Now, if this was his own prejudice (all because the women booed McGovern for invoking Eve), still one had to recognize that the best was usually bent like a line to the worst. So Aquarius had to contend more than once with a recurring recognition that Women's Liberation had given birth to some revolutionary ideas which he had to respect: the first was their view on abortion. If he had supported the legal right to abortion for as long as he could remember, even took an unadmitted intellectual pleasure in the way the problem buttressed his political philosophy as a left conservative, it was because he found himself in favor of abortion but opposed to contraception; even, by his logic, more opposed to the pill than the pharmacological reek of the diaphragm. The latter offered, at least, a choice each night, whereas the pill removed the dignity of such choice, and so invaded the undeclared rights of the fuck whose romantic imperative is to prevail —against all odds! Something had to be lost when there was no last possibility for lovers to declare, "This fuck must be apocalyptic—why else reach in, remove the plug, and try to have a child?" Yes, upon such remote and unendurably sentimental possibilties did any larger dignity of a fuck depend, for the act of love which discharged into chemical fences of the pill bore the same relation to capital punishment as the old California gas chamber, whereas the apocalyptic fuck owed a little at least to the early Christian who survived the lions.

Of course, abortion, in its turn, was a classical curb against excesses of the romantic spirit. Embryos extinguished by abortion were more likely to be the product of extraordinary fucks than the legal infant who saw the first light in a hospital—all too often embryos who were to be aborted had been conceived in the first place by too many good things happening not to conceive them. Since it is hard to imagine an optimistic view of human nature which would not assume that those who are born out of apocalyptic fucks are more likely to be rich in potential than those conceived from a dribble, abortion is tragic. (In clear opposition, it is exactly the logical premise of the technological society that artificial insemination is the perfect equal of any great fuck, so much so that readers can recognize themselves as advocates of a technological society if they believe such a proposition.)

Seen by this perspective, there was the real possibility then that abortion killed off more than an average proportion of superb babies: if so, advocates of the Right To Live had a powerful argument. Aquarius, nonetheless, would remain in favor of abortion; he thought the argument had only been raised to a higher level. For if at its most tragic, abortion is the decision to kill the memory of an extraordinary night, and so can be cruel and unendurable, close on occasion to creating insanity in the woman, still abortion is the objective correlative of sanity. Even in the abysmal condition of much love lost, it always speaks, it says: "My nature is divided between the maximum of my romantic moments and the minimum of my daily self-calculation, too divided to permit this child to live. Finally I prefer to be loyal to my working habits rather than to the recollection of magic." Abortion is therefore an act of self-recognition (which is a step to sanity) even as the decision not to have an abortion is another kind of sanity which states, "I am committed to the best moments I have known and take my truth from that." (Which is why the pill like all other technological concepts is an insulation against sanity for it inhibits the possibility of those confrontations which might reveal a woman to herself.)

The real argument to be presented then to advocates of the Right To Live is that if a woman had the ability to begin an extraordinary conception, she had also the right to terminate it. Who could be certain that a more virulent pollution was not given to existence every time a child was born with remarkable potential and failed to fulfill it than when a soul of such potential was murdered in the womb? Nobody had a deeper sense of what could be provided for a future child than the woman who carried it. If she knew she was not ready to devote herself to such a creation, then why not assume she was in her right to deny the life? For who could ever calculate the violation left on life, or the extinction of karma, which resided in the loveless development of souls who had been conceived in love? So he thought abortion of even the most apocalyptic fuck was still the measure of a woman's right. Therefore, when it came to the question of abortion for conceptions which had never been wanted (creations emerging out of such resolute mediocrity of impulse as to shatter every romantic idea that conception was a serious product of human state), well then Aquarius could find no argument against abortion at all, not when the world was in danger of being overpopulated with a new wad who promised to be as uninteresting as the mass architecture which would house them, no, better to let abortion have its legal status and become still another social hypocrisy that it was not murder even if, indeed, it was.

The women of the liberation had come up, however, with an idea which went further than his own, and he admired it. Abortion legislation would of course be equal to giving women a new right to control what went on within their bodies. The extension of that principle was wondrous! It might give patients the right to die in peace when doctors were determined to extend, stupefy and therefore shift their last meditations before death. It might even open the idea that soldiers had first rights over their own bodies and need not go out on patrol if in their opinion there was an unreasonable or foolish chance that they might die. That was equivalent to saying soldiers could demand the right to military actions in which their death would not be in vain, an altogether stimulating idea, for in nations of one hundred million men would there then be ten thousand willing to die in an army? What a fine inhibition upon the power of mammoth countries to wage mammoth war if this became a principle of the world, which of course it would (just so soon as the Age of Aquarius arrived).

So one did not quit the thought in a hurry.

Still, this was no Age of Aquarius, but the summer of 1972, and the McGovern forces, thinking of the choleric priapism of the wad forced to contemplate all those vaginas open to abortion, had an understandable caution before the language of the plank. Mild almost to the point of being inoffensive—"In matters relating to human reproduction each person's right to privacy, freedom of choice, and individual conscience should be fully respected, consistent with relevant Supreme Court decisions," the plank would still suggest that the right to abortion was part of a proper election campaign. So McGovern's platform man, Ted van Dyk, sent out word to McGovern delegates that if they felt "strongly," they "should feel free to vote accordingly." The vote for the platform change on abortion would be free. Of course, not entirely. There were 250 whips on the floor for McGovern, each with a half-dozen delegates to contact, and some of the whips were employed to discover those delegates who would switch their vote "in an emergency" or abstain. Something like an emergency may have developed, for Rick Stearns was reported later to say, "If we hadn't sent out our word, the abortion plank would have passed." It failed by a vote of 1,569.80 to 1,103.37, and so a switch of 250 votes, or less than one McGovern delegate in six, would have been enough to pass it. The women were furious. First South Carolina, now abortion. Of course, there is always the parochial masochism of politics which is ready to welcome betrayal for the pleasure of the bitterness it provides. Some people are in politics to find a focus for all their latent bile, and nothing generates bile like betrayal. So the women were acting like women—in a fight with the husband: they were now superior to male arguments of priority and proportion. McGovern would be nominated the next day—they were not so furious as to interfere with that—but in the weeks to come when the Eagleton affair would weigh down an election special which was perhaps doomed never to ride and hardly to fly, Aquarius would think more than once of the unvoiced curses of OMEN POWER.

15

Wednesday, he gets to see Shirley Chisholm. She has doubled the glory of her campaign overnight by telling the Black Caucus, "I'm the only one among you who has the balls to run for President," her barb so perfectly splitting the shaft of the last arrow she has fired into their ranks (by accusing some of the delegates of being bought) that the Black Caucus gives her a standing ovation. Now in her room on the twentieth floor of the Deauville (which is guarded by a young woman in the Secret Service, blond and attractive) Shirley, who weighs 98 pounds, is ordering a meal, soup and meat and spaghetti and a Key lime pie (gift of Rocky Pomerance) for dessert. It is enough to put weight on a 200-pound man. "Oh, I burn it all off," she says. And she would. She moves as quickly as a sparrow when she speaks and her arguments pile out nonstop—she is as related to politics as the air is to the wind, and she is soaring on a zephyr now: after coming to the convention with 25.4 delegates, no more, it is obvious she is going to gain ground. And each time Mr. Chisholm, a man whose features and build are as round and reserved and benign as Shirley's are pert and to the point, comes into the room, it is to tell her she is wanted again on the phone. Shirley is having dreams as delegates keep coming to her. It is Wednesday afternoon and she says, "McGovern is in more trouble than he realizes. We're going to give him a surprise tonight," but it is not as if she believes she will stop McGovern, more as if her arguments on any subject must come from a positive base. So now, in response to a question, she calls McGovern a decent man and says she will work for him, "but you know he made a real error in underestimating the innocence of those gay liberationists.

He should have told them he would let them down." She nods her head. "He just assumed they'd understand he was running for President and couldn't afford them. But they're new to politics. Now, they're mad, and they're all flocking to me." A white delegate obviously gives her just as much joy as a black delegate. "You see, I was salty with them from the start, so they trust me now. I started talking to them about bank presidents who are homo and hide it, and I said, 'Don't pretend you speak for your whole group, or that homosexuals are some kind of an elite. Half your people aren't with you, don't even want to be identified as part of your constituency.' I let them have it straight and they like it. Same with the black delegates when I lay it on them. I don't mind getting their vote bought. They're poor people, and poor people always need the money. I just say to them, 'Take the money and run—don't let them fool you. Use them, don't let them use you,' " and when the interview is up, a film crew is moving in, and she is finishing her meal and getting ready to meet some more delegates. In her office, Helen Butler her secretary has put up a sign which is perhaps designed more for the white girls than the black— "We left our maid in Washington, so everybody has to clean up."

16

We can pass easily over Wednesday night when McGovern was nominated. Senator Ribicoff who put him up in Chicago four years ago was here to do it again, but the occasion was quieter. No need on this night for Ribicoff to speak of "gestapo tactics on the streets of Chicago," nor was Mayor Daley there to shout "Fuck you" across the floor. The demonstration while vigorous was brief, it had been coordinated to be brief—something like a total of half an hour for nominating speech, seconding speeches, and demonstration was allotted to each candidate, and Jackson, Chisholm, Wallace, Terry Sanford of North Carolina, McGovern and Mills had all to be nominated. So the demonstrations were cut. It was a bow to the Media; for years the newspapers and TV had been mocking the sight of red-faced heavy-paunched Democrats cavorting drunkenly in the aisles as they blew their noisemakers, and McGovern with his taste for restraint doubtless agreed with such a verdict. But no convention had ever seemed more like an endless litigation before a worn-out jury of thousands, no convention had ever been more in need of the primeval hysteria of an all-out demonstration which might remind the delegates of the fires which resided beneath. A convention had always been a court of political process, but it had also been a circus—which had been part of its value—a fair measure of the American desire to move back and forth between vulgarity and justice. But the old-fashioned demonstration was too hot a phenomenon for the cool shades of TV. That depended upon a shift of narrative line controlled as carefully as the rising of yeast. TV could not bear shifts in tone which were too abrupt. No more could it tolerate a series of images which progressed to no development. Besides a screaming caterwauling demonstration for the candidate ruined any illusion that the event had entered the living room of the viewer; demonstrations obviously took place in somebody else's house and you were alone with the set. Media executives didn't work at giving a careful wipe to the bottom of every last viewer in TV land in order to remind them that watching TV was an essentially unsatisfactory act. So there was no brassy, wild, nor overextended demonstration. A pity. Who knows how many points the Democrats dropped to the wad by offering no circus?

Later, there was a victory party at the Doral where McGovern kids wandered happily about. The final count had been 1,864.95 for McGovern, and Frank Mankiewicz smiled happily on TV when he mentioned the sum, for it was possible he came as close as anyone at the convention to knowing how each vote was gotten. For the rest, Wallace had received 377.5, Jackson—in a fever of activity once Humphrey and Muskie dropped out—had 486.68, Chisholm 101.45, Sanford 74.5, Mills 32.8, and other votes were scattered for names not placed in nomination: McCarthy, Muskie, Humphrey, Kennedy, Hayes and Mondale. There was no move to make the nomination unanimous. Indeed it would have failed. And the streets were quiet on the way back. The helicopters had gone home, as well as the solicitors on the street. Gone were the Jesus freaks with their broken teeth, a lightning zigzag of sharp and broken teeth and lightning in their eye, but then they looked like an improbable mix of rednecks and Zippies. They sang out to every delegate "You're here to raise hell, I'm here to raise heaven." They sang on street corners. "Who does Wallace need? Jesus," they replied. "J.E.S.U.S." "Who does Humphrey need? Jesus," they replied and went by rote through each of the candidates. "What do the Democrats need? Jesus," they sang. "What do the Republicans need? Jesus! J.E.S.U.S. Go, go, go," they cheered, and cops waiting through the quiet hours while the convention inched its way into history were playing card games for small stakes on the grass behind the wire fence in the cool of a banyan tree. A kid in a denim jacket carried an anti-McGovern placard. Earlier that day a crowd of several hundred had invaded the lobby of the Doral to protest a remark McGovern had made the night before that he planned to keep "military capability—in Thailand and on the seas," and the candidate had taken the dangerous step of coming to the lobby to talk to them and say, "I'm not shifting my position on any of the fundamental stands I've taken in this campaign." Maybe the placard had been painted earlier, and now wobbled in the languid midnight air as a remnant of the afternoon action: "McGovern sucks." A black man in a dark suit carried the morose sign "Don't Vote '72."

Back at the Doral, however, was every incongruous mix of the McGovern kids, all there, Phi Beta Kappas with clean faces and clean horn-rimmed glasses, their presence to offer clear statement of a physiology which had little taste for liquor and much taste for good marks, as well as a horde of suburban youth with long hair and the sense of boredom of waiting on still another evening for some tribal Left wind to touch the hair of their nostrils. Out on the driveway of the Doral were kids wearing no more than white canvas shorts and copper bracelets on their biceps, their bare feet padding the asphalt to a beat which came to them out of Ravi Shankar by way of stereos in Scarsdale, and the mystery of America floated up upon Aquarius still once again. For the social phenomena of the country were as clear as the expressions on groups of faces, yet never a period of four years elapsed in which you saw the same expressions again, America kept shifting, growing more wild even as it grew programmed, more unbalanced as it became stable, the blood of the heart beating with thoughts of the frontier even as the suburbs choked the ponds and killed the trout, and now this latest phenomenon of the technological young and the drug-steeped young both out equally for McGovern, man of principle, clear-headed and altogether separate in mind and style from any vocation for drugs. It was enough to begin to brood on the nature of those reforms the Democrats had put into their party, new pockets for an old suit, but the pockets had become the cloth of the suit, and the young were wearing it. There was humor at the thought of those party bosses who had first agreed to cut the pockets in the comfortable cynicism that it would be an easy way to store the demands of minorities in the party, a sophisticated species of tokenism whose losses could be absorbed by the old pols in state-house committees. After the debacle of Chicago, it was also seen as a way of putting the party together. No old pol had seen reform as the instrument which would yet take his power away, nobody had been prepared for the possibility of a man laboring for years to set up a code of rules which would work to the benefit of his own candidacy. Nor had any old pol come close to the real meaning of the radicalization of the surburban middle classes (who were finally the parents of these children at the Doral). The country club gentry of ten thousand suburbs (cognoscenti of the golf course, the paddock and the beauties of the jury-rigged spinnaker—Republican, of course, to the bone) had been replaced, or was it swarmed over by millions of families newly prosperous, newly endowed with educations, specializations and professions, and absolutely alienated—or by their own view blissfully delivered—from the old inch-along eat-your-gut game of social advancement in country living under the inspection of one's betters. There were simply not enough betters left to go around. Nor was there anything left to respect. The war in Vietnam had done much to take away one's faith that lawn tennis, proper posting, and a nose for the shift of wind had any value in the training of leaders when the most powerful nation in the history of the world had squandered its moral substance in a war of massive bombardments, near to meaningless, a wholly cancerous war of the technological age. (Of course it is possible that the cancer cell, if possessed of a voice, would argue that it is trying to redesign a way out of the insoluble contradictions of the body.) But then if the Devil was devoted to destroying all belief in conservative values among the intelligent and prosperous, he could not have picked a finer instrument to his purpose than the war in Vietnam. If one continued to ask why America still remained in Vietnam, the final remark History might make was what exceptional power could be possessed by such a small Far Eastern land that it might preside over the slaughter of America's belief in itself, preside over it indeed to such a degree that our climate was finally prepared for peace with China and Russia, an event equal to admitting that America no longer saw itself as a hero facing two villains on a field of Colossi, but rather was ready to look upon itself as still one more corrupt and tarnished protagonist now as much in need of coexistence as any of the new found friends. Small surprise if the newly prosperous liberals of the suburb welcomed the idea that all principles of the Establishment—God, nation, family, marriage, patriotism, and the distinction of the sexes—were wrong or nonexistent: the social contract, far from being a mystical union between God and man, was a pottage of curds whose lumps were best dissolved by disbelief. Liberal with their money, and liberal to every idea which was anathema to the Establishment: women's liberation, welfare rights, minority rights, tax reform (it was their pride, their delight, and their levitation from guilt that McGovern's tax reform would hit them hardest), they were also devoted to every right and liberty which would make humans more equal in soul and body. Of course, the center of their aesthetic was the androgynous. A wonder that McGovern was their candidate! But a small wonder so soon as the law of political sex appeal is invoked, for if there was a man in America who was more of a Wasp than Richard Nixon did it not have to be George McGovern? A joy then that the minister was ready to join the swingers! And pick up the children of suburbia as well, those children who lived in a far advancement of the ideological confidence of their parents, for the children were rid completely of the idea that one's personal development might still be measured by the ways one could perform in relation to some code handed over by the cultural lights and sneaky vested needs of the prosperous community, no, one was a child of light, and the enlightenment was new—the sanction to act came from within the body. Did streamings of energy from the body reach out to that horizon where one could join the world stream of new consciousness stirring?—then one was part of a new historical process which no one could comprehend whose body was not part of the stream. If drugs were the inner circle òf the new world family and acid rock the second circle, sex the third, well politics, was always on the outside circle of them all, a condition of valence with loose electrons which could be picked up or shed at amazing speed. So the suburban young would plunge into politics until the disillusionment of events would strip all outside electrons. Then they wandered, inert, passing

through fluids of consciousness, waiting for the hypo-
dermics of social action to inject a few electrons they could
spend again. Be certain they were a curious force for old
pols to comprehend! One could never know in which
given season they would exhibit the dedication of the
damned or seal themselves back to apathy again—although
rare was the spring of a year for presidential election which
would not act as catalyst.

This year the suburban young had come out for McGovern, come out in all the muted arrogance of their world
confidence that there on the other side of the world, un-
known faces were closer to them than the compromised
tissues of squalor in the faces of the old pols. And if with
their much discussed tribal sense, they made a good army
of volunteers, it was not surprising. Their egos were tribal.
So their narcissism was for the group—therefore they could
for a period immerse themselves in the absolute lack of
vanity which routine political work will demand. And were
joined to a cadre of hard workers on the left of the Democratic party, a corps of schoolteachers and hard-working
professionals, who together with the socially-minded, the
community-minded, and the decent-minded, outraged by
Vietnam, helped McGovern to do well in the early primaries. After them came the money, the glory, the political
technology, and the winning of the nomination at last. Now
kids with long sunburned hair and bronzed bodies, wearing
copper bangles and spaced-out heavy eyes, sat nodding on
the steps of the Doral, kin across all the stages from Flamingo Park to the delegates to the hard-working Phi Beta
cadres, holding in common a species of belief in the man,
McGovern, even if they could hardly comprehend the gulf
between the mindlessness of the Mind which might have
brought them here, and the outraged motors overhead of
helicopters looking for some wildman or freak or assassin
upon whom the helicopter could charge with a beating of
blades and a reduction of pressure in the great gorged
military-American industrial choleric and McGovern-suf-
focated great American hard-fucking motor-heart. Around
the pool forty or fifty kids were sitting quietly on benches,
only two were in the water, and off to the side a boy was
playing a violin. Where was the bourbon and broads of
yesteryear? Yes, every sense of power in the Democratic

party had shifted. History had become a crystal ball whose image shivered so erratically one had to wonder if a TV set was transmitting the image or the underworld of crystal balls was in convulsion.

17

On Thursday afternoon, with McGovern nominated, and only the last night of the convention still to be enacted, a final press conference was scheduled at the Sheraton-Four Ambassadors for George Wallace. Yet when the Press arrived, the Governor did not appear. At his Sheraton headquarters there were always two opposed sets of reports on his physical condition. Some officials would speak of his splendid progress, of the hours he spent in calisthenics, his prowess with a medicine ball, the development of the muscles in his arms, his zest to get well, and his unbelievable stamina in talking to visiting delegates—other officials were always taking one aside with a haunted look in their eye (as if no one could describe the scenes of pain and torture they had just witnessed) to say that the Governor had to call off all meetings because he was feeling poorly.

In any case, since this was the last opportunity to see Wallace in public, the Press was furious, and a long delay in waiting for his Press Secretary, Billy Joe Camp, and his National Campaign Director, Charles Snider, helped nothing. When they finally appeared, Snider read a Wallace statement which Aquarius reconstructed from his notes. "We came to the Democratic National Convention to carry the message of the people. We would have hoped they would accept this message from the average citizen across the country. They did not. Now we will see the results of this convention's thinking in November. We know what we have done in Miami has been good for America."

"Does this mean the Governor is starting a third party?" came the question.

"It means what it says," said Snider. He was short and very well built with blond hair and the confident close-

cropped features of a man who has made his money early
in construction. But Snider being called away for a few
minutes, the Press Secretary, Billy Joe Camp, was left
alone at the podium, and he had a gentle manner, and the
unhappy look of a Ph.D. candidate who is in danger of
flunking his orals. Since the drama of the arrival had
ground down steadily all week, Wallace's appearance at the
convention muted and far from climactic, the majority of
the delegates receiving him with all the enthusiasm of marble walls, his changes in the platform rejected, and his own
politicking with the delegations kept carefully away from
the Press, there had been less and less to report. Wallace's
absence today was the final rebuke to the Media. So they
took it out on Billy Joe Camp, who stood there in his dark
brown suit and brown-and-white tie, stood there with his
soft and cherubic mouth hanging loose beneath his dark
hair and dark horn-rimmed glasses (which looked to keep
sliding down his small soft nose) and tried to field every
impossible question with Southern courtesy. The questions
were impossible because he had no answers to give. He did
not know what the Governor thought about this. He certainly did not know what the Governor thought about that.
No, the Governor had said nothing to him, no, he could
not satisfy the last question, no, he was sorry he had no
information on this particular topic. After much phumpher-
ing and several long silences which he could only end by
declining to answer once again, a newspaperman flicked a
whip. "Billy Joe, don't you ever get the feeling that you're
locked out of information?"

Snider came back to help him. Snider stood in front of
the podium with his legs apart, as if at parade rest, weight
on the balls of his feet. Wearing a pale cream suit, a yellow
shirt, and a well-chosen light-blue-and-light-brown figured
tie, he suggested the aplomb of a Marine who is wearing
the world's best clothes.

"Is there going to be a third party?"

"The statement will have to come from the Governor."

"Will Wallace talk to McGovern?"

"If Senator McGovern calls Governor Wallace before we
leave, I know the Governor will be polite to him because
the Senator now holds a position the Governor respects as
nominated candidate of the Democratic party which the
Governor respects very much."

"But do you, Charles Snider, think McGovern is a loser?"

"I, personally, do."

"Does the Governor?"

"I haven't gotten the Governor's thoughts on it."

"Will he start a third party?"

"I don't know."

"Will you advise him to?"

Snider looked back in scorn. "The Governor is the most astute politician on the face of the earth," he said in his Southern voice, "and I wouldn't presume to advise him on whether to start a third party."

"But yesterday didn't you make a statement that you wanted him to?"

"I made some remarks. A few may have been of that nature."

"Was the Governor displeased?"

"He wasn't too displeased, or I wouldn't be here right now. I don't have to go up to the twentieth floor to get the news if he don't like something. I get it right here on the third floor."

"So the Governor is thinking of a third party?"

"Now, look," said Snider, "I'm not going to answer any more questions on a third party. The Governor has more political intelligence in his little finger than I have in all of me. I wouldn't presume to speak for him. I'll just tell you this. If what happened in Maryland had not happened, and the Governor had been active through Oregon and California, I think you would have found a tremendous difference in the way we came to this convention and in the way we were received. And you all would have seen what the Governor is like in action, and there is no one who can compare to him, believe you me. He would have come in with all the power of all the people who believe in him which is a tremendous power because I believe that the Governor is the greatest messenger who has ever been on the face of this earth . . ."

"Including Jesus?" came a voice from the Press. The question was from a reporter with an aquiline nose and a beard like a Saracen.

Snider stopped as if he had just run into a pole. He bared his teeth in a good-boy grin. "I knew I could expect something like that from you and the fine magazine you work for," he said.

Hours later, catching him for a moment outside the convention, Aquarius asked if the reporter's question hadn't been legitimate. After all, Snider *had* said "the greatest messenger ever."

"Oh, I see what you mean," said Snider. "I should have said, 'the greatest political messenger.' " He shook his head. "Why," he added with shock, "I would never compare the Governor to Jesus. How can you? *Nobody* compares with Jesus."

18

There were arts to picking a Vice-President, and the first was the name. Your ticket became a company. Recognize that a man named Procter running for President would look for Gamble to go along. McGovern had the best of good monikers for a liberal since thoughts of the Conquering Celt had to be aroused in many an illiterate and reactionary head. At the least, could Mick Govern fail to give promise of Irish home rule? There was a percentage of voters (10 percent, 20, or more) who came to the secrecy of the election booth without a political thought in their head—they knew the name of the President and sometimes they knew the name of the man who ran against him. In the isolated terror of the booth, where voting was a religious act to inspire awe in the simple, God being closest to you when alone, the sound of the names on the ticket could be enough to catch your vote. The problem was to find the name to go with McGovern. Kennedy would of course have been acceptable no matter how, Teddy Kennedy belonged to a higher order of powers than euphony or the symbol of a word, but he was not available. If it was McGovern's first act upon being nominated to receive his midnight call, it was the Senator from Massachusetts' first response to congratulate McGovern and then to refuse. "For very real personal reasons." Despite every warning, McGovern's staff had hoped in common with the candidate that the ticket would bring them together but McGovern —according to Jimmy Breslin—now told his people that if he pushed Kennedy into the nomination and anything ever happened to Kennedy, he would be unable to live with himself. Faced with the loss of the best possibility, their choice was thereby reduced to Ribicoff, Eagleton, Mills, Leonard Woodcock of the UAW, Governor Lucey of

Wisconsin, Mayor Kevin White of Boston, Gaylord Nelson of Wisconsin and Sarge Shriver. Plus a few others. One was Reubin Askew, a perfect name! Govern and Ask-You. However, the Governor of Florida had already said no—his ideology and McGovern's were too far apart. After a flurry with Ribicoff who also refused (out of the fine political sense, no doubt, that he had been invited to show McGovern's solidarity with the Jews but was expected to say no—McGovern and Ribicoff as a product would be reminiscent of ambulance chasers) there came the hard business of picking that Catholic, from a big city or an industrial state, who could best warm South Dakota's prairie vestments. The difficulty was that fewer people knew Eagleton, Mondale, Lucey, White or Shriver were Catholic than believed McGovern to be. So there was also talk of Woodcock of the UAW because he could help to offset the cess of old George Meany and bring the unions in. But McGovern and Woodcock was a name fit for a company which put out a special variety of Tabasco, manufactured a fine grade of bronze casket, or catered to the Queen's grounds with croquet equipment. McGovern and Lucey was worse. McGovern and Shriver had a poor sound—stationers, old pharmacists, something pinch-penny!—otherwise, why not have picked Shriver after Kennedy had refused?

Now, McGovern and Mills was a fine sound, management and manufacture well combined, an aura of industry and competence rose from the words, but the ideological gulf was still not navigable. On the other hand, McGovern and Gilligan were Irish whiskey, McGovern and Bayh were depressing (too many millions would not know how to pronounce Bayh, and when they did, nothing was gained but subliminal thoughts of farewell). There was McGovern and Nelson of course but the Senator from Wisconsin had a first name of Gaylord—help! There was talk of Frank Church as well. McGovern and Church would be the equal of Dr. Pepper in the Bible Belt but could one sell it to the Jews? Besides, Church was no Catholic, alas. The list was reduced to Eagleton and White, and as between the two, White was in. Eagleton had connotations of the American eagle, a stern virtue, a modest plus. But the company of McGovern and Eagleton offered no particular ring—camping equipment! George and Tom might be fine, but both family names ended in *n,* a nugatory sound, reminiscent in the lower depths of the collective unconscious of the wad as no-no. It was down to Kevin White, Mayor of Boston, a Catholic, a jewel of a ticket to mollify the most ignorant of the Wallace voters, Govern in a White way, yessir. If you were close to Black aims in your program, then it was wisdom to choose a man named White. But calls to the Massachusetts delegation were reputed to close that choice. They threatened to revolt on the floor. Kevin White was a fine Mayor of Boston, which is to say, a Boston pol and in politics up to his neck and sheepish with the memories of a deal or two, and ready by repute to stand up and shake a hand when told to, a superb Mayor of Boston but the thought of him as President—White was the size of a mayor. The choice moved back to Eagleton who was conceivably the size of a Senator, and there were warm stories that night on TV how Eagleton had become so nervous waiting that he drank many a gin and tonic and wore two different shoes. Indeed his first appearance on TV was excessively modest—a white damp and vastly perspired face swam into focus. "Sparrow Who?" said a reporter staring at the set. But first impressions shifted. Eagleton had a nervous running humor which was sweet-tempered, then agreeable: he borrowed from the style of Carson and Cavett—sparks of wit were struck from the gait of an ongoing patter. *The New York Times* would later give him the Quotation of the Day, "Senator McGovern called me, and he said, 'This is George McGovern'—and I recognized the voice. And he said, 'Tom, I'd like you to be my running mate,' and I paused and it sounded like four seconds, and I said, 'Well, George, before you change your mind, I accept.' "

He was to do even better before the night was out. His family was seen in their box at the convention and his son who was ten or eleven had all the charm of the bright and assured, and spoke particularly well out of a delicate face. Later, Eagleton would give his speech of acceptance, and another side would show—he was a good and polished speaker, with considerably more power at the podium than in the sweat of interviews, something practiced and successful was now in his voice. That, however, did not take place until five hours later. It was two in the morning when Eagleton was nominated, and the run of bad luck for McGovern, which had begun with California in June, con-

tinued still. For the effort to win back the 151 delegates
had exhausted the resources of the staff every day before the
convention and through the first night, created the ill repute
of the lost South Carolina challenge and the insufficiency
of time to deal with Daley and Singer. Then maneuvering
over the platform used up their attention and energy on the
second night. By the time the nomination was won,
McGovern's staff needed sleep. Not until Thursday had
there been time to pick the Vice-President. Then—given
the mediocrity of the choices—it took until close to four
in the afternoon. So there was no opportunity to ask for
an afternoon session. The best television hours of the last
night were consumed nominating a number of candidates
who had no chance. McGovern, ready for the occasion of
his acceptance with a superb speech, was able to give it at
three in the morning. America had gone to sleep. Nobody
could ever calculate if the votes he might have gained
that night would tally in the millions.

As the small compensation, there was some action. Given
a political convention's definition of open—which is to say
cracked so wide as a slit—there was *open* action. Many of
the delegates' resentments broke open. Too few had heard
of Eagleton, and he was a Muskie man. There was annoy-
ance that McGovern was engaging in the old style of politics. Besides, the women, balked by failure to get the plank
for abortion, were in no mood not to nominate a female,
and gave their support to Sissy Farenthold after Shirley
Chisholm, out of the niceties of political decorum, refused.
Shirley might have done very well, but she was wise in the
political values of a single clear impression; her candidacy
had been a sentimental success. A second effort following
immediately on the first would have to be exceptionally
successful to improve the elegance of her status. So Farenthold, who had run well but unsuccessfully for Governor
against Dolph Briscoe in the Texas primary, became the
woman to enter the list. Against her, among others, was
Stanley Arnold, the businessman who campaigned with
full-face photographs of himself in horn-rimmed glasses
decorating all the hotel lobbies, a comic candidate despite
himself, and Endicott "Chub" Peabody who had traveled
through thirty-seven states looking for delegates and talking
of the need for a Vice-President who would be selected by
the people and thereby armed with a mandate from the

people. He had worked hard, harder than many a presidential candidate, but had the foul fortune to be immortalized by the old Kennedy court jester Dick Tuck who declared that Chub was the only man who had four towns named for him in Massachusetts: Endicott, Peabody, Marblehead and Athol.

Then there was Mike Gravel who provided considerable excitement in the first hours of the evening, the young Senator from Alaska, good-looking enough to have played leads in B films (if the Casting Director could decide whether to cast him as hero or villain). Gravel was regarded as something of a lone gun, a wild man from the West ever since he had read portions of the Pentagon Papers (which were Classified) to his Subcommittee on Public Buildings and Grounds. It had been a direct violation of the code of the Senate which looked upon Classified—that is, secret, documents as sacramental objects. Perhaps it was the thought of endless small punishments, or some large ones like censure that weakened his composure, but as Gravel read the following lines to television cameras in the Subcommittee room: "The story is a terrible one. It is replete with duplicity, connivance against the public. People, human beings, are being killed as I speak to you. Arms are being severed; metal is crashing through human bodies" he began—to his absolute horror—to weep. He had, he said afterward, passed through the nearest experience he had known of a vision, for as he spoke it was as if those bodies he described in Vietnam were milling about him; the flesh being rent was real; before his eyes, severed arms flew across the line of sight. He was overcome.

In the Senate they lauded him for courage, he was scalded for exhibitionism; the Department of Justice worked to convene a federal grand jury to investigate any possible violation of federal statutes; since the case involved the separation of powers between executive and legislative branches, it had already gone to the Supreme Court.

This proved no check to Gravel. He had already known that sensation of political transcendence which when it comes to senators leaves them ready to run for the highest office; invited to the White House soon after election to hear Nixon discuss the ABM, "it just dawned on me that he didn't know any more about it than I did." Even to politicians who are bold, there is still an instant when they let go of the modesty that men who run the world are possessed of qualities superior to their own. Gravel was bold. Winter nights in Alaska gave a man daring: even to visit a friend who lived ten miles away took daring. For if your motor stalled in the middle of the trip, you were alone on an empty road, the cold was down to fifty below, and you were therefore soon dead if the motor didn't start.

Gravel ran. Like Peabody, he cut across the principle that the choice of a Vice-President was an occasion for the nominee to exercise his art and add those strengths which would balance the ticket, unify the party, and ideally give some sense of excitement to the years ahead, a principle, obviously, which believed in the lore of the politician, subscribed to his craft, and honored his ability to live between privilege and justice, honesty and corruption, idealism and an adroit employment of the cynical—it was finally a view to suggest that politicians should not be morally better than other men so much as more skillful. Perhaps it was a sound principle. One could begin to measure its importance to the electorate by the disfavor McGovern's choice would yet bring upon him when it became evident he had exercised no more art than the use of crude rule of thumb.

Gravel, of course, was working on the opposed notion that a Vice-President, selected separately from the President, should serve in effect as an Ombudsman. "A person of the caliber of George McGovern would realize," Gravel remarked, "that having an in-house adversary within the executive would be an asset. Not a vicious adversary. The Vice-President should be pushing for the same programs and backing up the President. But I think he could back up the President much better as an independent agent than as a vassal."

An interesting idea. Its time, of course, had not quite come. The McGovern staff, now running the convention after nomination of their man the night before, were ready for all practical purposes to treat Farenthold, Arnold, Peabody and Gravel as, precisely, vicious adversaries. How account for the phenomenon which occurs in every political campaign once victory is in? The staff immediately discloses its secret passion is to get a good glove for the iron hand. No politician was kinder or more decent than McGovern—so said all. Who could say the same of his staff?

Not Gravel. On Thursday night when the vice-presidential
candidates tried to raise the issue of an open convention
for the nomination, their representatives could not get recognized. For to do so, they had first to phone the podium
and describe their purpose. The voice of the podium replied
that their motion was out of order, it could not be considered when it failed to be relevant to the business at hand.
But that, they protested, was exactly the issue on which
they wanted the convention to vote—whether to suspend
the rules. No, replied the podium, such a motion was at
the discretion of the Chairman. Where was the Chairman?
He was not available to come to the phone.

In the old days, a maverick could grab a microphone
and shout loud enough to get the floor. Now, the power
supply for all microphones was controlled by the podium.
So were passes to the floor. Eagleton's operatives had easy
access, the other candidates had next to none. Gravel's
workers sat outside the hall in their trailer, and were obliged
to communicate by phone. Friendly delegates called in to
report an anti-Gravel movement. Why, was it asked, had
Gravel voted for the ABM, Carswell, and the Alaska pipeline? He hadn't, cried his workers on the trailer phone.
Pass the word—he voted against ABM! and Carswell! and
the pipeline never came up for a vote at all!

A political tactic can now be absorbed: in a fluid situation, waging a quick war for delegates, it is obviously essential to have crack troops on the floor to serve up as many
lies about your opponents as they are spreading of you.
Access to the floor is access to that sea of prevarication
where the nomination may be launched. Gravel, now aware
that in an unsuccessful floor fight a man had nothing to
lose but his anonymity, succeeded in the high maneuver of
reaching the podium to speak for himself. His name scheduled to be put in nomination by Bettye Fahrenkamp, Democratic National Committee-woman from Alaska, the Committee-woman pretended to be faint with excitement at the
magnitude of her speech. So Gravel came along to give
support. Medical emergencies being always the best franchise to cross borders, they let Gravel approach the base of
the podium, where, unseen by the floor, he might smile at
her. But the lady's nominating speech was short. "The best
way for you to judge," said Bettye Fahrenkamp, "the next

Vice-President of the United States is not for me to tell you about him, but for you to hear and judge for yourself. My fellow delegates: Senator Mike Gravel."

He stood up to thank her, advanced to the podium, began to speak, and was stopped by the Co-Chairman, Yvonne Braithwaite Burke, a young black woman who was alternating with O'Brien. For hours she had delighted the convention with her wit, her speed, and her vivacity. She had been offering an unmistakable zap to parliamentary life. Now she was annoyed. The cool of the chair had been invaded.

Burke: Thanks a lot. Sorry. We just can't do it.

Gravel: You're telling me I can't talk to the delegates of this convention on behalf of my candidacy?

Burke: I'm telling you that I'm here to follow the rules and the rules say you can't talk.

She was still saucy and confident. But when he did not step down, her charm was withdrawn. In the instant, something palpable as stone came to her skin. She was a tough lady. Her eyes were empty of expression. Clearly they said, "Kidding is kidding, but get your ass off my pillow!"

Gravel: And I'm—I'm here to correct you on the rules. The rules say—the rules say very precisely that the person who seconds does not have to be a delegate. And I am therefore entitled to speak to these people.

Burke: Okay.

"You're making me look," said her expression, "like I don't know how to deal with a drunk. You have now gone and asked for it good." But she looked backstage for a legal interpretation. A general uproar had begun to rise from the floor.

Gravel: Is this an open convention? (*Cheers from the floor.*) If there is a parliamentarian let him come forward. . . . I'll be happy to hold my peace until we can get a ruling from the leadership of this convention.

Now, however, Yvonne Braithwaite Burke had gotten her signal from the rear. "Go right ahead," she said, and gave him the podium with a sidelong look, as if she had underestimated him.

He gave his speech. It was a good speech and might have been a better one. But he was perspiring from the hazards of first reaching the podium, then drilling into the formidable displeasure of Yvonne Burke's eyes. Now, as though lightly sandbagged across the kidneys, jostled just a hint in the high corner of the testes, Gravel went on with his plea to the convention:

"Select a person for the vice-presidency who is your choice, not a person who's been dictated to you. Pay no mind to the last-minute smears—whether against me or anybody else.

"The spirit of reform which has brought us all together will fade, this spirit will be compromised if you give in to a selection other than one of free and open choice.

"The vice-presidency belongs to the people of the United States."

There were cheers and boos.

"A little over a year ago, I released to the American people the Pentagon Papers." Cheers and applause. "What I did—was to give information to you, the American people, so that you could be more qualified in the exercise of your franchise.

"How can you get involved in government if you don't know what your government is doing?

"Let me paraphrase to you a dialogue between Senator Robert Dole, the head of the Republican party, and myself. Senator Dole said when I was attempting to introduce the Kissinger Papers—said, 'Senator Gravel, you're going to have to live with what you've done.' I answered back angrily: 'Senator Dole, I'm proud of what I've done. You're going to have to live with what you have not done.' "

His point was powerful as he declared, "Secrecy is the reason we're in Vietnam today committing genocide," but some of the juice was undeniably gone. He was, comparable to half the delegates on the floor, still a romantic—he had grown up in the belief that a great speeech carried fortifications before it. So had Gary Cooper spoken in *Mr. Deeds Comes to Town* and James Stewart in *Mr. Smith Goes to Washington*. But in politics even a great speech had to raise such a wave as to wash over the mountain, and Gravel could feel the defeat of such a possibility even as he came to the peroration.

"George McGovern had a magic that swept this country in the spring of this year. George McGovern can be the next President of the United States—not by doing less of

what was done in the spring, but by doing more of what
was done in the spring with George McGovern, and I hope
myself on the ticket.

"I thank you for your consideration and hope that you'll
consider my candidacy."

When he was done, well-wishers mobbed him as he descended from the podium. The floor of the convention was
alive. But it would never last. Hours of nomination of other
candidates were to follow, and the rains of prevarication
would muddy his ground. Gravel's troops, bereft of floor
passes, would molder in their trailer. No act on earth was
necessarily more difficult than to take a convention by
storm. Gene McCarthy had tried when he nominated Adlai
Stevenson in 1960, and it was the greatest nominating
speech in memory; the demonstration which followed gave
promise it would never cease, and didn't for sixty minutes.
Hours later, passions ground down to common meal, Jack
Kennedy was nominated without trouble. Tonight, with
just as powerful a machine, so would Eagleton get his required total on the first ballot and Gravel finish back of
Farenthold, and the incident be near to forgotten in the
agreeable force of Eagleton's speech, and the cornucopia of
cheers for Teddy Kennedy when he said, "There is a new
wind rising over the land. In it can be heard many things,
promises, anguish, hopes for the future, echoes of the past,
and our most cherished prayer. 'America, America, God
shed His grace on thee.' " Then came George McGovern,
speaking with animation to each roll of cheers, calling for
an entrance of democracy into the secret councils behind
the closed doors. "I want those doors opened and that war
closed." Cheers came again to him. "Let me inside the government and I will tell you what is going on." They ended
in the signs and tokens of unity, Humphrey, Muskie, Jackson, Chisholm and Sanford all holding hands with the
nominee. The mood was warm. The convention had run
before winds and beat through waves. Now they were done
and the ship would be put to bed. Up came the high medieval note of the hands marching off to the strains of "On-
ward Christian Soldiers."

Weeks later, Gravel would say with a grin, "The pioneer-
ing consumes you. The next guy walks on what you build."

19

Having come down now to the final minutes of the convention week with the speeches done, and the huge hall closed, the convention's aisles finally empty as if the echo of the chairman asking the delegates and Press to clear the floor had finally taken ghostly effect, having returned down Collins Avenue in the early morning for the last time, and having come in the final hour before dawn to the entrance of the Doral where hordes of the young, half-dressed in the heats of a late Southern night again gave an exotic sense of disarray while they lounged on the steps of the hotel (as if one were transported beyond Bombay to some future where Americans to come would sit half-naked in Lotus position before the gates of the American palaces), and having ascended the elevator and been brought and issued by the good will of Shirley MacLaine into the room of a private party in some roof garden of the Doral where McGovern was accepting the congratulations of some of the people of means who had helped to finance his campaign, Aquarius was able to take up position at last before the nominee and live in the charisma (or lack of it) his presence might convey. If there was all the warmth of a quiet and winning mood, and the sense of a vast relaxation as McGovern chatted for a few words with first a friend and then a sponsor, his tall body planted on legs which must have felt like posts of concrete after these two long years of campaigning, and these tense days of dealing and refusing to deal in Miami, the wealth of fatigue which came off McGovern now was happy and compassionate as the last rose-colored velvets of evening before the night was in, and it occurred to Aquarius that if he had stood next to many

politicians over the years, he had not ever before had such
a splendid sense that he was standing near a man who had
a heart which could conceivably be full of love—something awfully nice came off McGovern—and that was an
extraordinary gift for a politician to give. It clearly returned
Aquarius to the events of the convention and restored a
knowledge of why these days had been so agreeable and so
boring, and why the faces of the delegates massed in ranks
on the floor had been like no faces any political observer
had ever seen before, not in a convention hall, for they
were in majority the faces of men and women who had
come to have a good and serious time, like the faces of a
crowd who have gone to the most important basketball
game of the year in their home state, and so felt honored
to have the ticket of admission, and happy, and there to
squeeze the goodness in their will and determination out
across the air and into the bodies of their players—a sense
of *innocence* lived in more than half these faces as if they
had yet to learn of the deaths within compromise and calculation. One had to be partial to a man whose delegates
had the fair and average and open faces of an army of
citizenry, as opposed to an army of the pols, and Aquarius
knew then why the convention was obliged to be boring.
There was insufficient evil in the room. With all the evil he
had seen, all the lies and deals and evasions and cracks of
the open door, with the betrayals of planks and the voids of
promises, still there had been so little of real evil in the
room.

So one could know none of the fascination one found
at other conventions, when a walk on the floor was a promenade through vales of malignity or a passage through cor-
ridors of vested bile, and a study of faces was equal to a
study of American corporations and crime. There, in those
old conventions, the posture of political fixes came out in
the set of the hips when a deal was in, and the skill with
which it was once possible to read the moves of a convention (because the faces of the leaders and the gargoyle
heads of the minions had been as dead and carved and
fixed and ornamented forever as the pieces in a set of
chess), such skill was lost. There was now no leader to follow as he put a finger to his nose to tip the vote to the
leader across the aisle. The spell of drama when an evil

piece of political property was traded for a more or less
equal piece of profitable position was also gone, all gone
except for a delegation here and there, as old in appearance
with their baffled old-pol stone-set faces as the portraits of
another century, and of course one was ready to laugh as
one walked down the aisle because the count was already
in—there were more live faces than dead ones on the floor
—so McGovern was in, simple as that, and how different
a sensation and how less compelling than in the days of
other conventions when it was one dead face against another, and which of the candidates for nomination was best
equipped to enter the sinuosities of negotiation with evil,
for evil was the law of politics and the provender of the
floor.

Now there was a convention where delegates had come
to work. How diffident they were at parties and how good
at work—it was as if the animation of being at a party
came to them on the floor—their politics was their pleasure, and the tide of those faces returning to him as he
stood near McGovern now, there came to him as well the
first strains of that simple epiphany which had eluded him
through these days, and he realized it, and it was simple,
but he thought it true. In America, the country was the religion. And all the religions of the land were fed from that
first religion which was the country itself, and if the other
religions were now full of mutation and staggering across
deserts of faith, it was because the country had been false
and ill and corrupt for years, corrupt not in the age-old
human proportions of failure and evil, but corrupt to the
point of terminal disease, like a great religion foundering.

So the political parties of America might be the true
churches of America, and our political leaders the popes
and prelates, the bishops and ministers and warring clergymen of ideologies which were founded upon the spiritual
rock of America as much as any dogma, and so there was
a way now to comprehend McGovern and enter the loneliness which lived in his mood, for he inhabited that religious space where men dwell when they are part of the
powers of a church and wish to alter that church to its
roots. For yes, the American faith might even say that God
was in the people. And if this new religion, not two hundred years old, was either the best or the worst idea ever to

shake the mansions of eschatology in the world beyond, one knew at least how to begin to think of McGovern; if he had started as a minister in the faith of his father, he had left that ministry to look for one larger. When it came Aquarius' turn to speak to the new candidate of the Democratic party he felt content to say no more than that he had liked all three speeches at the end of the night. Eagleton, Kennedy, and the speech of the candidate himself, which was the best he had ever heard him give. And McGovern listened with that charisma which was finally and indisputably his own—which was to listen—for if his voice had no flaming tongue of fire, his power to listen surrounded everyone who spoke in his presence, and so had the depth to capture many a loyalty before he was done. Then the words of the speech came back to Aquarius:

"From secrecy and deception in high places—come home, America. From military spending so wasteful that it weakens our nation—come home, America. From the entrenchment of special privilege and tax favoritism—come home, America. From the waste of idle hands to the joy of useful labor—come home, America. From the prejudice of race and sex—come home, America. From the loneliness of the aging poor and the despair of the neglected sick— come home, America. Come home to the affirmation that we have a dream. Come home to the conviction that we can move our country forward. Come home to the belief that we can seek a newer world. May God grant us the wisdom to cherish this good land to meet the great challenge that beckons us home."

"I thought Ted Kennedy gave a very fine speech," McGovern said.

"He did. All the speeches were good. It was a fine mood, it was strong and tender," and McGovern nodded (as if it might be his own observation as well) and it was only after they had talked for another minute and Aquarius stepped back to listen to McGovern talk to others again that he realized he had used the word "tender" in speaking to a presidential candidate and felt no remorse and, agog on this realization, headed slowly for the exit with the rueful admission to himself that for the days left in which to write his piece he must leave out much in order to be able to put this little in, and thought McGovern was the first tall minister he had ever really liked, and so must have a chance to win the election. He kept his good mood until getting in the elevator when it happened that a dreamy Mc-Govern kid started to approach the car ahead of a Secret Service man who gave the practiced equivalent of a karate chop with a small quick blow of his shoulder—for nothing!—and the kid bounced off to the side and the Service man, carrying his drink in his hand, went in first and stared morosely into his glass as though those waters went all the way back to the raw seed of the hurricane. And if Aquarius had been a man to pray, he might have thought of the embattled God he discovered years ago. But then who had the right to ask the Lord to let America have one election which went all the way down the rails without a wreck? He shivered. The idea next to the unexorcised nomenclatures of Oswald and Sirhan left a discomfort on his back.

PART TWO

Politicians and Princes

1

Not ten days were gone and the derailment had occurred. With no deaths and no blood. Just a broken wheel on the election special, and the assailant proved to be one fine political fellow, Senator Thomas F. Eagleton of the railroad state of Missouri, indeed not even an assassin but a harried mechanic in a hurry to grease that golden axle on which his own wheel was going to be installed. He had neglected to mention the bit of grit in the bearing. A tortuous metaphor, but there may be torture in the idea that not all political assassinations call for death; there is also bloodless slaughter in the Media.

Once a politician used to work on his constituency to gain power in the party. Then the party worked to win election. The Press reported the result. While they led a number of the blind by editorial hand, more numerous were the legions of the unseeing carried to the polls by the party. But that was still in an age of Herbert Hoover and Roosevelt and Truman. By the time Eisenhower was first elected, the Media was beginning to make history as well as report it and Richard Nixon was its foundling. By the year of Goldwater's nomination, the Media had already become a mirror which reflected every curse back upon its sender, a Holy Ghost to intervene with every political conception. At its most palpable, the Media had *droit de seigneur* in its pocket, and had become a force between the party and the public with a license to rape the candidate or his party. Media would even create giants so that it could listen to the sound of their fall. In the groans of the dungeon, Muskie might give testimony to this. It was even possible that Nixon was the gymnast of the dungeon and the only man to scale the Media wall, for Nixon had survived! He breathed a summit air the Media did not inhabit. In recompense, Media dominated the levels below. One could not give issue to an event before the Media explored the potentiality of the event. Like a doctor who overadministered to every wheeze, the Media interrupted each national symptom until the specific ill was wasted and the general malaise was general. So a clear-cut discovery of buried secrets was aphrodisiac. On the instant, Thomas F. Eagleton's medical history became the best political story to come the Media way in many a month, and if one looked for a criticism of McGovern when all was done, it was to question the final acumen of a man who could assume that such a story would not engorge every issue before it and quickly become the center of the campaign.

2

Interviewing Eagleton on the afternoon of the morning
of his resignation as vice-presidential candidate, Aquarius
finds him changed from the diffident politician who perspired before the television cameras on the night of his
nomination and looked too furtive, too nervous, too quick,
too quick-tongued, too bright, too unsure of himself and
finally too modest to be Vice-President. Now in the two
weeks and more which had elapsed since nomination and
through the last seven days of disclosure the nightmare of
his most secret life has blazoned every breakfast table, as
well as the political shame of his treatment in a mental hospital for electric shock, not once but then and again, 1960,
1964, 1966, all kept so secretly by the family and skillfully
over the years that even the worst of the whispering cam-
paigns against him hinted at drink as a serious problem—an
excusable vice in a politician. But never shock. Shock spoke
of incarceration, not treatment, of manacled hands and the
possibility of a blasted mind. For there was the public
prejudice and who to refute it? A man who drank too much
could be wrestling for his soul and losing it—implicit was
the idea he might yet regain it. A heavy drinker could still
carry on a political life—the impost of booze spoke of a
war against too much of some powerful quality in oneself,
too much perhaps of passion, talent, or pain. But shock
treatment spoke of the irrevocable. Cures derived from a
machine, when the cure itself was not comprehended, left
an aversion. Nobody could argue that the cure had not
come from blinding the innermost eye of the soul—so went
the unspoken weight of public prejudice, and who to refute
it? Not Eagleton when it was obvious he had made the
choice to let rumors of drinking hang him first. (His disap-

pearance into the Mayo Clinic had even been once announced as a visit to Hopkins for gastric disturbance.)

Now, in the last week, the secret of his life disgorged,
he sat behind his desk in the New Senate Office Building,
with a change in his looks. He was bigger today, heavier,
stronger and more relaxed, somehow not unreminiscent of
a quick and nervous boxer who has finally gotten into a
punchout, been hit hard for ten rounds, and now sits around
in the next week with lumps on his head, welts on his face,
even a certain thickening of his wits, but manhood has
come to him. He has a new kind of calm. So sat Eagleton.
Yesterday, after a week of desperate campaigning to win
public approval of his candidacy, crowds cheering him in
Hawaii, and Jack Anderson confronting him on TV like
an older brother with evidence of busts for drunken driving
which Anderson didn't have, and apologized for, after a
week in which half of America took Eagleton to its heart
like a wounded puppy, while half of the top brass in the
Democratic party threatened to boycott the election if he
wasn't dropped from the ticket, and campaign money went
dry, McGovern had the fell political embarrassment of
asking him to withdraw, this after making the needless
remark at the first height of the disclosure that he was
behind Eagleton "1,000 percent," a phrase which entered
the language so quickly that 1,000 percent might yet live
as the conclusive way to let someone know they must certainly not count on your word. A whole disaster for
McGovern which had not been helped by Eagleton's un-
willingness to withdraw—anyone familiar with politics
had to know that McGovern was counting, if it came to it,
on just such a voluntary withdrawal to safeguard that 1,000
percent. But Eagleton had been riding with all the energy
of that cyst being lanced, a buried horror released and
himself still alive, crowds cheered him, strangers (from
states other than Missouri) grabbed his hand, he was a
national figure for the first time in his life, and with a brand-
new constituency—all of that Wallace folk who liked a candidate with a flaw they could recognize, something homey
and down to rights, a skeleton in the closet at which they
had had a peek, what pleasure! That threw a cunning
shadow into the soap-opera light. Just as the folk loved
Wallace because Lurleen had made the sacrifice to run for

governor knowing it could not help her dread disease, and folk loved Wallace again for recovering from her loss and marrying a young woman—renewal was the precise salvation of which the soap opera sang—so now Wallace folk loved Eagleton because he was a rich boy with a bad secret who was going through a crisis and not giving up. (If Aquarius had any doubt of this last hypothesis, it was demonstrated to the detail while he sat in Eagleton's outer office waiting for the interview, and a file of tourists kept coming by to pay their respects to the Senator, murmuring in intense throat-filled voices to the receptionist that they sure were sorry the Senator wouldn't be running and didn't know if they wanted to express their feelings about George McGovern but leave it that they sure wouldn't vote for him now—Wallace faces, every last one of them, clear in their election plumage to a face-watcher like Aquarius, equal after such years of practice to many a bird-watcher.) Eagleton had lived in politics all his life, could smell the turn of one's luck in the sweat of the work. So he knew better than anyone else that he had become a species of new political dynamite, and he didn't want to quit—how could he? But the less he wished to withdraw, the more livid and enormous became the wrath of the party at the caper he had pulled. "Get that mother fucker out," had to be the sweetest message on the hour to McGovern from all the boss and divergent forces in the party he was trying to unite. By refusing to withdraw, Eagleton had the largest play of his life available to him—and if ever elected might just as well have served as an Ombudsman—but the odds against him were huge, and the bulk of his own party would treat him like a leper. So he met with McGovern, and they came out, Eagleton's arm on McGovern's shoulder, using the old senatorial wedge as they drove into a press conference, and Eagleton announced he would withdraw, and did this morning, and now sat back on his chair, his legs on his desk, and talked in a deep politician's voice which still vibrated with the pain of loss and the pleasure of relaxation. Of course, he was far from wholly relaxed as yet, soon jumping to his feet to read aloud an item from the *St. Louis Post-Dispatch* which had just come in, and read (in the loud throw-it-away tones of an actor picking up new lines just handed him) that McGovern was "spineless."

"Spineless," Eagleton repeated. "A little too extreme, don't you think?" he said, but he was obviously enjoying himself.

"Oh, oh," he added with mock pain as he picked up another paper, "they're still misspelling my name. My God, they've called me everything and I don't mean dog catcher, I mean Eggleston, Eaglesworth, Eggnog, you call it." His secretary now handing him a take-out menu from the Senate cafeteria, he groaned at the familiar items, "Darn it, I'd like something more glamorous than cherry pie," he complained, as if finding his stomach convalescent, he would call for a taste tender and cozening to the palate.

Back again behind the desk, Eagleton replied to the quick question, "Do you play chess?" with the answer, "No, I wish I did, why do you ask?"

"Sometimes in chess games between masters, a move comes up which is so unprecedented and therefore so good or so bad that the people who annotate the game put both an exclamation and a question mark after the move. And I thought if you had not withdrawn, it would have been such a situation."

"I see what you mean," he said heartily. "No, I must say I never learned chess, but I wish now that I might have gone in for it." It was a politician's response. Complimented the questioner, but did not answer him; took pains to praise what might be a hobby. A hobby commended is usually worth a vote.

"Granted this may not be the day to ask such a question, but wouldn't you say that on balance you're still in pretty good position? The nation is aware of you, and there are new friends . . ."

"Oh," he rumbled, "I'm not bitter. Hell, we could say it was the cheapest campaign I ever ran. They gave me a free charge for my batteries. Think of it. All that publicity, and I didn't have to spend a cent."

It was an interview which so far had persisted in remaining out of focus. Not twenty-four hours ago, Eagleton had still been running; now with the proper politician's love for a meaty role (even the role of a loser done well is fertilizer for future votes) he was already working out the tone of new lines, but it was the first day, he was probably a slow study after all this pounding and so he had to sound a fraction off on every reading. The problem was to work

out how much he could speak against McGovern—
which would be tonic for his blood—and how much he
should support him, a professional decision which might
take weeks to work out. So now he chose to get away from
any suggestion of bile, and also gave up the forced and
hearty gallantry he had been exhibiting of a man who is
being good about his pain. Instead, he said in the voice
of an absolute good guy, "I'm really not bitter—George
McGovern was wonderfully decent to me last night." This
line was delivered with no more or less conviction than the
others. The new role was going to take work.

"Senator, could I ask a question which might be a little
presumptuous?"

"After what I've been asked these last seven days, you
could bounce the worst insult off my head, and I wouldn't
even know I'd been hit."

Well, one thing did confuse him, the questioner admitted.
He had read the reports of Eagleton waiting for hours on
the last day of the convention to find out if McGovern
would pick him for Vice-President. The former candidate
nodded. And it had also been reported that as he waited, his
good mood naturally began to go down. Eagleton nodded
again. "Well, Senator, forgive me for entering your head,
but didn't there come a moment when you said to yourself,
'They're turning me down because of that electro-shock
business.' "

Eagleton looked thoughtful. "Earlier in the week when
my name first came up as a possibility, and there were still
twenty names in the hopper, I talked about the shock
treatments with my wife, and we felt it was over and done
with. I don't know if you'll believe this, but I then forgot
about it."

"You didn't think about it once all that long day of
waiting?"

"While I can't vouch for my unconscious, it was not an
element of calculation in my conscious head, no sir, strange
as that may now sound."

It was preferable to believe he told the truth, that somehow it had not been in his mind when Mankiewicz asked
him if there were skeletons in the closet. But who could
know what was in Eagleton's mind? Probably he did not
know himself. When our motive is imperfect, the flaw is
whipped like a pea from mental shell to shell. We smuggle

our honesty just out of our reach while keeping an eye on the other man's game. Maybe Eagleton had built so many reflexes on his ability to whip a miserable recollection from shell to shell that he had lost the power to think of the hospital episode when questions were asked, just as a murderer living in a respectable world must manage to forget his murder and feel as much indignation as anyone else at the thrashing of a cat.

Leaving, Aquarius asked, "Anyone ever told you about a resemblance to Scott Fitzgerald?" He was thinking of photographs in those late years when Fitzgerald was handsome still but growing heavy.

"I've been compared to Jack Lemmon, but never Fitzgerald." He smiled. "Do I want to look like Fitzgerald? Didn't he have a drinking problem after all? I'm in enough trouble without being told I remind people of a drunk."

"Not just a drunk. A fine Irish poet."

"Well," said Eagleton, *"The Great Gatsby* is one of my favorite books."

If he was not telling the truth now, there was a fair chance good George McGovern had just disengaged himself from a congenital teller of the worst fibs.

Walking down the hall, Aquarius felt as if he had been talking to a nice friendly reasonably hard-working gooddrinking congressman who in another term would be ready to run for senator. No matter how many times it happened, it was unnerving to meet men who had been near to high office and recognize they were no more magnificent than yourself. Perhaps there were mysteries to charisma he would yet do well to ponder.

3

In McGovern's office in the Old Senate Building, the staff was digging out from their disaster. An unprecedented bout of political foul weather, it was hardly at an end, for in days to come Teddy Kennedy would again decline the vice-presidency, as would Muskie (while Humphrey and Ribicoff would state they were not available) before Sargent Shriver would take the ticket. The first Gallup Poll since the convention had been announced, and McGovern was riding low, Nixon ahead 58 percent to 34, but even the ripping velocity of such bad news had to be read as even worse, since McGovern's percentage had dropped as a result of the Democratic Convention, dropped! When it should have risen after four days of exposure. All those liberated faces and somewhat adenoidal voices of the articulate young telling America how to live right over the tube had obviously brought no good reaction from the Jews of the wad and the Italians, the Polish and the Irish—go through the minorities, go through the unions—the polls were terrible, they would get worse. For these last polls had been taken before the bad news about Eagleton was released; McGovern was in twice poor circumstances now —it was as if the political virus which wrecked your timing had been passing among the Democrats and he had caught Muskie's disease. The timing could not have been worse on Eagleton. Having supported him 1,000 percent when the first reaction was negative, McGovern decided to drop him just as Eagleton began to capture America's affection. Probably it had seemed like good timing—allow three or four days for the cut-off to take place, habituate Eagleton and America to the impending change, and give time also for

the breezes of ambition to stir again in prominent Democrats' hearts. Instead, there had come Jack Anderson's disclosure that he had "located photostats" of arrest records
on Eagleton for drunken driving. So, it looked like Mc-
Govern was dropping Eagleton just when his troubles were
at their worst. Then, it developed that Anderson's charges
were false. No photostats. No arrest records. Eagleton's fortunes were now ready to zoom and climbed instead up to
the low ceiling of McGovern's decision already committed
to dozens of Democratic leaders that he would definitely
drop Eagleton. It was worse than the worst moments in
"The Short Happy Life of Francis Macomber"—once again,
the protagonist was getting killed just when ready to become a man. What a direct reflection in polls to come! (A
month later, Nixon would lead 64 to 30.) But then the timing and retraction of Anderson's charges had been so bad
for Democratic fortunes that more than one sinister interpretation was passing around in Washington. For as political intelligence was quick to point out, Jack Anderson didn't
make that kind of mistake. Aquarius, who sometimes
thought it was his life's ambition to come up with evidence
that the CIA was tripping on American elections, might
have loved the story, but since even men like Anderson
could have lapses, it was possible astrology offered as much
revelation. Whether a plot, Muskie's political flu, the fine
hand of the Devil giving a stir of the broth for Richard
Nixodemus, or the worst zodiacal concatenation ever
handed a presidential poker player, McGovern had just
managed to stop a series of haymakers by the forceful motion of his head against his opponent's glove, and, true
fighter, was not yet necessarily aware how totally he had
been hit. (Pete Hamill indeed had described him as reminiscent of "those old Irish heavyweights like Braddock who
catch everything and still go fifteen.") Maybe McGovern
would go fifteeen, but no big Democrat was running up this
day to second him; it would be a week until Shriver was
nominated in full assembly of the Democratic National
Committee.

Waiting in his Senate offices to get an appointment with
the candidate, there was opportunity to talk for a while
with Warren Beatty in a corner behind two file cabinets,
and Beatty who had carried the reputation of being a not-
altogether-manageable movie star, heir among others to

that surly mix of pride, wit, benightedness, bumps, lumps, and independence which had been legend for Brando, was in the position of having been working hard for months and year for McGovern, and he spoke from that unmistakable base of centrality which sits in the chest when you are part of the team. So it was like talking to a halfback who will explain why his coach, the best coach, can still lose a game. "You got to understand, naturally. There's been work here in this place. I mean some of the people in this office were with McGovern back out there two years ago when he had 2 percent of the vote in the polls, and figure this—they were lying. It was not a *solid* 2 percent." From time to time Beatty moved his head the way an animal might, as though to take stock of sounds not heard but sensed—shifts in the ringing of mood. "People like that, back there working so long at 2 percent, think how they feel now their man's all the way up, and boom, low bridges, the newcomer, *this* newcomer has his flaw which is going to louse up the campaign, smash all the good work they've been doing for two years. People were incensed at Eagleton here. Cause you know he wasn't exactly telling the truth. He made Frank Mankiewicz look incompetent. And it isn't so. Frank didn't say, 'Ho, ho, fellow, any skeletons in Daddy-O's closet?' Frank questioned him. I was in the room. Frank asked *all* the questions. I mean, he didn't say, 'Any mental difficulties?' but he was *thorough*. The man had plenty of time to search his own mind. And that leaves Frank on the spot now. He's had to keep his lip buttoned. Cause we didn't know if Eagleton was going to stay or not." Beatty gave that hint of wry balance which was his smile, and went on in his slow, off the beat, laconic voice, not Clyde so much as some dry variant of the syncopation Brando first brought to phrasing when he played psychopaths and gave a mix of the old man's stern salts with the delinquent's softened voice, yes, the sociology of half of America was an Oriental rug, and actors were a legitimate part of the cadre. "It all," Beatty said, "goes back to California. If we'd known we were in, we could have done a full check. But the way we had to do it! Look, even the *St. Louis Post-Dispatch* had no stuff on Eagleton. That's the clue to the kind of search we couldn't make. Just think —we're back there where we don't have the nomination yet, and we're trying to make that search, poking in

Rochester, Minnesota, for *medical* records? And Eagle is
still a *Muskie* man! Think of the stink."

"But when did word first get to you about Eagleton?"

He shrugged. "A couple of reporters called."

"How did they know?"

"There was a phone call to them from Rochester."

"Was it anonymous?"

He nodded.

Why bother to look for the CIA when there was always
the FBI? But, as if the sense of excitement he felt at this
possibility quivered across the air and was seized instantly
by Beatty, the actor gave a wooden look in return. The
interview was abruptly over.

"Are you sure of this?"

"No."

"Is it a secret?"

"No matter. It's not said."

"What do you mean?"

"The rain in Spain."

"What?"

"Doggerel."

Now Beatty got up. The interview was certainly over.
Aquarius made small talk with the staff for a minute. Yet,
before he left, Beatty tapped him. "It's okay. You can use
that story. It's been in print."

He was not to get in with McGovern for an interview
this day but had an opportunity to say hello as the candidate passed through his office, and it was the first time
Aquarius saw fatigue on his face. The Senator had been
defeated that day in the attempt to put a ceiling on the
defense budget, defeated (like an index of the polls) by
59 to 33—19 Democratic senators defecting to Nixon for
the vote, and it had been McGovern's first important effort
on the Senate floor since winning the nomination. Then,
the candidate's plan to offer over nationwide television a
full account of his reasons for encouraging the resignation
of Eagleton had been refused for that night by the networks
on the ground his remarks would not be newsworthy, not
unless he could name the new Vice-President. A rebuke.
For whatever the legal merits of the networks' position, it
was also Media's way of telling him he had been demoted:
His thoughts and emotions in coming to so agonizing a
decision were without the content of real news. Obviously,

he was a candidate whom the Media had concluded was not going to become President.

We may leave aside the attack on his vanity. He was in the worse frustration of not being able to present his side of the Eagleton affair for another week, just that crucial week in which opinions would be hardening. Yes, McGovern had just had the kind of news which stirred fatigue.

Next day, there was still no interview, but all the opportunity to watch him from the Press Gallery in the Senate Chamber, for there was one close vote after another on a series of amendments to a bill for military procurement. And after two hours of watching the floor and observing McGovern as he wandered around Senate desks, so could the character of any sentiment surrounding him also be observed. But the Senate Chamber was not the most cheerful place in which to make such a study, for with its inset black marble columns along the beige walls, and its colorless dingy lavender-gray carpet, the great room despite its high and noble molded ceiling still looked like one of the grimmest of grand old hotel lobbies. The sofas in the corner of the floor were of the dark brown of office leather which can only be found in the oldest banks and hotels, and the desks of the senators were as old and dark as a Havana cigar. Upstairs, the seats in the visitors' gallery were red and pink as if some small-town decorator had been called in on a change of management to warm the mezzanine and had only succeeded in firing the essential loss of connection between the heaviest habits of decoration in Establishment past and present. If, on reflection, it was not a badly designed set considering how many times it had been called the most powerful and exclusive men's club in America (99 of the 100 senators were men), still never had the appointments of a Men's Club been more in need of Women's Fumigation; the rules of the club, as if grown in the logic of the décor, were chiseled enough to suggest that the code for senatorial manners must be filed in aisles of marble. That severity of air which arises when the banker's rights of money are preeminent to the rights of men (McGovern was later to say, "Money made by money should be taxed at the same rate as money made by men") sat in judgment over the Senate like a palisade of cigar smoke on a counting-house floor, and one had not been in the precincts of that chamber for an hour before a few new observations were clear: The fortitude of Gravel in defying Senate protocol to read the Pentagon Papers had not been rated sufficiently high; the view of other senators toward McGovern was cool. He might be running for President, but in the eyes of his peers, he was an upstart, or was it nearer to estimate that he was regarded more as a fellow who had taken the pledge and next year might even live in the fraternity but for the present his only fame was that he had won some sort of sweepstakes off the campus.

A huge simplification, but analogous perhaps to the kind of notes anthropologists might take on the goings and comings of baboons in the brush. There were flurries to the passages of senators between their desks, men they made a point to greet, others they passed with a nod, and the desks of particular senators came to seem like stations on the line. The Democrats' half of the chamber was beneath his perch in the Press Balcony, and after a period it was established that the desk of Teddy Kennedy while in the last row and to the side might as well have been the center of the floor —everybody stopped there!—not even his worst detractors would ever claim that Ted Kennedy could not become the president of any fraternity to which he belonged: one could define the prerequisites of an ideal fraternity leader in Kennedy's qualities—to be rich, hearty, handsome, cognizant of tradition, witty, and not without independence. Charisma glowed like aurora borealis about his desk.

And Humphrey, peripatetic this day, moved like the most expensive tropical fish in the tank, and was greeted everywhere and was obviously loved, and as obviously loved the Senate—he had never looked so well campaigning for President as he appeared this afternoon, younger, slimmer, the bloat gone, the career now finally in balance again— warm were the greetings they gave him as he visited from desk to desk. And warm were the greetings given to Eagleton. He remained in the seat he occupied, chatting with senators who came by, and was altogether at ease—his life, ideally, would move from club boy to club man—it was obvious after a period that the oldest and most venerable of the senators were making a point to stop and accost him, a set of avuncular buttresses to remind him that he was back in the place where he belonged and could spend his life, and it was only after a period of observing him that the realization came home that Eagleton was occupying McGovern's seat! Many of the senators could be found at strange desks, maybe more than half were not at their own, but the query which would remain unanswered was whether Eagleton's move had been accidental or chosen, and if the second, then was it a way to declare allegiance to his former running mate or just a casual means of reminding him that ghosts last longer than corpses.

And McGovern? Even though he is running for President, there is a difference between him and other senators, an absence of rich greeting, a delicate air of the cool, as if they cannot forgive him for succeeding when he has still not learned how to move in these halls. He wanders through the Senate as if he attends a somewhat strange campus function, looking perhaps like that affable and lonely graduate student who holds two jobs and gets the best marks in class, and walks on flat feet as the price of working those nineteen hours a day he can remove from the tyranny of hours lost to sleep. Now although he knows everyone here (he has worked with them on other campus functions), he does not know how to time the weight, duration, and splendor of his greeting to individuals of different merit, knows that the function of the particular job he has at this minute is to be friendly, and is of good will, but something in his manner speaks of that prairie poverty which teaches decency and good manners, yet always leaves one circling outside the intimidating pauses and rich thrusts of successful manner. If the Senate had been a roaring abbey with a blazing fire, McGovern would have been the monk who prayed in the chill at the rear—something of the transcendent passion of the poor graduate student now came clear. For out of five decades of American graduate students, he must be the one in ten million who had successfully taken the vow to rise above every closed circle of elegant establishment he would never enter. Movies had been his forbidden fruit not country club dances. If men run for President out of a hundred motives, certainly a good one for McGovern was that it would be easier to become Commander in Chief of America than be accepted in the Senate. Aquarius wondered if part of McGovern's readiness to pick Eagleton had not come out of the simple social pleasure that he would have allied to himself the kind of man who was born to an inner club—what McGovern did not know is that poor graduate students tell the truth when questions are asked (for examinations are their Olympics and their triumph), whereas rich boys are in need of cribs and there is always some family secret to snake away with charm.

4

Next morning when he went in to have his interview, McGovern was not visible in his office. So his secretary, Pat Donovan, stayed and talked for a few minutes. If one could judge the caliber of men by the presence of their secretaries, then all the qualities already perceived in McGovern were fortified. Pat Donovan had one of those modest pleasant and turned-up faces which used to speak of the integrity of Americans, as if something in the lakes, the pine woods and the prairies bred honesty in American flesh as naturally as vitamins in grain—if she were the young teacher sent to meet a parent on the first day a child was put in school, the mother might surrender the first-born without a qualm. Still, the most honorable people are not always the easiest to talk to. Conversation worked against a certain embarrassment. "Two days ago," said Pat Donovan, continuing a fumbled set of remarks about politics which Aquarius had begun, "I even spoke to Hubert Humphrey on the phone. I could hardly believe it. There I was being pleasant to him, saying hello as if nothing had happened." She shook her head at the peculiarities of the profession she found herself in. Politicians could forgive each other, but not the women who worked for them—he could remember the ice picks in the eyes of female workers when McGovern's name was uttered in Eagleton's office.

Still he did not know why Pat Donovan, confessing how her days since the nomination were never removed from the phone, took one precious minute and then another to fill silences with sound—why did she give him this attention he did not need, and could not use nearly so well as a minute to himself the better by which to note a detail or two of the furnishings in the room.

And the answer came in a flushing of the john. McGovern's private bathroom was next to his office. Miss Donovan had simply not wanted a reporter to sit in a state of open ears while her boss had that obligatory few minutes to himself. What a delightful sense of protection she had! Aquarius wished he could have told her how, out of the depths of his own political career, he knew no candidate's bowels were ever in condition to be eavesdropped upon!

So began his interview with McGovern. They shook hands on the human ground of the Senator emerging from his bathroom door. Then McGovern took a seat some fifteen feet away, a good distance for what was only a fair-sized room, yet the distance was comfortable, for once again Aquarius felt a sensation not altogether separate from that mixture of eminence, near-levitation and dread one breathes (in the lightening of the weight of the heart) as one walks on the edge of a cliff. McGovern seemed so unlike a politician, and so much more like a man of some inestimable goodness sitting in one's living room and emitting a free current of moral decency which proved to be as strong as the agreeable sense of awe one could know at the best of times in a church. Yet the office in which they spoke now, while a nice office—no more had he observed it!—seemed to be in his own service as much as McGovern's: part of the Senator's most exceptional quality as a politician was that he did not even appropriate his own surroundings. Of course, if one sat literally in one's own living room, and was confronted by a man of such superb moral worth, there would be all the discomfort of not knowing what to offer for conversation, except that McGovern's power, perceived all over again! was in his grave and pleasant quality of attention as if all that was said could be of value. So Aquarius made the error of not interviewing but of talking for too many of his precious minutes on a theme he envisioned for the campaign, and recognized even as he spoke that these ideas were too subtle to be reported properly if ever inserted in a speech. The admission of this—his own discouraging reaction to his own ideas—seemed to come as some function of the attention McGovern offered, much as if Aquarius had been abruptly endowed with the power to apply any critical spirit he used for others upon himself. So he shelved the catalog of these once dear ideas, and recognized that he had no real questions to ask.

There was no form of inquiry on earth more unwholesome to him than a face-to-face interview—truth could emerge no more easily from that than statistics on the sum of British Guiana's arable acreage, gotten up for a test, might bring some cognition of life in British Guiana.

Since the office day was beginning, however, the phone began to ring. Between two calls, Aquarius managed to suggest that one of the obstacles to election might be the desire of China and the Soviet Union for Nixon to win; any progress achieved with Republicans would be concrete and not easily reversed, whereas fine relations with a Democratic President could always be overthrown four years later.

"Well, there may be some element of truth to what you say," McGovern offered. He pondered it. "I've never heard the question put that way before." Was this a compliment to slip away from the need to answer? "Let's leave it," said McGovern, "that while I don't necessarily have a rebuttal, we can still contend with the idea that history takes place in an *atmosphere*. The prevailing tone in the world might be somewhat different if I can win."

Once he had been described as "not modest but humble," and the phrase was comprehensible. He was certainly not modest since he obviously thought he could make a good President, but he was humble in his unstated confidence that it would not necessarily be himself who accomplished such a wonder. There were human forces powerful as waves in which he believed and they would yet carry him. It is only, his manner seemed to say, that there may not be time for people to recognize I am probably sincere.

Yes, in the silences after he spoke, something in his manner spoke again, and better.

Then the phone rang once more. When he was finished, McGovern began on his own accord to speak of Eagleton, doing this with the painful smile of a man who has always trusted his candor and now must trust it again. "I think," he said, "it may have been the hardest decision I've ever had to make in my life." He spoke in the self-removed tone a man would have to employ after an automobile accident in which he had been the driver and others had been hurt. "It was bad not to be able to give him a chance, and yet the division in the party would have been total. And the money stopped. Nothing has been coming in. And then in

all this time we couldn't get to see his medical records. We
still don't know how serious it was. Although, of course,
no matter what the records said, they're old. He could
now be more stable than any of us. There are no guides
in this."

"What would you have done if he had mentioned the
shock when Mankiewicz asked?"

"I don't know. Maybe we would have asked for the
direct release of the records, and seen if they were the kind
of thing we could announce and proceed to live with." But
that could hardly be the answer. How would they ever
decide at four in the afternoon on the day a Vice-President
must be nominated, a monumental question whose edges
were undefined?"

"You picked a nice man who just doesn't give the impression that he could ever conceivably be a President. With
due respect, I think it was your fault."

"Yes," said McGovern, tall and sad and brooding, "it
was my fault," and Aquarius thought that if they had only
talked of the mistakes he had made, and the flaws in his
powers, still he had never looked more and sounded more
like a President, for it was as if his error now leaned against
all the wounds of that world he hoped to mend, and the
wounds leaned back on him.

But, indeed, being next to McGovern was like being in
a movie film next to Gary Cooper. No man could give off
such an impression of strength, fine attention, and guarded
concern for the vulnerability of existence itself without
posessing something of those qualities. For how could any
actor offer a decency in his face which was greater than
the decency he might be capable of attaining at certain moments in his own life? One can simulate many an emotion
altogether, but not decency. Perhaps this could explain why
actors like Cooper were loved as if their roles were real.
In any case, whether the nicest politician he had ever met,
or the unheralded matinee idol of splendid Westerns never
made, Aquarius had just known the most disturbing sentiment one could feel for a politician—was it something like
love? Or was McGovern the living embodiment of a principle which was only new to the Age of Technology: the
clear expectation of democratic government that good and
serious men of honorable will were ready to serve.

5

The calendar being never so orderly as the requirements
of literary form, Aquarius had his conversation with
McGovern on the day after an interview with Henry
Kissinger, but in memory the occasions were reversed, as
if he had shifted from observing Democrats to covering
Republicans on the precise hour he crossed over the parties
and went to visit Dr. Kissinger in the White House.

Since it was an interview which had been scheduled
weeks in advance and confirmed the day before, with all
option given to meet at Sans Souci for lunch or the White
House, he had naturally picked the White House. How
often did such opportunities arise? Still, it took fifteen long
minutes and then five more to pass through the special police at the gate. Interrogating him through a microphone in
a plate-glass facade, they claimed at first to have no record
of his appointment, and then informed him he had been
due at nine in the morning, only to discover they were
looking through the schedule of the resident White House
physician, Dr. Tkach. Kissinger! now that was better! but
before they could announce him, he would have to complete a questionnaire. There was something as reductive as
a steam bath in this colloquy through the glass. Already
he was perspiring at the minutes being lost for the interview.

Once admitted to the kiosk, however, he was freezing in
the air conditioning and fuming at the questionnaire. When
he handed it back, the Sergeant who conducted the inquiry
through the window, scolded him. "I told you not to use
abbreviations, didn't I."

"Why don't you have a form which gives you space to write out the full word," he snapped back, and was apparently accepted at last by the Sergeant as a man of sufficient self-importance to visit the White House, for he was invited to take a chair.

Still, he had to wait while they phoned for clearance. In the meantime, he listened to the Sergeant and his assistant, a bright-eyed and wiry Southerner, who said, "I just reduced crime in my neighborhood by forty percent."

The Sergeant jeered; the other policeman, a young Black with a ramrod posture, smiled uneasily.

"Hell, yeah. The other night I talked my wife out of hitting me on the side of the head with a skillet. That's forty percent right there. But when it comes to armed robbery I'm helpless. I come home at the end of the week with my pay check and she holds me up for all fifty-one cents."

"Why," said the Sergeant, "don't you study the life of George Washington and stop telling so many fucking lies?"

"There's an example. George Washington cut down the cherry tree and they gave him ten thousand dollars a year. Why, way back then he was making more money than I am right now."

"What are you complaining about?" asked the Sergeant. "He was the first President of the U.S. What was you ever the shit first of?"

But a young Secret Service man had now come up to the kiosk, and conducted him across the North Lawn. Inside the West Lobby a receptionist apologized politely for the delay. Ushered through a door into a hallway, he was met by Kissinger who gave the greatest of broad smiles, pumped his hand, and said in a deep and gutty German accent, "Today must be my day for masochism since I dare to be interviewed by you."

Almost immediately, they were in his office, large and full of light. "We have a momentous decision to make instantly," said Kissinger. "It is: where shall we eat? I can offer you respectable food if you wish the interview here, not exciting but respectable, and we won't be interrupted. Or we can go to a restaurant just around the corner where the food will be very good and we will be interrupted a little although not very much."

Similar in height and build, it was probable they would not wish to miss a good lunch. So in much less time than it took him to enter, he left the White House (that most placid of mansions!) with Kissinger, hardly noticing the same Secret Service man who unobtrusively—it was the word!—had stopped the traffic on Pennsylvania Avenue while they crossed. If not for just such a rare American pomp, he could have had the impression that he knew Kissinger over the years. For as they walked along, chatting with no pain, it was much as if the learned doctor had been an editor of some good and distinguished quarterly, and they were promenading to lunch in order to talk over a piece.

In fact, that was the first topic—his piece. "We must, from the beginning," said Kissinger, "establish ground rules. We may make them whatever you wish, but we have to keep them. I can speak frankly with you, or not so frankly. But if I am frank, then you have to allow me the right to see what you put into my mouth. It is not because of vanity, or because of anything you may say about me, you may say anything you wish about me, in fact"—with the slyest grin—"you will probably hurt my position more if you say good things than bad, but I have, when all is said, a position I must be responsible to. Now if you don't wish to agree to such a procedure, we can do the interview at arm's length, which of course I'm used to and you need show me nothing. Either method is agreeable, provided we establish the rules."

They had by now reached Sans Souci, and Kissinger's advance to his table was not without ceremony. Since he was hardly back twenty-four hours from Paris and some talks with the North Vietnamese, the headwaiter teased him over the pains of quitting Parisian cuisine. Passing by the table of Larry O'Brien there were jokes about Watergate.

"That was good luck, Henry, to get away just before it hit the fan," said O'Brien.

"Ah, what a pity," said Kissinger. "You could have had me for the villain of the sixth floor."

And a friend intercepted him before he could take his seat. "Henry, what truth to the rumor that McGovern is picking you for Vice-President?"

Kissinger chuckled. "Twenty-two thousand people in the

State Department will be very happy." He was animated
with the pleasure these greetings had given him. While not
a handsome man, he was obviously more attractive to
women now than when he had been young, for he enjoyed
what he received, and he was a sensuous man with a small
mouth and plump lips, a Hapsburg mouth; it was not hard
to see his resemblance to many a portrait of many an Aus-
trian archduke and prince. Since he gave also every sign
of the vanity and vulnerability and ruddy substance of a
middle-aged man with a tendency to corpulence—the temp-
tation to eat too much had to be his private war!—his
weaknesses would probably be as amenable to women as
his powers, and that German voice, deep, fortified with an
accent which promised emoluments, savories, even meat
gravies of culture at the tip of one's tongue, what European
wealth! produced an impression altogether more agreeable
than his photographs. So one mystery was answered—Kissinger's reputation as a ladies' man. And a difficulty was
commenced—Aquarius' work might have been simplified if
he liked the Doctor less. A hint of some sinister mentality
would have been a recognizable aid.

Yet even the demand for ground rules was reasonable.
The meal ordered, Kissinger returned to the subject—he
repeated: he would obviously expect the rules to be clarified
before he could go further. Nor was there much impulse to
resist him with argument. Secretly, he respected Kissinger
for giving the interview—there was indeed not a great deal
the Doctor could gain, and the perils were plentiful, including the central risk that Kissinger would have to trust
him to keep his side of the bargain. Since his position not
only as Assistant to the President on National Security Affairs but as court favorite must excite the ten thousand
furies of bureaucracy—"this man who can't speak English
that they keep hidden in the White House" being a not un-
common remark—the medium of this interview was not
without its underlying message: Kissinger, in some part
of himself at least, must be willing to function as a cultural
ambassador across the space of mind between the con-
stellations of the White House and the island galaxies of
New York intellectual life. So Aquarius made his own
speech. Like a virgin descending the steps of sexual congress, he said that he had never done this before, but since

he was not unsympathetic to Kissinger's labors, and had no wish to jeopardize his position, which he would agree was delicate . . . so forth. They set up some ground rules.

"Now what should we talk about?" asked Kissinger.

Well, they might talk about the huge contradiction between the President's actions in Russia and China as opposed to Vietnam. "You know, if not for the bombing I might have to think about voting for Nixon. Certainly no Democrat would have been able to look for peace with Russia and China. The Republicans would never have let him. So Nixon's achievement is, on the one hand, immense, and on the other ghastly." Kissinger nodded, not without a hint of weariness to show his familiarity with the argument.

"If I reply to you by emphasizing the difference in our styles of negotiation in each country, it is not to pretend that these negotiations preempt moral questions, but rather that I'm not so certain we can engage such questions properly if they're altogether stripped of context. For instance, it would be impossible to discuss the kind of progress we made with China and Russia unless I were to give you the flavor of those negotiations for they were absolutely characteristic and altogether different. For instance, I was not unfamiliar with Russian matters, but my ignorance about China was immense on the first secret visit, and I had no idea of how they would receive me"—a hint of the loneliness of his solitary position now passes across the table at Sans Souci—"nor even what we necessarily would be able to talk about. In the beginning I made the mistake of assuming that they negotiate like the Russians, and they don't. Not at all. With the Russians you always know where you stand. If, for example, you are hammering out a joint statement, you can be certain that if you ask them to remove a comma in one place, depend on it they will ask you for a comma in return. Whereas the character of men like Chou must emerge to a great degree from experiences like the Long March, and so I discovered—and not immediately— that you always had to deal with them on the real substance of the question. I remember when the President visited China, and I was working with Chou on the joint statement we would issue describing our areas of agreement and difference, I asked if a certain point the Chinese had brought

up could be dropped because the wording would be difficult for us in America. In return I would give up a point
to them. Chou said 'Explain to me why this point causes
you difficulty, and if your explanation makes sense I will
cede it to you. If it doesn't convince me however, then
nothing can make me give it up. But I don't need or want
your point. You can only give your points back to *your*
President, you cannot give them to us.' So he shamed me,"
Kissinger finished.

"And the Vietnamese?"

"They could hardly be more different. The problem is to
convince them we really want peace."

"Don't you think a million tons of bombs a year makes
it hard for them to believe?"

"No. I know this has to sound unendurably callous to
you, but the North Vietnamese are inconceivably tough
people, and they've never known peace in their lives. So to
them the war is part of the given. They are able to
live with it almost as a condition of nature. But when it
comes to negotiation, they refuse to trust us on the most
absurd little points. Let them feel if they will that we are
not to be relied on in the larger scheme of things—that is
not my point of view, but an argument can obviously be
advanced—it is just that they refuse to trust us on the
pettiest points where it would not even be to our interest
to cheat them. So they are not easy to comprehend. On
the one hand they have a fortitude you cannot help but
admire; on the other, they are near to little lawyers who
are terrified of the larger processes of the law—and so cling
to the most picayune items. That is one difficulty in dealing
with the North Vietnamese. The other is their compulsion
to the legalistic which bears no relation to reality, nor to
the possibility of reality. In effect they expect us to win
their war for them for they want us to write up into the
peace agreement their literal investiture of the government
of South Vietnam. And that obviously we can't do. There's
nothing we want more than for the war to end, but they
must take their chances too. They have to win their own
war."

"When they began their offensive in April, why then
didn't the President just let them drive ahead and solve the
problem for you? Why, just at that point, did he choose to
escalate the bombing?"

Kissinger did not reply. The difficulty in continuing the discussion was that they would now be obliged to talk about the character of Richard Nixon rather than the nature of the North Vietnamese; given Kissinger's position, that was hardly possible: so the character of the interview changed. If it was easy for Aquarius to have the idea that Nixon and Kissinger were more in accord on Russia and China than on Vietnam, there was no evidence for it. Kissinger took pains to express his respect. "The President is a very complex man," he said, "perhaps more complex than anyone I've known, and different from the public view of him. He has great political courage for instance."

"Yes. It was no ordinary gamble to go to China."

"And he made moves in Russia which would take too long to explain now, but believe me he showed extraordinary decisiveness."

"Still, don't you think it's a vice that he has a personality which is of no use to the country?"

"Nixon is wary of exhibiting anything personal in himself. You have to consider the possibility it's for very good cause considering the way he has been treated by the Media."

"Still his wariness creates contempt."

"And a spirit of debunking which I don't find very happy. It was like that in the Weimar Republic. Just the kind of wholesale debunking that may yet lead to totalitarianism." Kissinger shrugs. "I wonder if people recognize how much Nixon may be a bulwark against that totalitarianism."

"Can he be?"

"I'm not certain I know what you mean."

"As people grow up, don't they form their characters to some extent on the idea a President gives of his person to the public. Nixon may give too little."

"Is it your point of view then that in the presidency one needs to have a man it is worth being like?"

"Yes. Nixon offers nothing authentic of himself."

"You would argue that he is not primarily a moral leader. I do not wish to agree. But perhaps you go along with me that he has political genius," Kissinger said.

"Absolutely."

It was indeed Aquarius' opinion. Still, that was a thought he could return to. Their lunch broke up with the passing of their table by Art Buchwald who announced to Kissinger that Dobrinin was coming to his house one night soon to play chess, and schedules permitting, he thought, granting Dobrinin's status as a chess player, that they should make a date to team up against the Ambassador. Kissinger agreed.

On the way back to the White House, they talked companionably of the hazards of working life, of jet-lag and fatigue. "How much sleep do you get?" asked Aquarius.

"I am happy if I can average five hours."

"Is it enough?"

"I always thought my mind would develop in a high position. But, fatigue becomes a factor. The mind is always working so hard that you learn little. Instead, you tend to work with what you learned in previous years."

They said good-bye in the white office in the White House with its blue sofas, its Oriental rugs, and its painting by Olitsky, a large canvas in blue-purple, a wash of dark transparencies with a collection of pigment near the center as if to speak of revery and focus. "I've only come to like modern art in the last few years," Kissinger remarked.

Aquarius was to think again of focus. Because Kissinger opened to him a painful question on the value of the act of witness: lunch had been agreeable. Yet how could one pretend that Kissinger was a man whose nature could be assessed by such a meeting; in this sense, he was not knowable—one did not get messages from his presence of good or evil, rather of intelligence, and the warm courtesy of Establishment, yes, Kissinger was the essence of Establishment, his charm and his presence even depending perhaps on just such emoluments of position as the happiness he obtained in the best restaurants. If there was a final social need for Establishment, then Kissinger was a man born to be part of it and so automatically installed in the moral schizophrenia of Establishment, a part of the culture of moral concealment, and yet never was the problem so perfect, for the schizophrenia had become Aquarius' own. Kissinger was a man he liked, and in effect was ready to protect—he would even provide him with his own comments back to read. So Aquarius wondered if he had come into that world of the unendurably complex where one gave parts of one's allegiance to men who worked in the evil gears and bowels and blood left by the moral schizophrenia of Establishment, but still worked there, as one saw

it, for good more than ill. It was a question to beat upon
every focus of the brain, and he prepared with something
near to bewilderment to go down to Miami again and see
if there were moral objects still to be delineated in the
ongrowing blur of his surest perceptions.

PART THREE

Program

1

He has even gone down early, and finds himself in Miami so soon as Wednesday for a convention which will not begin until the next Monday, and then promises to be an exhibit without suspense, conflict, or the rudiments of narrative line. If the selection of the Vice-President might have offered drama, Nixon announced his choice of Agnew much in advance and the V.P. in reply to a reporter who asked if the Republican Convention wasn't going therefore to be dull, replied, "Very well, then, we'll be dull," a way to point out that the values of the Media and the values of Republicans might by now be as separate from one another as opposed political systems.

Aquarius was early because he wanted time to think, and lie perhaps in the sun, but in fact he was not at the Fontainebleau a day before he was working. The Platform Committee was meeting, its subcommittees were meeting, and already a parade of speakers had come and gone, Senator Dole (the Republican National Chairman) and George Romney, John Ashbrook the conservative who had run for President against Nixon in the primaries, and John Gardner of Common Cause, Senators Buckley and Javits of New York, and Frank Fitzsimmons of the Teamsters who was successor to Jimmy Hoffa.

There was of course no need to catch much of this. Hours of reportorial prospecting would pan very few grains of gold; most of the prepared statements were read in the La Ronde Room, which was so large that one would not get near enough to see the faces (not when Platform Committee workers occupied most of the floor). Besides, the statements would hardly matter. It was taken for granted that the platform was being written in the White House and

the hearings were going on because conventions had platform committees which were bound to listen to speakers.
But he could legitimately miss the pleasure of not having
heard John Ashbrook's voice speaking as the spirit of the
Republican Right when he called for the U.S. to restore
its "clear-cut military superiority" so that it might take the
lead in resisting the "spread" of Communism. (Which
genius of the Right, Aquarius wondered, had divined that
a cure for cancer would not be found until there was a cure
for Communism?!?) Of course, Ashbrook also called for
"the government to live within its means" and bring an
end to interference "with the freedom and self-reliance of
the average citizen." Such reasoning would not be equaled
until a politician called for the absolute enforcement of
absolute monogamy with no restriction upon pornography.
But then Richard Nixon had once spoken in much the same
way—if twenty years ago! Was this the law of historical
progress?—that it took two decades for the ideas of the
center to be evacuated to the Right? Well, a good healthy
body plus fat-shit for a head might be the indispensable
stock of a patriot. (And proceeded to play with the pun-
nings of fascism, fetishism, and fat-shit.) Like a fighter
getting mean in the last days before a bout, he was obviously ready to work, and so plunged in to witness the
best hearings he could find on Wednesday afternoon, Subcommittee II on Human Rights and Responsibilities, not
the worst way to spend an afternoon—his powers as a
witness could even feel temporarily restored.

He had chosen II because a representative from the National Coalition of Gay Organizations was listed to speak—
Human Rights and Responsibilities was his fair category!—
and Aquarius had naturally looked for a confrontation between flaming youth and fierce-eyed Republicanism, an ap-
petizer to tempt his jaded political palate! but the schedule
was running behind, and there were other speakers to
come first. After a time—perhaps he was just enjoying his
work—he relaxed into the somnolence of an atmosphere
of visiting speakers reading very rapidly from concentrated
reports (fifteen minutes for statement and questions) while
members of the Subcommittee read along with mimeo-
graphed copies, working with their pencils to make that
diagram of trunk lines, private lines, and shunts in the

brain which is called doodling. The Subcommittee was invariably bored. There was a platform to be gotten out and fifty impossibilities to be eliminated first. So it was as if they all agreed there was a marble statue back in the barn which bats were juicing with rabies spit; the aim of the committee was to let the bats beat their wings, flare their gums, then thank them for spreading that rabid saliva. Once the bats were gone, the Subcommittee could wipe the saliva off. In a few days, their work would be done and the statue could be unveiled. No one could say they had not worked on it. If no Subcommittee hand had guided the chisel, who was to say that Chase and Honaman, Jackson, Olson, Victor, Brake, Ramey, Hansen, Ashcraft, Sullivan, Hopkins, Weston, Babcock and Heckler had still not done their bit by holding a seat through long neon-lighted air-conditioned summer afternoons while catching spit? Counting Peter Frelinghuysen from New Jersey and Alice Perry from Mississippi, Chairman and Co-Chairman, there were four men and twelve women on the Subcommittee and the value of the sex quota was established forever since one could not begin to see how a shift in the virtues of the atmosphere would take place if there had been twelve men and four women. Doubtless it was only the title of the Subcommittee which had dictated the particular ratio of vagina to penis.

Donald W. Riegle, Jr., was the first speaker he heard, Congressman Don Riegle of Michigan, the anti-war Republican, and he was young and personable with blond hair which he wore at a generous enough length to reach his collar.

Perhaps in reply to Chairman Frelinghuysen who had opened proceedings the day before by saying, "We intend to have impact on the writing of the platform [and] want to assure each witness appearing before us today that this is where the action is," Riegle gave this forthright beginning. "As you know, certain Republicans have been banned from appearing before the full Platform Committee, including Paul McCloskey, John Gardner, and myself. When I raised this issue with Platform Committee Chairman John Rhodes he said to me: 'You're crazy if you think anyone is going to appear before the full Platform Committee that would say anything that would embarrass the President.' As a result . . . full and open discussion of the issues has been denied. . . . I hope that what I say here to you will find its way back to the full committee."

The Subcommittee members were now a hint ill at ease and they studied Riegle covertly in the light of the Bonaparte Room (a most ordinary hotel meeting room, considering the weight of its name), shifting their study to other faces or back to their fingernails whenever Riegle looked up to make a point.

"Today the U.S. wages undeclared, automated war in Indochina—using weapons' technology that . . . is the most savage, brutal and inhumane the world has ever seen. . . . In the past three and a half years of our Republican Administration, the President, with the silent acquiescence of the Congress, has dropped some 3.6 million tons of bombs in Indochina—the equivalent of some 200 pounds of bombs for every man, woman and child in both North and South Vietnam. . . . In three and a half years of bombing under our Republican Administration, some 4.5 million additional Asians have been killed, wounded or made homeless. Over 12 million American bomb craters under Nixon have left much of the land torn and useless. Some would respond with the statement—'But we're winding down the war—our ground troops are coming home." The truth is that we have taken our troops off the ground and put them in airplanes. The war goes on—and our bombing policy makes it a bigger and more destructive war than at any previous time."

Now he tried to touch into the center of their attention. "Innocent people are this minute being blasted and burned to bits—their families and homes are being destroyed. And these people are innocent of any wrong doing. There has been no declaration of war—because none is justified." Good Republican faces looked back at Riegle in the uneasy bewilderment of bankers who listen to an attractive client apply in well-ordered and reasonable style for a most sensible loan, but they know they will not grant it because there is a note in the file "Do not lend this man money!" So their attention had a tethered look. They were obliged to listen as this articulate maverick congressman went on with his simple unendurable facts, "200 pounds of bombs on every man, woman, and child" (people poorer than the dirtiest Mexicans on either side of the Rio Grande). What species of masochism to listen to an argument when they have lost the thread which goes back all of twenty-five years. They have married, and some of their children have married, they've gone through the meat of a life and it's all been built on the rock of one certainty—America is the only country which can stop the "spread"! The nation has gone through a cultural revolution in the throes of that faith and suffered the third worst war (by casualties) in its history and certainly the most expensive, and then their own Republican President has stopped the spread by virtually joining the spread. China and Russia are practically our friends! And still we are massacring Gooks who never dropped a bomb on us. So perhaps the contagion is not a worldwide conspiracy but a conspiracy which is piecemeal, a rabies where even the poorest peasant is a menace. Good Americans, contemplating the national motive, had nothing to lose but their minds. (So, too, did good Germans come to believe that if Hitler was not right about the Jews, they were all mad.) Of course, Republicans had always lived with the generally unstated premise that if there was a logic to things, it was to live one's own life with decency and not try to contemplate the starving Chinese. Now, however, we weren't just ignoring the empty bellies of people we had never seen, we were burning those empty bellies. Even the thought of leaving four millions of fish or birds dead, wounded or homeless would have made the Subcommittee ill. Riegle was going to win no popularity contest here. He finished by saying: "If we wish to destroy our country, destroy its meaning, corrupt and destroy our capacity for moral leadership in the world, then we need only shut our eyes and ears and our minds to this inhuman bombing policy. If any of you dare speak out—dare ask the President to stop the bombing—then something important will have happened here."

One of the ladies of the Subcommittee was waiting for him. Possessor of a nervous mobile face with prominent eyes, a full head of iron-gray hair, and chiseled features, she was quivering with the nearness of her anger as she announced that she was Jean Sullivan (of Alabama) the wife of Ira Sullivan, who had been a PT boat commander in the Navy—here the words coming so fast that Aquarius could only gather that her husband was the brother or close relative of the five Sullivan brothers who had all been killed in World War II (which had provided the story for a box-office movie on the family disaster) and she and her husband had three sons in the Air Force, or so Aquarius heard, and Jean Sullivan wanted to know if the witness thought maybe they were murderers, her contained wrath tightening the taut flesh a little more over the prim bones, and Don Riegle answered that he was working to end the war so her sons would not have to be overseas, and was certain they would not be happy to prosecute a war like this one. And Jean Sullivan having been answered to that point where she could rest in the momentum of her wrath—how like a flywheel must such an anger once aroused keep turning!—Riegle was queried next by C. Tucker Weston of South Carolina, a heavy-set man with the honest moon face of a farmer or a judge, and he wanted to know why nothing had been said of the atrocities of the Vietcong and the North Vietnamese upon the South Vietnamese, and Riegle gave a courteous reply which referred to the corruption of the South Vietnamese and their profits in drug traffic, and to the fact that the last man to run for the highest office in South Vietnam, and lose, had been imprisoned since 1960 for just that crime, no more, and could one conceive of what America would be like if Richard Nixon had been in jail since 1960 for the crime of losing to Jack Kennedy? And when Weston's face went suddenly thoughtful, Riegle said deftly, "I think this country was founded on the idea that we should be better than others."

They thanked him, and he went out, and it was late in the afternoon, he had been scheduled late so as to keep him out of morning hearings which might get TV prime time or newspaper deadline time. Somnolently, the Republicans listened to the next speaker who was now Martha Rountree, the head of Leadership Foundation, founded "for the purpose of acting as the catalyst for organized women's groups, clubs and organizations," and she was a pale and delicate blonde, no longer young, and her body had gone toward the edges of irreversible rounding and plumping—perhaps as an insulation to her nerves. She was nervous, read nervously, droning on as she told of Leadership Foundation "waging a crusade against what we call Moral Pollution," uttering up that ongoing whine which indifferent orators make when they worry at consuming the time of others. Perhaps she had not been listened to in childhood but now she was there to speak on the issue of putting prayer back into the public schools. "Show me," she said, "one young person who has ever been harmed by acknowledging God. I cannot concede for one moment a position which will accommodate the atheistic point of view in our American society. . . . Today we are beset with drugs, with crime, with rioting and with an obvious moral breakdown. . . . Many people are comparing the problems of today with the Rise and Fall of the Roman Empire," and she was almost petulant as she said, "Will the first nation to put foot on the moon be unable to keep its feet on the ground?" The Subcommittee listened to her politely, but the word was doubtless down on this as well—forget prayer for '72— there was no sense in stirring up liberals and getting the technicians into a crusade against even the faintest hint of hick irrationalisms in the Nixon Platform, the President was calling to Democrats this year and prayer in the schools had the smack of pure Republican piety. So the Subcommittee contented itself by showing open sympathy for Martha Rountree's nerves but had an embarrassing pause when they could find no questions to ask just as the lady finished by saying in a tremulous tone, "I am eager for your questions." She had been obviously affected by her own speech but still no questions. While they might be sympathetic, they were hardly suffering those wretched nerve chitterings which have one sleepless and brooding on Moral Pollution in America in the middle of the night while the distant sounds of automobile exhausts come in the window like the blasts of flame throwers and the cries of drug-heightened rapists stir a dream horizon where bestial yellow eyes glow in the awful world of all moral work undone! The pause went on until Mrs. Honoman from Pennsylvania, a substantial genial woman, thanked Mrs. Rountree and reminisced about Martha's energies and powers and kind favors as a good Republican in a bygone Rockefeller campaign, and Rountree left with hope in her eye but the wisdom on her mouth of a speaker who knows the words failed to reach the hearts they were supposed to touch—failed the Lord again!—and a minister was next, Dr. Elwyn A. Smith the Provost of Eckerd College, speaking on behalf of the General Assembly of the United Presbyterian Church in the U.S.A., and the Provost was a dry and formal man who would have looked well in high collar and a pince nez, but he read a paper which called for "complete withdrawal from Indochina, normalizing relations with Communist governments, support of the United Nations, renewed social services, tax reform, ecological responsibility and compassionate criminal justice" among a schedule of other liberal items, and the Subcommittee listened and let his words buzz like flies passing through the stone grotto of their ears, and when Elwyn A. Smith of Eckerd had finished, Mrs. Nancy B. Chase of Michigan, a middle-aged lady with a face as stern and proper as her name, was ready to say she knew now why a Methodist member of the Subcommittee had complained yesterday about a Methodist minister who pretended in these hearings to speak for all Methodists. She, a Presbyterian, could now make the same objection. Did the speaker really think his views were representative of Presbyterians? The Provost, as gravely composed as when he read his paper, said that he had explained carefully already that the General Assembly for which he had been selected to speak was "composed of seven hundred commissioners, half ministers and half laymen elected from 188 presbyteries in all the fifty states," representing three million United Presbyterian Church members, and Mrs. Chase while silent had a face which spoke eloquently of the intrigues and trickeries of front organizations which led good church groups down the pinko drain, no, she was not impressed, and Smith had done his duty, and the next speaker, long awaited, would speak for the Gay plank.

There had been several homosexuals in the room with long shag haircuts for hairdo and hip huggers for pants. They tossed their hair as if they had read all the paperbacks about faggots tossing hair, and they *minced* with good awareness of that word, and *worked* on the Subcommittee, looking for eye contests while they tingled the air with the Christmas tinkle of their love beads. Yet when the time came, their spokesman was wearing a dark business suit, a conventional hair cut, a shirt and tie, and introduced himself as Dr. Franklin E. Kameny who lived in D.C. and appeared "before you, with pride, as a *homosexual American citizen*. If, throughout my remarks, and in your later deliberations, you will keep constantly in mind the second and third words of that phrase—*American citizen*—instead, merely, of the first word—*homosexual*—you should

have no problems at all with implementing our needs and
with incorporating our concerns in the Republican Party
Platform. In fact, if you keep that phrase in mind, it will
be difficult indeed for you *not* to incorporate our concerns
in your platform, if only because it is so outrageous that
ANY group of *American* citizens, in this day and age,
should still have these concerns unmet and requiring attention."

If God gives every man a bonus, Kameny's voice was
not the bonus. Probably, he had not been born with it, but
cultivated its character, the community tone of the didactic
homosexual who speaks clearly, contemptuously and pity-
ingly to his audience (with just enough effeminacy to establish credentials) and with just enough of the finest strain
of exquisitely insinuated vulgarity to remind you that homosexuality goes back to the childhood root of the stinky
pinky and, hee-hee, your asshole is showing, but now the
vulgarity was reduced to a veritable dingle-berry beneath
twenty mattresses of homosexual pride, born to all purple
princemanship. How the Subcommittee loved Dr. Franklin
E. Kameny for the way he presented his ideas! He might
just as well have inserted sixteen thermometers up sixteen
Republican channels of rectitude.

"I could easily devote several times my alloted quarter-
hour to a full and detailed recital of those of our grievances
which our government at all levels should be considering.
I will not try. Even an adequate treatment of our abuses
at the hands of our federal government alone would take
far more time than I have, even were I to limit that, in
turn, to the indignities visited upon us just by the executive
branch."

It was written with all the polemical indignation of a
thousand conversations over the years between his friends
and himself, homosexual citizens. It was a cultural docu-
ment, a recitation of woes in lofty language which he read
in a haughty voice, he *deigned* to address them, and all the
while some wistful underpull of the human desire to vault
the void put a touch of stridency into his invincible air.

"Our country's birth certificate, the Declaration of Independence, grants to us—ALL of us—the inalienable right
—*in*alienable—to the pursuit of happiness. That is really
what America is all about. To guarantee that right to all
Americans is one of the major functions of our government.

That right is one of the unique glories of our country. And, of course, that right is meaningful only if it refers to the happinesses chosen by each individual citizen for himself, not merely those happinesses granted him by his government or allowed him by society. But when *we*, as homosexuals, wish to pursue *our* happinesses—interfering with no one else in the pursuit of their happinesses—we are hounded, harassed, and presented with often insuperable obstacles at every turn. And not only do we get no redress from our various governments, but they are the most rabid zealots of all in doing the hounding, harassing, and placing of obstacles, with a singular ferocity rarely equaled elsewhere.

"Our society takes pride in its pluralism. But you had better realize just what pluralism means and where it leads. . . . In a pluralistic society, every minority group can properly say—and we do say—that for us as homosexual American citizens, this is OUR society, quite as much as it is yours as heterosexuals, and it is OUR country, and it is OUR government, and he is OUR President, and they are OUR political parties—and this is OUR Republican party. That places an inescapable obligation upon you, as an *American* political party. We ask—we insist—that you shoulder your obligation, and do so NOW."

Was it fifteen years ago or more that Allen Ginsberg, the prophet, had written, "America, I'm putting my queer shoulder to the wheel"? On went Kameny, scolding the Subcommittee.

"And so we have come here to ask for no special favors or dispensations, for no crumbs from your table, for no condescending, patronizing, demeaning, degrading and dehumanizing compassion or pity. We are asking for—and ever more of my people would say that we are quite properly *demanding*—that which is OURS, *by right* to begin with, and which we should have been enjoying all along, not fighting to obtain."

He had read for many minutes at a great rate, but he had all his life to tell, so he moved on without pause. "And that brings me to the stuff and substance of politics: votes.

"The Democratic party was fearful lest those Democrats who might find it offensive to cast their votes for the candidate of a party supporting rights for homosexuals, might defect and vote Republican. Nevertheless, they did include

us. Therefore the Republican party need have no corre-
sponding fear, because a defection from the Republican
ranks for this reason would gain these bigots nothing, since
they would now have no place to which to defect. In any
case, however, the argument is specious for either party,
since there are enough of us so that every vote lost through
supporting us will be offset by several gained."

Yes, his argument was specious said the faces of the Subcommittee. What he preached was *license,* the granting of
franchise to sin and disease. The country was indeed in a
state of advanced Moral Pollution (when poor Martha
Rountree could not get her prayers into the schools) and
the Republicans were here to safeguard America's spirit.
So the promise of ten million votes would not sway them.
Indeed the votes were not there. Let McGovern have all
the political homosexuals, and in return the G.O.P. would
be pleased to pick up all the homosexuals who kept their
private lives in some kind of closet and were probably more
than proud of their Republican ties, high church was the
party of elegance, when all was said!

"Severe limitations of time have necessarily forced this
to be a somewhat superficial and simplistic presentation,"
said Kameny. "I have left a few minutes, and will welcome
questions, comment, dialogue and discussion for as long
as you may wish. I will be pleased to discuss these matters
with any of the Subcommittee members who may wish,
more informally later on today. We look forward to seeing
a gay rights plank in the platform of the Republican party.
Thank you."

He was done, there was one question, a mild one, and
then he went outside to be interviewed, not a very handsome man. His sex life may have been no accommodating
bed of pleasures, for his hair was thin and graying, his
nose was large and not excessively distinguished, and from
the strain of having appeared before so *dim* a group with
such urgency of purpose and pride of deportment, his
eyes has a restrained but wild and marbleized look, staring
blue eyes with raw red rims as though he had been up
all night and all this morning and afternoon working
on the speech and looking for support on the plank, he
was perspiring profusely from fatigue and effort, and now
his assistant, a quiet pleasant-faced young man also dressed
in dark drab clothes (together they looked like fund-

drive solicitors for some rural charity—Northern-Midwest Lutheran Orphanage Association, some such!), was telling the few members of the Press ready to listen, about their difficulties in trying to reach Republicans who might be sympathetic. "We expect very little from these proceedings. Why, even when we managed to reach Paul McCloskey, who is after all by reputation most liberal of the many Republican figures here, the *paragon* of Republican liberalism replied when asked if he would offer us support on the gay plank, and I repeat Congressman McCloskey's remark exactly, he said, quote, 'Oh, shit!' unquote."

2

Now the faces began to move faster, and promise arose of a convention which would be interesting after all, not for its conflict, and never for its surprise—rather, for the promise of design. Slowly, as if one were studying a huge canvas inch by square inch through the glow of a pencil light, a composition of splendid grasp began to reveal itself, a portrait perhaps of the faces tending that great and impeccable computer which measured the pulse and politico-emotional input and emoti-political output of those millions of votes which lived like algae on the rivers of history—the wad in the hour of decision!

If while speaking to Kissinger, he had called Nixon a genius, he meant it. For a genius was a man who could break the fundamental rule of any mighty sport or discipline and not only survive but transcend all competitors, reveal the new possibility in the buried depth of the old injunction. So Nixon had demonstrated that a politician who was fundamentally unpopular even in his own party could nonetheless win the largest free election in the world, and give every promise of doing considerably better the second time! What Aquarius had not realized until this convention began however to disclose its quiet splendors of anticipation and management was that Nixon would reveal himself not only as a genius but an artist. What had concealed the notion of such a possibility for all these years is that it is almost impossible to conceive of a literary artist who has a wholly pedestrian style. It was possible that no politician in the history of America employed so dependably mediocre a language in his speeches as Nixon, nor had a public mind ever chased so resolutely after the wholly uninteresting expression of every idea. But then few literary

artists proved masters of the mediocre. Nixon was the artist
who had discovered the laws of vibration in all the frozen
congelations of the mediocre. Other politicians obviously
made their crude appeal to the lowest instinct of the wad,
and once in a while a music man like George C. Wallace
could get them to dance, but only Nixon had thought to
look for the harmonics of the mediocre, the minuscule
dynamic in the overbearing static, the discovery that this
inert lump which resided in the bend of the duodenum of
the great American political river was more than just an
indigestible political mass suspended between stomach and
bowel but had indeed its own capacity to quiver and creep
and crawl and bestir itself to vote if worked upon with
unremitting care and no relaxation of control. He had even
measured the emotional capacity of the wad (which was
vast) for it could absorb the statistic of 4.5 million civilians
and 1.5 million combatants being killed, wounded, or made
homeless on all sides in the three and a half years Nixon
had continued the war, yes, quietly accept it as a reasonable
cost for the Indochinese to pay in order that we not lose
our right to depart from Vietnam on a schedule of our own
choosing. Better than that—Nixon had spent more on the
war than on welfare, not far from twice more—and so had
taken the true emotional measure of the wad which calculated that two dollars expended on burning flesh in a foreign land was better than one dollar given to undeserving
flesh at home. But if this was the major work of Nixon's
intellectual life, to chart the undiscovered laws of movement in the unobserved glop of the wad, it had been a
work of such complexity that it would yet take the closest
study of the design he had put upon this convention, this
masterpiece of catering to every last American pride and
prejudice going down the broad highway of the political
center. However, there were also smaller perceptions to
make each day, and the growth of political excitement in
a political student like Aquarius at the size of the bonanza
being offered: a course in the applied art of politics by the
grandmaster himself. That this convention would be studied
for years by every political novice who wished to learn how
to operate upon the insensate branches of the electorate was
clear to Aquarius by Sunday when Pat Nixon arrived and
certainly by convention time on Monday when the linea-
ments of superb design had emerged, but that was still later

—his earlier days of watching Republican faces provided
only the small pleasure of suspecting that a design would yet
be here to find, and at times he despaired, obtaining, for instance, very little from a press conference Elliot Richardson
gave, since he had gone to hear Richard Kleindienst explain
his lack of relation to Watergate, but at the scheduled hour
Kleindienst had been replaced by Richardson who offered
himself as a bewildered substitute. Richardson was the
Secretary of Health, Education and Welfare—HEW, as
the initials went—and he had a face for the job. He looked
somewhat like Clark Kent wearing his glasses, a fine example of a Harvard Club man on the bureaucratic hoof, tall,
lithe, vigorous, awkward as a crew man, but *hew!*, he had
a face as keen as the blade of an ax. While obviously a
quiet wit, he first chopped down the tree assigned to him
in the Democratic woods: Richardson was there to state
for newspaper leads that there were 12,000,000 people
now on welfare rolls, whereas under McGovern's plan,
97,000,000 would receive benefits—only Clark Kent Super-
man could stretch a point like that! But the Press preferred
to hear about Watergate. Richardson smiled to himself. He
couldn't resist suggesting (with the grin of a man who is
contemplating the principals all caught in the act) that if
the Committee to Reelect the President had actually pulled
off Watergate, Richardson, for one, couldn't believe that
they would be so inept. He used the word as if the first
Republican sin was to be inept. Yet at another press conference, with Black Republican politicians now in the same
room where the Platform Committee had originally met,
with the same powder-blue tablecloths (now wrinkled
for the Blacks), there are few of the Press and no excitement and an air of things close to the edge of the inept.
Even the Black Press is a hint hostile. The first speaker,
Paul Jones, Executive Director of the Black Voter Division of the Committee to Reelect the President, a pale
moon-faced Negro with a worried purse of his lips and
a genteel Afro, is wearing Republican clothes, dark suit,
gray-blue shirt, a blue checked tie. In answer to a black
heavy-set reporter who asks what he thinks of the atti-
tude in the Black community that Black Republicans are
back-stabbers to their people, Jones says mildly that this
administration has at least delivered on the promises it
made to Blacks instead of offering a hundred years of

rhetoric and Democratic pie in the sky. "What I'm saying is in 1972 the Black vote is not in the bag." Next is Ed Sexton, black member of the Republican National Committee and his rose-pink shirt and white silk tie give *statement* to his gray suit. Since he wears horn-rimmed glasses and keeps his gray Afro high on his head and shaved near his ears, he suggests a black English barrister wearing a court wig on top of his head. But he is *crude*. It is by choice. "Our so-called Black leaders are now all in bed with McGovern. Why he had to buy a king-sized bed to get them all in! We might have fewer black delegates here, but Republicans don't play the numbers game. We're content that we have our people in now in responsible positions whereas McGovern has the lousiest civil rights record of anyone running!" Then comes the third spokesman, Robert Brown, half bald, with silver-rimmed glasses and a white suit with large lightly indicated blue checks, a gray shirt, a maroon tie. He is substantial as he says, "Law and order is one of the biggest issues in the Black community. I don't need anybody to tell me about law and order, I got mugged last week. I can assure you the Black community is behind the President in his desire for law and order." But now the first speaker, Jones, is asked what he thinks of Haynesworth and Carswell. The Press snickers as he answers that his choice "might" have been different. "Still the background does not necessarily indicate the performance. The Supreme Court can change a man. In terms of looking at the overall track record of the President—which is what I go by—I don't know of anyone who has been better for Blacks." The cynicism in the Black Press is audible. "Better for *you*, Nigger," is the mutter.

By all estimates, Nixon will do well to get one Black vote in five. It is tokenism in action, a black face or two to pop a word for him on the tube, and yet, it is more, an elucidation of the political principle of scraping the bowl for whatever vote is there to be scraped. If Nixon had a hole in his heaven, it was in that Black hole of space where all the gravity of American patriotism disappeared with our moral worth. Long before Vietnam, we had had a species of moral Vietnam for fifty years in the Black ghetto and the South, yet this past is going to be nobody's politics if Nixon can help it. So you blow on the faintest glow of

every fire, concentrate on the glow of the one coal among
the dead coals which you might be about to save when
election comes up. So Nixon blew on the remnants of the
old ideology of the Black bourgeoisie (before sympathy in
Black communities for Black militants preempted the scene)
and if he blew the Black vote from 19 percent up to 22
percent well that was half a million votes he did not have
before.

Of course, if Aquarius had seen no more than Elliot
Richardson or the Black press conference, he would have
done well to suspect even a hint of design, but the next
speaker is very much on time (probably so that the
Black press conference will not go on beyond its means)
and is Pierre Rinfret, the economist in residence to the
White House who gives a fast hard-pounding sell on Nixon's
economics as opposed to McGovern's. Rinfret who looks
like a chubby British M.P. wearing a very broad gray-on-
gray pinstripe with immense and elegant lapels, a broad-
striped blue and white shirt with a broad dark-blue silk tie,
is, despite a round face, straight gray hair, a pointed nose
and a receding chin, nonetheless not bad-looking. There
is something in his booming voice, utterly confident and
wholly reminiscent of the autocratic child at the nanny's
breakfast table which gives him all the heartiness of a
spoiled Member of Parliament; his voice resounds out of
a chamber which holds no dusty files of doubt, why he
could be a hard-sell television salesman for some expensive
foreign make of car giving five hard real incontestable
reasons why his product is superior to the competitor, yes,
he says, the "economic position of Senator McGovern must
be considered not free enterprise but socialist in character."
It is, he virtually burps with disdain, "Alice in Wonderland
economics" and has the following characteristics, five in
number, wholly regrettable he would assure the Press.
"McGovernomics" moves, one!, toward equality of income
"the numbers-game way of getting into socialism," and
he holds up a finger. "Secondly, it is the most inflationary
set of proposals ever presented to the American people—
there will be a 130 billion net increase in government
spending." Now, in preparation, the third finger goes up—
"this does not mean tax reduction but a *massive tax
increase.*" Rinfret looks down at his audience, thus collar-

ing his young first chin in the beginnings of a second. "Since stagnation and recession will prove a function of a new calculated 17 billion dollars of corporate taxation, we can be certain that point four involves nothing less than a reduction of American capital investment, which with its inevitable retardation of the rate of increase of the GNP (if not its absolute decrease), means nothing less than the fifth and fatal point—an increase in unemployment." This Walpurgisnacht of transfer from Nixonomics to McGovernomics having been delivered by Rinfret in one long oratorical breath as full of gusto as a head waiter in a heavy eatery recommending the pot roast tonight with its gravies and magnificent roast potatoes just like Mommies used to make—Rinfret loves his job!

On the other hand, here is the record for Nixon's economics. "In the last quarter of this year, we had one of the highest expansions of the last seven years. There has been a substantial increase in the private sector. If the Press would like a 'fun' statistic, this country adds on in two months what the Swiss economy adds to its GNP in twenty years. Our growth alone is equal each year to all of Canada's economy and nearly equal to Britain's. The Confidence Index of the American People is rising—from 74 percent to 90 percent in the last two years according to a study at the University of Michigan. The President has defended the integrity of the dollar whereas"—he speaks loftily—"McGovern never talks about the concern of retired people for a stable currency. And if in this picture of growth, prosperity and a controlled dollar, the 5.5 percent rate of unemployment is still too high, let me assure you the reasons for this are to be found in the winding down of the war in Vietnam and the reduction of jobs in defense industries by 1.5 million plus the fact that 1,700,000 youths join the labor force each year. So the rate of unemployment conceals the fact that the administration had actually created 3 million new jobs in the last year, a vigorous creative statistic! Nixon economics is sound, stable, dynamic and progressive economics, not Alice in Wonderland McGovern economics."

They asked him questions and he took pains each time to find a way to compliment the query—a technique he must have learned from the boss. After a while, Aquarius' mind began to wander. In their turn when the time came, the McGovern economists would speak in the same positive terms of their economics and would deride that Nixon economy which had just been praised. They would take the same figures and draw opposite conclusions. It seemed to him that economic arguments were invariably reminiscent of court disputes on sanity. On such occasions, the only certainty was that an expert for one side would always be matched by an expert for the other. Perhaps morality and money, equal mysteries, might yet prove to be mutually antagonistic systems, and much like matter and anti-matter calculated to destroy each other on contact. For morality, carried to its logical development, might have to insist that one soul was worth all the coin and credit in the world, whereas money might have to argue that nothing should finally prove alien to its measure. Since each economist, however, tainted the pure science of his economic analysis with moral weightings so subtle as to be unperceived by himself or even by his colleagues and critics, and since producers and consumers moved slowly by times and sometimes quickly through shifting moral evaluations of their work and consumption, for which moral displacements there was as yet small recognition and no units nor instruments of measure, it seemed to him that one's only legitimate confidence was that economics was famously unpredictable, and might yet prove more so since the pollution of the world's ecology had begun to invade the natural wealth of the five senses—those same five senses for which all products of consumption were finally intended. It was this thought he had tried to present to McGovern, but so poorly!—tried to say that Nixon had impoverished the real wealth of the land (by his personality first) but also by continuing the straight-out pollution (by the economy) of the five senses: the sight of urban and suburban sprawl, highway glut, and bad and monotonous architecture; frozen and chemically fortified food on the palate; a touch of plastic in all of one's intimate environment; the noise of motors, electronic whine and static; and the smell of inversions and smog had taken one vast if undetected bite out of the Gross National Product, indeed had grossed out the sweet and marrow of any average good life in the second-third of the Twentieth Century—part of the rage

of the wad was that life did not feel as good as the sum of
their earnings encouraged them to believe it was going
to be. But he smiled at the thought of presenting such
notions in the form of a question to Rinfret, that raging
bull of the economic pampas! Long live Nixonomics. It
would poison us no faster than the rest.

3

Later that day, Clark MacGregor is giving a press conference at the Doral just one hour after his arrival in
Miami. A big man with straight sandy hair and dark horn-
rimmed glasses, a big friendly nose, his manner is there to
suggest that if only there were no Blacks, no Latins, and
no slaughter in Vietnam, then America could be a country
where Republicans administer government for other Republicans, and they would be superb at it, for collectively
(MacGregor's presence is there to suggest) Republicans
are better able to give off that necessary aura of confidence,
good management and impersonal courtesy which the man-
agers of successful corporations are also able to convey.
Of course MacGregor is no corporation executive but a
former congressman from Minnesota appointed recently
by Nixon to run the Committee for Reelection of the
President after John Mitchell has resigned, and in fact he
dresses with just a little too much hint of the lost Square
to work for an *Eastern* corporation, he is wearing a gray
suit, baggy from travel, a pale-blue shirt *and* a black tie
with little red diamonds, but these are unworthy items—
what he fairly promotes is the geniality of high confidence.
Behind him, reminiscent of Rinfret, are charts. "Rate of
Inflation Is Down," they say; "Real Earnings Are Up";
"Total Civilian Employment Is Up While Armed Forces
Man Power Is Down!" and they stand in front of the
powder-blue curtain (TV-blue in every press-conference
room) while underfoot is a blue-green carpet and gold-
painted chairs for the Press. Mermaids and sea horses look
down on MacGregor from the ornate ceiling of the Mediterranean Room as he is asked if there is any way the
Republicans can lose the election.

"No," he says. A smile. "Although I think it will get closer. Let me say that we are gearing up for a close fight, and absolutely on the watch against overconfidence."

"But you think the polls are good?"

"In Minnesota, my home state, 96 percent of the Republicans are for Nixon, and that's an incredible figure if you know anything about party breakdowns."

"How many Republicans for McGovern?"

"2 percent. We're ahead in the state 58 percent to 31. Exceptional statistics for Minnesota." In 1970 at Nixon's request, he has run for senator against Hubert Humphrey, an impossible campaign and lost by 2 to 1.

"How big is your budget for the election?"

"We're aiming—the figure is not yet fixed—but we look for a total budget between 35 and 38 million." (The Democrats have announced 25 million for their budget, and nobody thinks they will reach it.)

"What about Watergate?" comes the first voice. "Will that hurt you?"

He is unflappable. "I am absolutely satisfied that the so-called Watergate caper will have absolutely no effect on the election of Richard Nixon." His doughty air suggests that he could be hired equally well as a sales manager or a police commissioner.

"In relation to Watergate," says another reporter, "is it possible you've set up your tight security in this hotel because you expect the Democrats to bug it?" There is mocking laughter, for the Press is much irritated. A security tight enough to guard the President has been installed at the Doral, yet the President won't even stay here!

To get to see even a minor Republican official, it is necessary to obtain a special folder and look up his room which is listed in it, get the official's permission by telephone for an interview, then look to obtain a pass in the downstairs lobby in order to get on the elevator. A woman reporter cries out that the Republicans call themselves the Open-Door party. "Will you please open the door of the Doral a little?"

"Well, look," says MacGregor, "I just got off the plane. Let me look into the situation."

"Will you ease it?"

"Let me see." He thinks he is done with this, but another reporter asks, "Any truth, Mr. MacGregor, to the rumor that the security is so tight because the Republicans already have the 35 million in the hotel?" MacGregor laughs heartily. "I knew it was the dog days, but not the silly season."

Now the conference is moving to its point. If there is a single flaw in any Republican presentation of themselves, it is (except for the six million killed, wounded, and homeless) to be found in Watergate. What a mess. Five men have been caught trying to remove the bugging devices they have installed (by breaking and entering) in Democractic Headquarters in Washington, and the two leaders not only have had links to the CIA but to the Committeee to Reelect the President, indeed have worked for a more important team with the modest name of "plumbers" who were set up to investigate White House leaks to the Media: the "plumbers" include mem bers of the White House staff, and a former Assistant Attorney General, are even connected to a special counsel to Nixon. One of the plumbers, E. Howard Hunt, formerly a high official in the CIA and White House consultant. has now disappeared. Two weeks before the Watergate arrests, however, Hunt has flown to Miami to meet Bernard Barker, leader of the five men who were caught in the middle of the night at Watergate, and Barker has deposited four checks totalling $89,000 to his account. the money reputed to have come from wealthy Texas Democrats via wealthy Texas Republicans, but none of these names will MacGregor agree to divulge (at the request of the contributors, he says) and then there is still another check for $25,000 which has gone through Maurice Stans, former Secretary of Commerce, and Hugh Sloan, Jr., treasurer of the Nixon campaign (who has since resigned for personal reasons). Allegedly this check has been given to G. Gordon Liddy, a former White House staffer, who became the attorney on the Committee to Reelect the President's Finance Committee—Liddy—it is the same allegation—has converted the check to cash and given it to Barker. Liddy has been fired for refusing to respond to questions. "You know I can't answer that," is the reply everyone hears him making to his sympathetic inter- rogator. What a mess! Rumor in Miami, Washington, and New York suggests Martha Mitchell's last ultimatum to her husband John that he must dare to choose between the government and herself is no curious coincidence. Certainly, not since the writing of *El Cid* has such a conflict between love and duty been presented to so high an official with such perfect timing. Is it true that John has been told he could not do better than to choose Martha? Some go so far as to suggest Martha has been encouraged to be Martha. Whatever! MacGregor has replaced Mitchell as the head of the Committee to Reelect the President and now can dodge the worst of the questions by saying that he has only been on his new job since July 1. So he has no first-hand knowledge of what has gone on before, "Although, I am convinced, let me say, that no one in the White House, or in high responsible position on the Committee to Reelect the President, has any prior knowledge of, or gave sanction to the operation generally known as the so-called Watergate caper. I will say," MacGregor stated solemnly, pushing his glasses up on his large nose, "that I have talked to the White House principals in this affair, and Mr. Stans, Mr. Mitchell and Mr. Colson have all assured me that they were not involved, and I am convinced that they are men of honor. I can only say that they have satisfied me."

"Will you agree that if any of them were lying, there was no way you could know?"

"No, I cannot agree. The word of men of honor is good enough for me. More than that, I cannot say. We have been warned by Judge Richey to employ all necessary discretion against impinging on the rights of the defendants by making disclosures which would then hurt the government's case."

"But since you were not there before July 1, you have only the word of these high officials to go on?"

MacGregor has a temper, and he is containing it now. The straight sandy hair suggests some fire at the root, for his face is getting red. "I have endeavored to be as forthright as I can, given my lack of knowledge before July 1 of the activities of the Committee to Reelect the President."

No one quite dares to suggest he is saying that he knows but he doesn't know. "In public life," MacGregor says, "you have to learn when to trust the word of other people." But what he can't know is when an honorable man has overpowering motive to lie. So, too, for motive something less or somewhat more than this, have public officials already created the highest euphemism for an official lie—

the credibility gap. MacGregor gulps and reddens and his
temper singes his hair, his glasses slide down his nose and
are pushed up once more, the sea horses and mermaids
look down on him, the Press looks up from their golden
chairs and he does not move. He doesn't know and he
does know, but he is a man who has been picked to
weather more than one storm, and it will be no trick at all,
here today, to ride this out. The Judge, he repeats, wishes
to restrain them from talking of the case. ". . . necessary
discretion . . . you fellows are trying to get me to impinge
. . . rights of the defendants. . . ."

4

Were counter-espionage and Christianity the good true poles of the party? Next day—what could possibly restrain him from going?—Aquarius attends the Sunday Worship Service of the Republican Convention. It is being held in the Carillon Room of the Carillon Hotel, a supper club room which moves in a crescent of coral curtains and gold fringe around the room, with golden seats arrayed for more than a thousand guests and these seats are filled. American flags cover the wall on either side of the stage. Sitting there, he thinks there is probably no act on earth more natural to Republicans than going to church on Sunday. That bony look which seems to lay flat white collars on ladies' clavicles, that Wasp look bony with misery (when they are merely tourists eating in some jammed Johnson's off the boiling reeking superhighway during family summer travel (the windshield shellacked with the corpses of bugs numerous as dead Vietnamese), yes, same gangling bony lonely pointed elbows) comes instead into its inheritance and stands out in all the decorous composure of characterological bone when Republicans get to church. Then their virtues live again—hard work, neat clothes, patriotism, and cleanliness become four pillars of the Lord to hold up the American sky.

This church service, however, is being held in the morning as balance perhaps to the Republican gala of the evening, a veritable panorama of worship with celebrities to pray and Mamie Eisenhower for Honorary Chairman, plus the wives of Cabinet officials to compose the Advisory Committee. Senator Tower, tough little John Tower, right-wing Republican from Texas, gave the welcome as Worship Leader. Once, when he first came to the Senate,

Tower had the mean concentrated take-him-out look of a
strong short welterweight, but the Chamber laid senatorial
courtesies upon him—now this Sunday morning he was
mellifluous and full of the order of dignity as he whipped
out his reading glasses, intoned "Almighty God," and
delivered the prayer written by President Eisenhower for
his first inauguration, "Give us, we pray, the power to
discover clearly right from wrong." There was no hitch in
the words for him. Tower was a hawk, and the operative
definition of the hawk is that they do not have trouble
with moral discernment.

Then came Frank Borman, the former astronaut, who
had read Genesis on Christmas Eve as the capsule of
Apollo 8 circled the moon. There were a few (liberals and
Democrats in the main) to whisper that Borman read the
familiar words like a grocery list, but this morning, wearing
the shortest haircut still left on a good-looking American,
he read the same way, comfortable before the audience—
he was a man who always occupied his own volume—and
it was clear that he came out of all that part of America
which knows that to read with expression is suspect.

George Romney offered a prayer. "Help us to help those
who most need help." Was he praying to the 12 million
bomb craters in Vietnam? "A crisis of the spirit requires an
answer of the spirit."

Cliff Barrows who was the Music Director for Billy
Graham now led the singing of "America the Beautiful"
and for once Aquarius listened to the words.

> O beautiful for patriot dream that sees beyond the
> years,
> Thine alabaster cities gleam, undimmed by human
> tears!

John Volpe, Secretary of Transportation, gave the Con-
gregational prayer "Through your goodness, the sustenance
of life is always flowing," and thoughts wandered again,
mindless once more, over the concrete, macadam, asphalt,
sand and gravel which had poured and flowed across ecological cuts in the land since Volpe first came in to build
more roads, and then spoke liberal Senator Brooke from
Massachusetts. It was only in some inner suppleness which
suggested the tricky reflexes of a ball player like Maury

Wills that one could sense he was a Black. Otherwise Brooke looked more like a respectable young Jewish businessman as he read from Corinthians "and the greatest of the three is charity," his liberal contribution to Sunday morning.

But it was left to Dr. Elton Trueblood of Earlham College, Richmond, Indiana, to give the sermon, and Aquarius later wondered if Richmond, Indiana, was looked upon as a swing vote in a swing state; in that case, local Hoosiers might be loyal to the honor that one of the town clergymen had addressed the assembled Republican mighties, loyal at least for a few hundred more votes—Aquarius had already begun to admire the thoroughness with which Richard Nixon looked for such votes—quite the equal of any first-rate housewife on the hunt for ants during spring-cleaning. (It is the innocuous corners which must never be overlooked.) So, even on this nonpolitical and nondramatic occasion, this *un*political and highly Christian convocation, care had been taken to invite the President of the Synagogue Council of America, also serving as rabbi of Temple Emmanuel, Miami Beach, to offer an Old Testament meditation. Then Maryland's Junior Miss, Miss Cathie Epstein, soon offered the song "Amazing Grace" which was harsh on the ear for its amazingly tortured sounds, he thought, but the crowd gave Miss Epstein such a spontaneous whip-out of the sound, "Amen," and so much hand-clapping that they had obviously heard something else—score one for Jews-for-Agnew. No, Nixon did not miss any corner with an opportunity for amazing grace, and the Reverend James A. McDonald who sang next with the deepest pleasure of the ages since Paul Robeson, was also black, blacker than Brooke, and the benediction being given by Father Ramon O'Farrill who was Cuban, his name in the Miami Beach papers would do no irreparable harm with local Cubans, no more than Rabbi Lehman, Epstein and Jeannette Weiss would offend nearby Senior Citizens. Of course, Jeannette Weiss, an alternate delegate from Michigan who read the Pledge of Allegiance, might have been German as easily as Jewish, but all the better—she could gladden both kinds of newspaper readers, and certainly would not hurt the pride of women, alternate delegates (so often ignored) and a few hundred near neighbors in Michigan. But since Jeannette Weiss proved when she stood up to be black, it could be said that Nixon was tickling every straw in the broom. Now, there was not much chance that the President had literally been able to bother with such detail as this, but of course it was not impossible he had actually put the program together for the sort of relaxation others take in crossword puzzles—it didn't matter—his hand was laid so finely upon the palpitations of this convention's breast that from the thought of his presence came all the necessary intimations of *intelligence*. Even the least of his assistants must acquire a sense of how to place each potential use in its slot. Not every evidence of harmony in the Vatican issues directly after all from the Pope, but who would say he is not the center of all its political spirit!

Along came Dr. Elton Trueblood then to give the sermon, and in fairness to him, he was there for more reasons than to swing a corner of Indiana; the Doctor was a sermonizer of invention—he fulfilled that Sunday function which requests the preacher to give the parish something to think about from Monday to Saturday for he said, "Government ought to be a holy calling, a divine vocation. We ought to speak of the ministry of politics." And he quoted Romans 13:6, "The authorities are ministers of God," and so decided that, "Whatever your occupation in politics or government, you are called to be His ministers." As he spoke, his features too far away to be discerned, only his white hair and glasses, his balding head, dark-blue suit and starched white shirt visible in the distance, he looked nonetheless like a compressed whole bully of faith—small surprise that Faith was his favorite word. It was as if he was the first to know that this worship service was not part of the convention so much as the convention was going to be a service of worship. Nonetheless, Trueblood touched something of confusion in the Republic heart, which he did not necessarily put to rest. No more than the good decent average Republican would admit that he loved to fuck his wife (those who did) in a voice which might ever be heard aloud—as if blight must immediately descend on the marriage—so must many Republicans have thought in private over the years that they were doing God's work and being *His* ministers in the world of corporation and government, *His* ministers to work for the salvation of this tortured and troubled Republic, as divided as two souls residing in the same heart, this Republic of order and bar-

barism where the young would, if given their way, yet walk
with naked breasts and faces hidden by matted hair and
trampled flowers, timeless droning drug-filled young with
filthy feet—they would yet walk upon the heart of America.
And now Aquarius knew suddenly why good Republicans
would never mind the bombs, for the blood of the North
Vietnamese was the smallest price to pay that America
might be saved from the barbarisms beating in the young
—yes, it was Nixon's genius to know that every bomb
dropped somehow extinguished another dangerous hippie
in the mind of the wad, evil was a plague of creeping
things and the bombs were DDT to the cess-dumps of the
world. It was America which had to be saved—the heart
of God resided in the living life of an orderly America,
and this passion was so deep, so reverential, and so in terror of the harsh light of the word, that his congregation
listened to Elton Trueblood with respect but not com-
fortably, staying at the edge of that bolt of comprehensions
he would loose, for if good Republicans might think of
themselves privately as ministers of God protecting the
homeland by their acts and their presence from every
subtle elucidation of Satan, still they feared the loss of
magic, like primitives they feared the loss of magic once
the thought was declared aloud. Fierce as the fever of
discipline which holds the heart in righteousness is the fear
of the fire beneath—what a fire is that compressed American combustible of love and hate which heats the stock of
the melting pot.

And Aquarius, carried along by the flux of some of his
own thoughts, began perhaps to comprehend the certainty
of these Republicans whose minds never seemed to reach
beyond the circle of favors, obligation, work, courtesies and
good deeds that made up the field of their life and the re-
pose of their death. That was the goodness they knew, their
field was America, and they seemed spiritually incapable of
hating a war they could not see, yes, sentiment against the
war had eased even as infantry had ceased coming back
with tales of the horrors on the land—yes, Nixon was a
genius to have put that war on the divine national elevator
high in the sky where nobody could see the flowering in-
testines of the dead offering the aphrodisiac of their corruption to the flies. So, was it then a compact with the
Devil to believe one was a minister of God and live one's

life in work and deeds and never lift one's eyes from the nearest field? Or was that all any human could dare to comprehend, his own part of the patch, and leave Nixodemus to be divided by Satan and Jehovah, no, impossible! the miserable truth was that men and women, willy-nilly, were becoming responsible for all the fields of earth since there was a mania now loose on the earth, a species of human rabies, and the word was just, for rabies was the disease of every virulence which was excessive to the need for self-protection. One hundred seventy-six thousand tons of bombs had been dropped on Cambodia in the last two years, and that was more than all the bombs dropped on Japan in World War II. Cambodia! our ally! but on Laos it was not 176,000 tons but more than a million. We had in fact dropped more bombs altogether in the three and a half years of Nixon's reign than we dropped on Europe and Asia in World War II, indeed almost twice as many tons of bombs and there was no industry, military population, railroad yards, navy yards, or other category of respectable target to compare with Germany, Italy and Japan, no, finally not much more than the wet earth, the dirt roads, the villages, the packing-crate cities and the people—so the bombing had become an activity as rational as the act of a man who walks across his own home town to defecate each night on the lawn of a stranger—it is the same stranger each night—such a man would not last long even if he had the most powerful body in town. "Stop," he would scream as they dragged him away, "I need to shit on that lawn. It's the only way to keep my body in shape, you fools. A bat has bitten me!"

5

So, yes, carriers of a rabid disease the Republicans might certainly be (that same disease of the Twentieth Century which first had transported the victims to the ovens even as—a speaker in Flamingo Park would cry out—we were now bringing the ovens to the victims, Amerika!) but small evidence of the rabid was visible as he watched Senator Dole on Sunday TV after this worship service. Nothing appeared in Dole of the disease unless the rabies had been transmitted into Dole's private reserve of contumely and scorn. Dole was perhaps the best-looking of the Republicans, Senator from Kansas, Chairman of the Republican National Committee, a ringer to play Humphrey Bogart's younger brother, and he had taken something of Bogart into his style, that stubbornly created manliness which scorns any other man who cannot live on the wry edge of the code, "Yes," Dole promised, "I'm going to keep an eye on McGovern in the Senate—if he ever shows up." He gave every evidence of disliking McGovern personally (which is effective politically if you have the looks to hold your audience) although, for fact, Dole might be truly jealous of a senator from a sister state as equally unglamorous as Kansas who could still win a national nomination. "Yeah," said Dole, vintage Bogart wit to the jugular, "he's always 1,000 percent certain until he changes his mind." Of the running mate, Dole was heard to say, "Shriver's always available," which was kinder than his comment on Pierre Salinger who, subject of anathema for a trip to Hanoi, was described as a man who "can never do much but smoke a cigar." Dole had all the sharp bite of the proud and crippled—a little later, greeting Pat Nixon, it was evident that his right arm was paralyzed for he shook hands with his left, and held the right to his chest like the wing of a wounded bird.

Then came Rockefeller and Reagan down the broad highway of the tube and they sat side by side, and jiggled each other in the soft inner flesh of the arm, the telltale flabby few inches above the elbow on even the most weathered old politician, teased each other for TV nearly so much as they teased the Democrats, Rockefeller and Reagan who had not been able to get together in '68 to stop Nixon, their ideological differences too much to right and left. Now, they were closer. Rockefeller was blooded. He had his right-wing dueling scars. Thirty-two convicts and eleven guards had been killed at Attica after Rockefeller refused to visit the prison and talk to the convicts about their demands, or even to be present to watch over the details of the attack to regain the prison. Something had gotten into his face since then—the look of a sour clown. Oh, was it a stale hero? So that face which once had been able to win votes for him, would now lose them. His honor was gone (if not his ambition) and it was possible he knew it.

Yes, Rockefeller had paid. He had the beginnings of a high-pitched whinny, he snaffled a little as he laughed, and Reagan had him going and coming, because Reagan had never wandered out of the arena of his own imagination, whereas Rockefeller had once traveled to such strange stadiums that he even tried to capture a nomination after obtaining a divorce, bold Republicanism! Rockefeller had had more to lose, and now within must feel older than Reagan, wearier certainly, and he argued with less wit on their point of dispute (which was over the reallocation of delegates for '76—were the big Eastern states to get them or the small and Western states?) Actually, they seemed fonder of each other's presence than with continuing the dispute because, now if they wished to try for the nomination in '76, they were indispensable to one another. By then, Rockefeller would be sixty-eight years old, and Reagan sixty-five, which is old for a presidential candidate. So the living presence of each would give sanction to the other's campaign. Indeed either one would prove a final disaster to the other if he died. No wonder Rockefeller spoke of Reagan as Ronnie. For a politician there is small distance between necessity and affection.

6

Pat Nixon arrives with her daughters at the gate of the Fontainebleau, up the driveway and into the crowd of Young Voters for the President. She disappears in a sea of white floppy hats with blue brims and straw hats with red-white-and-blue bands. A combo with red-and-white-striped jackets is playing middle-class weddings songs, pseudo Benny Goodman music (may be the term for its category), accordion, clarinet, flute, drums and electric guitar, and George Romney has been running before her arrival—he is excited—and Dole is now down to greet her. There is a flood of cheers when she comes up in her black Cadillac —much like the on-off hysteria you hear when the team hits the field, and all the signs wave. Now, the signs painted by the YVPers all begin to wave, these Young Voters for the President who in the eyes of the liberal Press will yet look as ears of goldenrod to hayfever sufferers. Somebody has provided all YVPers with the paint, no dark secret, Republican money can be spent for Republican posters and paint, but the kids have done the work themselves and the signs say "We stand for Pat"; "We Love Julia"; "Trish You're a dish"; "Miami loves the 1st family"—there is just a hint of the slovenly in the uncertain use of capital letters. "Welcome back, Pat"; "Agnew for peace"; "Vote for a WINNER"; "Nixon gives a damn"—here is one—"Nixon is For Love." Now kids are chanting "Four more years," "Hey, hey, whateya say, Nixon, Nixon, all the way." They are not the most attractive faces he has seen. Hundreds of young faces and not one is a beauty, neither by natural good looks nor by the fine-tuning of features through vitality or wit—the children

in this crowd remind him of other crowds he knows well,
and does not like. Of course!—they are the faces of the
wad!—all those blobs of faces who line up outside TV
theaters and wait for hours that they may get in to see
the show live, yes, the show will be more alive than their
faces. The genius of Nixon! Has he selected this gaggle
of mildly stunted minds from photograph files? Or had
they been handed applications as they left the theaters
after the live shows? Aquarius remembers the look of the
television set in his room at the Fontainebleau. It was up
on a small pickled-white dais and looked like some kind of
altar for a medico-religious event. Nixon may have drawn
the deep significance from such a sight twenty years ago—
how valuable must be the insights he could pass on to
McLuhan, well, Aquarius was frothing again and so came
near to missing the value of Pat Nixon's entrance.

Ergo, he went back to the opportunity to watch Pat
Nixon do her work, went twice that afternoon to see her,
once at her planned spontaneous tumultuous entrance with
Secret Service men who quietly, gently, steadily, *politically,*
forced an aisle for her up the steps and for a few hundred
feet along the lobby to an elevator up to a private room in
the Fontainebleau Towers while the band played (a trip
which must have consumed a half hour) and there after
a bath presumably—how much desire for still another
shower did such waves of human flesh arouse in a First
Lady?—she had changed and came down again with her
daughters to plunge into an orgy of hand-shaking and
autographing as she proceeded along a six-foot-wide roped-
off aisle to a banquet room of the Fontainebleau where a
reception party was being given for Pat Nixon, her girls,
and the Young Voters for the President.

What a rich opportunity then to study Pat Nixon, first
with her entrance to the hotel in a pink dress, then her
immersion later into the reception crowd with a royal-blue
dress, long-sleeved, straight-skirted, a light soft material
vulnerable to crowds, she was able to demonstrate that
particular leathery hard-riding sense of grace she possessed
which spoke of stamina first, for she could knee and elbow
her own defense through a crowd and somehow never
involve the dress, that was one of the straight-out tools of
her trade and she knew how to employ it—that material

was not going to get snagged on some dolt's ragged elbow or *ripped* any more than a seaman would get his feet caught in a rope he was coiling in a storm.

So, for instance, had she managed her passage through the lobby for the reception, pointing her head at an angle up to the glare of the Media lights poised like flaming swords over her way, the ears inured to the sound of another brass combo (with one black trumpeter) trombone, banjo, other trumpet, and drums), still she moves a little to it, just a flash, as though to demonstrate that dancing is one of the hundred and sixty-eight light occupations she can muster.

Earlier Clark MacGregor has come down the steps with his wife, he stands close, he is proud of her like a college kid with one smash of a keen steady! Indeed there are older people all through the lobby waiting with love in their eyes for Pat—she has worked hard and she is better off for it—they are ready to revere her for caulking the hull of the ship so well (it is their ship, too—the presidency residing somewhere in the awesome fall between one's god and one's parents) and the crowd is orderly, not pushing, the YVPers all stashed in the reception room, but Pat is still going slowly down the aisle through the older folks in the lobby, tarrying to say hello, and before her comes Julia, committed, determined to do a good job in a green top and white-skirted dress, black belt, and Tricia in a white and pink dress with her husband Ed Cox who looks gracious, as if he takes considerate care of her which she might need for she is near to beautiful and tiny, wearing perhaps a size 5 dress with blond hair all pulled back and sprayed into an immaculate pale-gold mass, but her dark eyes, nymphlike and lost, suggest the vacant remote and yet flirtatious look of a princess who has been told about life outside the castle. Then comes Pat. There are liver spots to perceive on her hands, and her teeth must be capped, she has obviously pinched and pushed and tightened her presentation of herself all her life, but she had ridden the beast of such discipline, she looks better now than when she entered politics. No, she has emerged as a pro, such a pro indeed with such a pride in having mastered every side of her occupation that one did not ask oneself if she liked shaking hands. Possibly the question did not exist for her, since it was a matter of indifference whether she liked it or not—she was not on earth to like things but to do them!

Still, for a politician, the love of shaking hands is equal to a writer's love of language. Ultimately that is the material with which a politician must work, yet not all politicians love shaking hands, nor with everyone, any more than Ernest Hemingway loved every word in the English language. Certain words like "gorgeous" brought out Poppa's snobbery—perhaps he was in this sense equivalent to a Republican politician who preferred to grasp the hand of the clean, the neat, the precise, and the well-laundered. (Hubert Humphrey, to the contrary, was a veritable Thomas Wolfe of a politician; just as no word was too mean or out-size splendiferous for the man who could write *Of Time and the River,* so Hubert would kiss Queens and scrofula victims with the same warmth.) Now, if Pat Nixon had been a writer, she would have gravitated to the commonest words that everyone used or the most functional words—she would have wanted to reach the largest audiences with ideas they could comprehend on first reading—that was how she shook hands. Like a *Reader's Digest* editor attacked a paragraph. She loved to work with the wad. Give her the plainest dullest face, no spark, no flair, just the urgency to get what it wants—her autograph, her handshake. She gave them out equally, like the bills and smiles of a bank teller. There are faces to greet, currency to handle, stay on top of the job!

In his own mayoralty campaign, Aquarius ended up by shaking hands wherever he could, had in fact to his surprise ended up liking that act more than anything else in politics, at least once he comprehended that the only way to do it was to offer as much of himself as was present with every greeting. The phenomenon was that energy came back, and the hand did not get tired. It was as if in shaking a thousand hands, six hundred may have returned a little more energy than they took, as if the generosity of a mass of people might be larger than their greed, a belief which was as it should be if one wanted to become a politician, for it gave, on balance, some confidence at the thought of working for others.

But Pat Nixon had obviously come from folds of human endeavor which believed the reward for service was not to be found in the act but afterward. Naturally she gave energy and she took energy, impossible not to, and was somewhat wilted if with a glow when she was done, but it was the muscles of her arm which worked, and the muscles in her smile, her soul was the foreman of the act, and so did not reside in her muscles, but off to the side and vigilant as she worked the machine. She no longer saw faces, no, she was a heavy worker on an assembly line, and bodies came her way, there were touches and taps, a gloved rhythm to keep —she moved in some parallel perhaps to the burden of a slim tight-mouthed Negress with heavy family worries on a heavy assembly line for whom the pay was good and so she was in it until death or double overtime. So, too, would Pat Nixon have no inner guilt before trade unionists or Blacks—she had worked as hard as any of them—in her own way, she moved as well. Afterward, her fixed expression stayed in memory for she had the features of a woman athlete or the heroine of some insurmountable disease which she has succeeded in surmounting.

A man getting an autograph from her asks, "How do you stay so young?"

She smiles carefully. "With hard work," she says.

7A

If it seems to be a convention with nothing but background, arrivals, receptions and press conferences, nothing in contention and nothing to commence, still he finds it more and more interesting for it is the first sustained clue he has ever had to the workings of Richard Nixon's mind and *his* comprehension of America, and it is a mark of Aquarius' own innocence that he has never recognized until now how Nixon's vision might be conceivably more comprehensive than his own.

At the Celebrity conference in the same Mediterranean Room of the Doral, three of the five most massive celebrities are not present. Charlton Heston, Sammy Davis, Jr. (Sammy for *Nixon!* all the pastrami eaters will scream), and Frank Sinatra, are somewhere else or not arrived. There is only good Jimmy Stewart and good John Wayne in a dark-blue yachting jacket and gray pants, his cheeks red, his dark hairpiece on, and his eyes as wide open, expressionless and sleepy as a lion digesting a meal. Later, when he makes his speech, it will be very short and he will say no more than that he wants Nixon cause he's the right man in the right office at the right time, a way of remarking that Nixon isn't his man under other circumstances, but he is also there to guard the flock—there is a herd of women, honey-blond soft-featured animated Ruta Lee from TV who will be seen at the convention Tuesday night with Kissinger—she has converted to Nixon from the Democrats, as has Mary Ann Mobley, former Miss America, now a "card-carrying Republican," and she is animated too. Mary Ann Mobley has obviously gone to acting classes where they taught her to use her personality, and so there is the unhappy suspicion that if you asked her how to cut a carrot she might say, "I take out my *cleaver* which is shining bright, for cutlery must *gleam* in the kitchen, and I wash my carrot, and then"—flash of her eyes—"I go chop-chop, chop-chop!" So she was using her personality as she spoke about politics until interrupted by Johnny Graham, a comic and/or gag-writer, a sawed-off man in a big yellow jacket who seemed to be serving as team shepherd and Commissar—Graham got her to sit down at which point she received cheers. At a press conference! But it was now apparent two-thirds of the room was filled with Young Voters for Nixon out to see their TV stars.

Graham had the floor. He was funny. "I see where all by himself Bob Hope raised as much money on television for flood victims as all the actors who worked to raise funds for the Democratic party on their telethon. I guess," he said with a grin wide as a barn door, "Americans are particular which disaster they give their money to."

Glenn Ford gets up to a big hand, but he is soft-spoken and very shy. He makes an inaudible speech three sentences long and goes back to his folding chair, but one of the rear legs inadvertently slides off the back of the platform, the chair collapses and Glenn falls down only to get up quickly in the middle of bales of his sheepish embarrassment.

"Get a stunt man," yells Johnny Graham.

"Glenn will do anything for publicity," says Ruta Lee.

Chad Everett, a TV star, ambles up and says, "I think if you got a big gun, shoot it. And Nixon's the man." He sits down. The YVPers scream. Somewhere in Nixon's Maxims must rest the observation that a TV star in a current series is worth two Hollywood evergreens.

Nonetheless Kathy Garver, TV star on a show called *Family Affair,* is trapped by the invisible imps of her motive, for she is suddenly unable to say Nixon's name and mispronounces it. Jerry Rubin in the Press section gives her the friendliest grin out of his wild red-and-blue T-shirt and full chestnut beard, and John Wayne glares at Jerry Rubin. Kathy Garver corrects her pronunciation, Mary Ann Mobley laughs wildly. The YVPers clap.

Ethel Merman takes a bow, and none of the young in the audience even know she was the madam in *Call Me Madam.* The speeches get shorter and shorter and say less and less. Jimmy Stewart humphs and phumphs his skinny presence all the way up and says, "I'm a lifelong Republican and not about to change now." Cheers. The actors have all borne testimony to the show-biz maxim which goes, "If you're doing a benefit, and it's a nothing mood, don't be the one to try to turn it around."

Still, how reassuring will the dullest of these actors seem in memory to the dullest regions of the wad, for they have demonstrated that even if one is famous, it is possible to be utterly uninteresting. Across our continent, the yaws of one soul will offer comfort to the voids of another. Bombs are fireworks to the sleepy.

7B

On the way back to the Fontainebleau, he stops off at a Black reception. Negro doctors, lawyers, and businessmen, delegates most of them, move around with their wives who are heavy-set. There is not a jive Black in sight, no smocks, sarongs, or flaring Afros. No prime evil. Nothing carnal. The mood, if boring, is absolutely safe. He has not felt so safe among Blacks in years. The spirit is sullen, long-suffering and secure. It is as if he has been invited to a gathering of pullman porters. Then some young Blacks come in. They are saltier in their stance for they are self-defensive. Still, there is no menace. Just safety. Will America be miserable when the streets are safe?

Later, he will hear about the Black caucus next morning. It takes place in a small pink room at the Eden Roc with wrought-iron black chairs and white plastic seat covers. Counting various whites and the Press, there are present two hundred people. Paul Jones, who had spoken at the Black press conference, walks in with Julie Nixon who is wearing a white dress with a sailor collar. Reportedly Jones has the sly look of a man who is pressing hard not to reveal that he is the first Black from his hometown to have a white lady on his arm. Of course the other Blacks look on it as a token—where is Pat? So when Julie Nixon starts speaking,

they are annoyed that her speech is prepared. (Indeed, it
is so prepared that next morning Julie Eisenhower will give
the same speech at the Latin caucus, only substituting the
word Latin for Black, etc., as she talks of the administrative
appointments of Latins to high-ranking position.) "We,"
she says, "will do much better among black voters," then
tells them her father has ended much discrimination in the
South. "Even if we had the most massive busing program
ever proposed, we couldn't reach all the children." Perhaps
it is her didactic manner (where spontaneous if halting remarks might have been more appropriate), but she is hardly
begun before there is a strong undertone of muttering. It
grows so loud that Jones from the podium is obliged to
hush the audience.

When Julie is finished, the Press start to move out, and
a short heavy-set woman on the podium pleads: "We
would appreciate it if the Press didn't leave now." En
masse, the Press goes away. They have come to see Julie.
A chairwoman announces the time of departure for the
bus which will take the Blacks to Convention Hall.

7C

That was Monday morning after Sunday night when the
Republicans had had their Gala, one thousand dollars a
ticket, and security as tight at the gate of the Ballroom in the
Fontainebleau as at the elevators of the Doral. He cannot
get in, and succeeds only in missing some of the street
action outside, for a few of the guests have been harassed.
Next day he hears of women whose dresses were spattered
with eggs. A mistake, he thinks, to inflict small damage.
Be able to shut a Gala down, or leave it alone—to a Republican lady, one egg on the dress can mop up the guilt of
five hundred bombs. Later, that evening, he stands on a
balcony and watches police twelve stories below form a
wall across the entrance to the Fontainebleau. On Collins
Avenue, the demonstrators, down to a few hundred, are
marching off. "Back to the Park, back to the Park" a girl
keeps shrieking over a radical bull horn. He wonders if

she is the same girl he has seen in Flamingo Park on Saturday night, one of the leaders of one of the groups. He has
been remiss about preparing to cover the street action. He
recognizes that he expects it to fail.

The Jefferson Airplane has been planning to perform at
a big free concert in Miami the weekend before the convention and other groups have promised to come if the
Plane was there. It would bring tens of thousands of kids
to the area. Which would bring more thousands of government troops to stop them. But there is a military principle
to public assembly. When the number of demonstrators
increases from hundreds to thousands, then it hardly matters how well they are policed, nor how quickly one moves
to disperse them. There comes a point of congestion where
traffic cannot move at all. So if the Yippies and the SDS,
the Zippies and the Vietnam Vets Against the War are to
be effective in their demonstrations, they need thousands
of youths to amplify their moves. But the big free concert has had to be called off. The Jefferson Airplane
changed its mind. It did not wish to come. Grace Slick was
supposed to have said that demonstrations are of no use
after the Eagleton affair because McGovern is sure to lose.
There were some who had thought the point was to embarrass Nixon and protest the war regardless of who won
the election, but in any case a lesson has been taught which
will not be learned. It is that one should not try to found
a revolution on musicians; because the delicate instrument
of their body can all too easily be damaged, they are all
too prone to desert.

In any case, there have certainly been no fine musicians
in Flamingo Park the night before. Hundreds of kids sat
on the grass and watched movies about atrocities in Vietnam, and listened to a boy with a black beard dressed in
red-white-and-blue overalls (and nothing else) sing a song
called "Revolution." Indeed even as he padded up to the
platform in his bare feet another boy in the grass shouted,
"Watch out for the nails in the board."

"No, man, my feet are tough," the boy said, laying down
his soles from step to step with inadequate caution but
some kind of heavy grace. Then he sang. His voice was
even flatter than his feet. "Revolution!" But the words
were so poor that hardly anyone could retain them long
enough to give back a chorus. The kid now made a speech

about everybody staying cool and not getting grassed out so they could *work* for the demonstrations, but put-on is the law of the revolutionary young, you are nothing if your head is not living in two places at once, and therefore half a minute later he announces "The revolution means sharing, so pass around your dope." A big laugh from the spaced-out throng. They sit there waiting in the night, an apathetic mass respectful of their own apathy, for Sunday, Monday, Tuesday and Wednesday they will be demonstrating.

Later, he walks through the park. A group called Sequoia are finishing on another bandstand. He stares at a sign near them which says, People's Independent Military Party—PIMP. Yes, support your pimp. The signs are good at least. One tent has a placard over the entrance. "JAIL for War Criminals" it reads. Beneath is a list.

1. Richard Nixon
2. Spiro Agnew
3. Richard Helm
4. Henry Kissinger
5. Melvin Laird
6. Nguyen Van Thieu
7. The Rockefellers

Now the next night, Sunday, watching the few hundred demonstrators move away from the hotel and begin the two-mile walk back to their tents and bedrolls in Flamingo Park, he thinks that Miami Beach is a splendid site for a picturesque war, but one would need an army of Mexicans to wage combat in its heat. Languorously, a few yachts are meandering down Indian Creek running parallel to Collins Avenue so they can study the demonstrators from the water. Rich and native Miamians on a sightseeing party. And he is observing from the balcony of the twelfth floor. He must have turned some corner in his life for he feels no shame whatsoever. Later he will go out and eat a good dinner and not think of the kids in the park. When the time came for the real war, if it ever came, and came to America, he would presumably be enough of a man to recognize it. If he was not, it would be his own karmic ass he fried. So, cheers to Hemingway, he thought, and a good dinner.

Still, over the meal he found himself thinking once

again of Nixon's genius. Of course, it had only been common sense, no more, to pull the convention out of San Diego. The scandal of ITT would be well averted, and so would all too many groups of musicians be averted. All of San Francisco would have come down to jam San Diego. Half of the experienced college demonstrators in America lived within a few hundred miles. How many California undergrounds would have mobilized? Rumor even had it that John and Yoko Lennon had been sheepshanked on citizenship and visa applications in order to keep them away. Slowly, the metastases of the totalitarian were setting up their new colonies and the Republic was kind enough to give Media a perfect seat for each non-event. What benignities might reside in the malignities to come. Muzak in the cancer ward. Tomorrow he must go to Vizcaya and study the reception for Agnew.

8A

He sees an example of typical Republican management. The strategy is excellent and the tactics moot. It is probable there is not a better place in Miami to exhibit the Vice-President than in Vizcaya since it is much too far away from Flamingo Park for the demonstrators ever to march to it. Besides Vizcaya, being an uncommonly luxurious estate situated in a mangrove jungle by the sea, proves to be a perfect setting for Agnew, yet it has been turned over by the heirs of the original owner to Dade County and is now an art museum which charges admission and even has a gift and snack bar (hidden away). Any group of one hundred people can rent the place for a private function and pay no more than $350, so the Republicans are thereby able to present a reception which will be distinguished, lavish, and symbolically resonant, yet need never be considered guilty of squandering money. The greatest single expense will probably prove to be the salaries of the Secret Service men, for a platoon, at least, must be on hand. The outlay, however, will certainly not be great for entertaining the Press: the costs here seem restricted to two bottles of whiskey, a tray of sandwiches on the patio (which will get wet in the late afternoon rain) plus a velvet rope drawn totally across the middle of the East Loggia so that reporters will not be able to touch Agnew or any of the guests whose hands he shakes, nor incidentally hear any of the conversation which is the probable purpose of the quarantine.

From Nixon's Maxims: Never make friends with the Press on a short-term basis. The sudden warming of relations will encourage their true nature which is spite. Cold relations create chilly stories whose details however remain correct since the Press is now afraid of reprisal. Then, if the office is esteemed enough, the "chilly" story may actually work to advantage since it is obliged to keep the central figure at a distance which is where he belongs. Warming relations with the Press must however only be undertaken during periods so long as a four-year administration and then should be conducted with great care analogous to the methods used in training intelligent dogs for the harsh routines of the circus. Reporters whose behavior cannot be predicted by any of the best methods once sufficient evidence is in must be maintained in a state of chilly relations.

Since Aquarius certainly had had no opportunity to work for the Prince, he could only assume that the wisdom of these neo-Machiavellianisms was coming to him as a species of spin-off from one of the more Aquarian manifestations of the century (which had to be the incalculable amount of telepathic transmission and reception now girdling the globe—a phenomenon doubtless ready to exhibit vigorous activity over Miami tonight what with the President arriving tomorrow and the young yearning the Cosmos over a little toward the vortex of their grassed-out heads in Flamingo Park). Psychotronics, the new science of the century, must be putting him on the same beam of RN Maxim Intuits that the Nixon staff was receiving. But who was serving as his antenna? It could not be Vic Gold, Agnew's press secretary, who kept a conversational ping-pong bing-banging over the velvet rope while reporters waited for some action to begin.

"Did *he* play tennis this morning?" a voice asked.

"Of course, you kidding? When doesn't he?" asked Gold.

"Vic, tell the truth. Where is *he* staying?"

"I don't know where he is staying, believe it or not. The Vice-President's residence in Miami is a secret even to me."

"How you holding up, Vic?" asked an old intimate.

"Lousy. Nervous. Look at these." He held out his hand and cocked the near Press a peek at his sedatives, four leaden-blue capsules, as impressive in their color as bullets.

Dr. Bill Voss, Agnew's personal physician, now said,
"These are Eagleton pills." Gold groaned. "Man, will I
be glad when this is over? You kidding? Will I be glad!"
he said, distributing his largesse of news to the ten or
fifteen members of the Press who had come all the way
out to Vizcaya. Abruptly, Aquarius was happy. Psycho-
tronically speaking, his unwitting antenna must be no one
other than the Vice-President himself. How else account
for the authoritative language in the maxim he had received. What a bonus. He has a plug into Agnew!

Since we may be confident that Aquarius only becomes
fanciful when he is frustrated, it will help to explain that
Vizcaya is a palace of exceptional beauty and he would
like to be able to explore its rooms and talk to the guests
Agnew is receiving, instead of being grateful for the bul-
letins Vic Gold has been providing in the roped-off corral
of the East Loggia. There is at last in this palazzo a sense
of the tropics and the high style of the tropics, of sunsets
turning from gold to the deepest washes in mother-of-pearl,
of orange flamingos and Spanish blood and coral keys,
patios which overlook the sea, even pirate chests buried
in the mangroves. Vizcaya! It is an Italian Renaissance
palace, planned in part by the first owner for its courtyards
and galleries, its pillars, its arches and its Italian steps, its
Great Stone Barge which serves as a breakwater and looks
as large as Cleopatra's float, standing off the terrace,
moored to the sea. Vizcaya's gardens are isolated from the
visitor today, and its statues of coral. It is altogether, he
senses, one of the few legitimate palaces in America, and
he will read afterward about its history, discover that James
Deering, the manufacturer and philanthropist, its creator,
has the peculiarly American history of being born in
Maine, growing up in Evanston, Illinois, where his father
has founded a fortune in harvesting machines, and is, our
capitalist-protagonist, a bachelor heir who dies an exotic
bachelor, a traveler, a collector, and the creator of the most
remarkable stage set ever arranged for an American
politician since the moment Agnew comes out and stands
in the loggia with his wife and daughter and the heirs of
James Deering to receive his guests—a move he has made
with no rush of ceremony at all—Vizcaya is transformed.
There is Agnew not ten feet away on the other side of the

rope in a dark near-black suit, a white shirt, and a black-and-white-figured tie, a stern mode of dress one cannot locate at first—it is not quite the costume of a banker nor an undertaker, and certainly not an executive. It is perhaps the suit a retired French hangman might wear, but he would have to be wealthy. The suit sits on Agnew with distinction. He stands there, his eyes heavy-lidded, narrowed down to slits—the writer Joe McGinnis will later describe them as looking like the slits in a tank turret—although it is possible Agnew closes them the better to pick up messages through his skin—but in any case Agnew is composed and remote as he shakes hands, a figure of distance and very well installed as he stands on an inlaid marble floor with marble busts in the niches in the walls behind him. Through the arches one can see a terrace with balustrades by the sea and the Great Stone Barge with its herms and gargoyles and nymphs of gray coral dripping in the waters of Biscayne Bay. A combo is playing on the terrace and black waiters serve drinks to the guests who have gone through the reception line and now take a buffet under a pink tent with white posts while white metal chairs and tables decorated with ornate patterns of holes seem to repeat the holes in the flagstones of the coral, the much-pocked look of a stone wall which long ago must have weathered a burst of bullets, yes the coral gives the impression that all of Vizcaya has been spattered with bullets, and then taking in at last the steel shutters cranked up high on the arches of the loggia, Agnew's suit assumes its focus. He looks, of course! he looks like he is wearing just the suit a Latin American dictator would wear in his palace by the tropical sea, and indeed has there ever been a man as high in American public life who has looked this much like the general who throws over a banana republic in a putsch?

The idea, while endlessly attractive for its sinister connotations, is nonetheless too simple for Agnew. He is a curious fellow, much more curious than Aquarius has ever realized, and not nearly so formidable as his pictures, a particularly quiet man on this occasion. As the guests go through, he shakes their hand with a peculiar impersonality much as if he is a spirit installed in some flesh-and-body machine which shakes hands. Perhaps his soul is away somewhere and his body is playing the equivalent of computer chess

as it shakes hands. It is not that he has lost his soul or is
a robot, it is just as if he understands this occasion so well
he knows there is no need for the soul to suffer with him.
An altogether unexpected reaction for Aquarius, and
cheers him as nothing else could on the virtues of covering
a convention in one's own body-and-flesh machine rather
than watching it on television. For example, seeing Agnew
come in yesterday at the airport, and be greeted on the TV
set by a solid and united wad of cheering YVPers, Agnew
had looked merely like Agnew. Now, ten feet away, across
the untransmitted air, there was this inexplicable sense of
his privacy as if no one in America knew the first thing
about him. There was even—was it with the faintest hint of
contempt—a suggestion that he was altogether aware of
how much people would regard him as like unto a South
American dictator, and therefore how much some would
need him, not *him* he would know, but the symbol of his
appearance. And again a suggestion arose from his presence
of something so shrewd and self-centered and private, so
recognizant of the possibilities life had thrust upon him,
so recognizant of the instrument the whole public idea of
his person had become, that it was almost profitable to
wonder what he thought of all that rich man's fear in all
that money and power of corporate America which had
settled so strongly on him as the successor to Nixon, settled
on him because he was reminiscent in appearance of Mus-
solini, Peron, and a dozen other prognathoid promises of
a man who would *run* the country and so shore up the
bottomless anxiety of those tropical rich who swallow
frontiers no more but live in the sun and fret—if their anxiety can be described—at the triple worry that the country
is on the edge of apocalyptic violence, the wife is readying
herself for a fling and if they weren't so old they'd be long
gone queer. The religion of the rich, like the religion of the
wad, was freedom from dread. And the reception line
moved forward, Republican delegates from all of America,
and Republican celebrities beginning to come, and rich
men from this region of tropical gardens and treachery
where revolution is an excuse for the letting of blood, and
strong men are more desirable than saints.

As Aquarius departs, the cops are feasting in the wood
on what is left of the sandwiches in the rain.

8B

From Nixon's Maxims: The ESSO Company is changing its name to EXXON for all of its 25,000 gas stations. We may say that there has never been a more deeply based compliment on the successful centrality of my name.

From Nixon's Maxims: Nixon-Agnew is the ticket whose sound best elicits voting response in the Silent Majority. This may be attributed to three factors. (1) The lack of specific meaning in the sounds. Explanation: Nobody can be offended in the absence of a specific statement, concept, or idea. (2) The rhythm of Nixon-Agnew, ONE-two, one-TWO, while irregular, is strong. Explanation: This tends to activate a similar sense of rhythm in the Silent Majority. (3) The sounds of Nixon-Agnew while not agreeable. are also not disagreeable. Explanation: Therefore they will speak of the middle, the recognizable, the monotonous, the daily. The Silent Majority will always vote for anything which suggests the maintenance of their daily life. Let me say that the more this daily life is without interest, the harder they will vote.

9

Of the convention itself, of the formal programmed activities of the Republicans in Convention Hall, nothing need be said, and everything can be said. The President was heard to remark, "It's like no convention has ever been in the world," and he was right if the function of a convention is to infuse the candidate into that part of the American brain which watches a television set. For three consecutive days it was inevitable to find the President's face on the tube, or the face of some Republican who was speaking about the President (not unfavorably!) or thinking about him (with a smile!) and if occasionally a demonstrator in the street would also be heard stinging the Office with an indictment sharp as pepper in the nostrils, still the reference was always to Nixon, and it was a fair assumption that the demonstrator's interruption of the benign mood was worth more to the President than whatever he could lose to the words. The medium is the message, and the fundamental message of television is an electronic drone of oscillating dots. Onto that psychic vehicle of almost unperceivable nausea upon which our sense focus is installed a rider—the content of the television program—but the content is to the nausea as the size of the rider to the size of the vehicle. People who sit before their television set for hours must use it as a kind of videotronic tranquilizer, a psychic poison whose uses are also medicinal; they sit there in order to receive the nausea —yes, to receive the nausea, exactly so that something unbalanced in the play of their appetites or the swoop of their fears can be vitiated a little, worn out precisely by that imperceptible nausea of drone and dots. Something animal washes out of them and into the cosmic sea. Reduced to less over the years, they are nearer to balance, even if such balance has been achieved by polluting the dread of their soul (which may be their only guide to Heaven!)—what an unnatural distance to come from reporting a convention. But perhaps no explanation of Nixon's success may suffice which fails to consider the possibility that this public personality, once young, near to rude, and self-righteous, has become a bland drone of oscillating ideological dots. In its impact as it comes over the tube, his personality is close to the nature of the tube itself, closer than anyone else in political life. (Which may be a way of saying that while Nixon is speaking, if the set should regress down from color TV with a clear image to nothing but the bare and vibrating gray screen offering no more than the drone and the glare of the dots, shock and shift of mood would be felt less with Nixon on that screen than with anyone else!) How tempting to rephrase such a thought into one of his maxims for is it not also a way of saying that a politician of the center does well to look for a personality which will cohere to the spirit of centrality of the television tube and so be part of the cure which is found in the reducing drone of the TV atmosphere?

Still, not everyone who watches television is ill. Healthy bodies (if not too many vigorous minds) spend hours before a set and take this all-but-unperceived nausea, as small price to pay for the pleasure of the content. So the art of television is to find a content which can sit agreeably with the nausea, a rider who can take the motion sickness of the machine. If we can conceive of books printed upon a paper whose texture is slimy and odor repulsive, it is evident that the fundamental art of the writer might then be to accommodate his topic and prose, so far as possible, to the paper. (Given offset printing and plastic pulp that day comes nearer.) How successful the Republicans had been at choosing a content with a high degree of nausea-accommodation may be seen in the pleasure of the President's reaction after watching much of his own gathering on TV. Complimenting Rick Reichstein who had overseen the production Nixon said, "It's like no convention has ever been in the world." We can take the existential meaning of his words, and assume he is really saying that other conventions have had their historical life confined mainly to the convention hall where their political war was being waged, and only a fraction of this history was communicated outside. Nixon, however, had conceived of a convention which would possess *no* history—since there would be no possibility for anything unsettling to happen in the hall. Therefore the *history* of this convention would exist immediately, but in the world, not the hall—the communication itself would be the convention. Whereas the happenings in the hall would have almost no legitimate existence in themselves—they could, for example, have as easily been photographed in a mammoth studio with superb mimics playing the principals, then have been edited into a spectacular. The shift in content and mood might have been minimal. Nixon had succeeded in composing an artwork with highly skilled actors who would not have to concern themselves with the perils of improvisation, ergo they could bring all of their energy, spontaneity and charm to prepared positions, an ideal situation for most skilled politicians since like professional actors they are happiest with familiar lines and a winning role. If there were also elements of opera bouffé in the mass entrances and exits periodically of an amateur chorus, the YVPers, there was also sophisticated comprehension of how to incorporate the antiwar demonstrators outside as an element of uncontrolled improvisational cinema left to the discretion of the television networks themselves, a freedom not so large as might first be suspected, since Republican orchestration of the major events would hardly be interfered with by the networks. On that Nixon could count. Indeed he had made the elegant move of turning the Media's resources against itself. Since he offered a paucity of conflict, the means and modes of television reporting—which are interviews with embattled principles and contentious delegates—were diminished; indeed many of the interviews had been all but scripted, then choreographed, since every lack of eagerness by Republicans to trust the Media resulted in a seller's market: the television interviewers—will horrors never cease!—had to apply for interviews, and thereby be screened out of the best questions while the subjects of the interview were prepared. With desperation, the Media discovered that their little impromptu interviews were more boring than events on the podium where anti-McGovern invective was winging and zinging. So they had to cover the podium more than they cared to, for that was the only continuing action Nixon provided. Thus his own script became the one which would finally be filmed. The occasional insertion of the street action, however, didn't hurt; in fact, it helped to spark the product which emerged as a species of new TV film (in effect!) as sophisticated in its mass wad-like way as a work by Jean Luc Godard—for if the actors virtually wore earphones through which the director could tell them how to respond to unforeseen reactions, there were also minor montages in this spectacular left open to moods of chance—yes, that is the very nature of sophistication in a highly controlled film; once in a while it is wise to put in a pinch of unlabeled herb for a classical sauce. So let us see Nixon as the first social engineer to harness and then employ the near to illimitable totalitarian resources of television. If the remark is not immediately comprehensible, its impenetrability can be reduced if we will recognize that every film director is totalitarian to the degree he exercises a near to total control over script and actors—it is just that he is a totalitarian competing alone against other totalitarians—he has no troops, is merely a tyrant to a few actors. It was Nixon's fundamental achievement to recognize the possibility of a three-day spectacular of *celebration*—the most difficult sort of script one can conceive—except that Nixon had the artist's wisdom to confine himself to those themes and audiences which were compatible; he would offer the reductions of his personality, warmed and *gemütlich*-ized, to the Silent Majority of both parties. Never before in history had a prepared tide of sentiments so similar in direction been washed for so long across the American brain.

Not for small effort had Nixon become the Eisenstein of the mediocre and the inert. A monumental arrangement of details and the most careful timing of their sequence had gone into the Program, as well as a host of materials and a hundred artful resolutions of his problem—which was to conduct all necessary business of the convention while catering to the audience's desire for direct or symbolic representation of their favorite organizations, military forces, their fifty states and all such small and large and variegated categories as: the local Florida officials, the

women, the parochial Republican organizations, the major
religions, the senatorial and congressional proprieties, the
police (local and national), and such unorganized groups
as children, teen-agers, the young, the middle-aged and
the old, Republican liberals, conservatives, athletes, and all
hordes of Democrats who detested McGovern.

The disposal of convention business could be handled.
While a bold solution might have been to show no business
at all (and so turn the convention into a telethon raising
money for the nation's most incurable disease—the national
vanity) Nixon was famous for caution and compromise!
so he merely reduced business to a concentrated minimum,
then employed the theatrical properties of business as a
tone for his palette, industrious hues of gray-green and
brown were occasionally established for background. The
party platform was, as expected, written in advance and
most modestly amended by the committee and subcommittees. No platform disputes reached the floor. There
were none visible. On Tuesday afternoon there was a floor
fight between separate liberal and conservative plans for
the allocation of new delegates among the states in 1976,
a matter of no importance or much importance depending
on whether a liberal and conservative might be in close
competition for delegates four years from now. Since no
one could be certain, the rules' fight finally was important,
but since conservatives had more representation in this
convention than liberals, it was evident they would win.
Nixon permitted the matter to come to the floor where the
conservatives won after a carefully limited hour of debate
by a vote of 910 to 434, and this proceeding provided a
thin and most useful red line of narrative strife to the
afternoon activities, delayed nothing at night, and gave
the delegates a half-hour of deliberation and balloting
which participation accelerated their cheerful faces into
greater cheer. Participating at last! And happy to laugh at
themselves. The Chief was so smart.

That was convention business. For representation of all
the American groups watching TV, the Jeannette Weiss
Principle (discovered during Worship Service) was
employed—wherever possible use a black lady with a
German Jewish name doing a patriotic bit. Thus Ray
Bloch, the Music Director of the Convention Orchestra,
had a name which at once might please Jews and Germans

as he played music which satisfied every gamut which ran from Dixieland through Lawrence Welk to Lombardo. Chad Everett, of *Medical Center,* the Special Guest, pleased TV fans, doctors and Californians; the United States Naval Sea Cadet Corps satisfied the military, the young, the patriotic, and Senior Citizens who remembered John Philip Sousa. The Pledge of Allegiance was given by Thomas Joiner of Rock Hill, South Carolina, winner of the 1972 American Legion Oratorical Contest, a choice which pleased Legionnaires, high-school debating teams, citizens with the first name of Rocky, or the surname of Hill, the state of South Carolina, and all the many Southern families for whom a name like Joiner was well-regarded. When one considers that all this did not occupy more than the first fifteen minutes of the first afternoon of the convention, while audiences still adjusting their sets were also being entertained by acting Chairman Senator Dole, the Republicans' handsome injured war veteran, engaged in his quiet understated resurrection of Humphrey Bogart, respect for Nixon begins to rise. It is the mark of great artists that they pay attention to those surfaces of the work to the rear of the niche. By Tuesday afternoon, the Jeannette Weiss Principle was being employed in full swing. Not only did Philip Luther Hansen of the American Lutheran Church give the invocation, but he was also Director of Alcohol and Chemical Dependency in a unit of Northwestern Hospital, Minneapolis, a lock thus on Scandinavians, Scandinavian Lutherans, Alcoholic Lutherans, Senior Lutherans on pills, and the formidable number of voters in America named Hansen or Hanson. But of course Tuesday afternoon was aided by a theme—it was Salute to Older Americans, and led by the Honorable Jacob K. Javits (winner of pluralities of so much as a million in New York State and obviously much beloved by Jewish voters of all ages), a double use of the distinguished Senator since he was honored by a place on the program and denied (or had relinquished temporarily) his position as one of the few liberal Republicans in the Senate who were articulate against the war in Vietnam. The super-function of the Jeannette Weiss Principle (like double and triple-word scores in Scrabble) not only connects the separate properties of a speaker, but manages to convert his negative potential to positive. To complement Javits, the salute to the aged was fortified by a lady named Church who could thus reassure some of the more bigoted Senior Citizens, especially since she was on the Planning Board of the *White House* Conference on Aging!—Tuesday afternoon had its buried arts to reveal.

So through the five sessions of Monday afternoon and evening, Tuesday afternoon and evening, and Wednesday night did the Jewish Rabbis, the Catholic Bishops, and Greek Orthodox Reverends give Invocations and Benedictions, so too did the Lutherans and the Methodists, and the Baptists. On the last night, Ms. Susan Savell gave the invocation. She was a former Chaplain Intern of Vanderbilt, thus delighting Liberators, youth, and the distinguished universities of the Middle Southern Conference. Indeed all the Protestant sects, including the A.M.E. Zion Church, were brought in but for Episcopalians, Presbyterians, Congregationalists and Unitarians. The Episcopalians and Congregationalists were bound to be so completely for Nixon that they could take a snobbish pride in not being called to a gang demonstration, the Presbyterians were so stubbornly divided that no one could unify them and not worth the effort to try. The Unitarians were long gone to McGovern.

It would be tempting to follow the order of appearance of Boy Scouts and Girl Scouts, 4-H, the Salute to Working Youth, and the Fellowship of Christian Athletes; to give an accounting of how often there was a mention of each state, or a study of the flattery paid to local officials in Florida, the honors paid to the police, liberals, athletes and the middle-aged—Ethel Merman would sing "The Star-Spangled Banner" on Tuesday night—but finally a college course in Government could devote a semester to the near to ninety items on the program over these five sessions. Better to concentrate on the higher applications of the Jeannette Weiss Principle in the Keynote presentation which produced the metamorphosis of an Eastern black senator into a Midwestern mayor with a resemblance to young Nixon, which then became an attractive former Democrat from Texas who was a woman. There was thus an Eastern-Midwestern-Southwestern Black Woman Nixon giving the Keynote speech who was also white and a mayor and a Massachusetts senator. We may pass over Senator Brooke who passed over his own disapproval of Vietnam—"It is the privilege of every American to differ with his President, but it is the obligation of every American to be fair in judging a President's performance." Fairness would suggest that no mention be made of the six million Indochinese who were dead, wounded, or homeless. We may even pass over Mayor Lugar of Indianapolis who indeed looked very much like young Richard Nixon first entering the Senate, in fact, Lugar was reputedly a favorite of Nixon's and thought enough of his resemblance to the Chief to announce, "I'm hopeful I'll be considered for President of the U.S. . . . in this decade." Like an earlier Nixon, he attacked. McGovern would "cripple our Army, Navy and Air Force," be found "begging, crawling to the negotiating table," "abandon prisoners of war and friends in Saigon," and we Republicans would not permit "radical new taxation plans to flatten hard-working Americans," or "perpetuate welfare into a way of life." Lugar was as tough as a pistol; he could go fifteen rounds with his own voice. Then came Anne Armstrong who could not be passed over.

She was attractive, she was agreeable, she was relaxed. She did not show any of that fatal political screw-tight at the corner of the jaws which disfigures so many otherwise good-looking women in politics; on the contrary, Anne Armstrong looked like a good liberal Democrat from Texas, humorous and brave. The worst of it was that she had once been a Democrat, and moved over to the Republicans. If the delegation she brought to the convention from Texas had no Blacks, one Chicano, and one delegate under thirty, small matter, she now gave her third of the Keynote speech which must have been worth hundreds of thousands of votes, maybe it was even a million-dollar speech (if a vote is worth a dollar) for one could feel Democrats sliding off the party wagon as she cantered along in her easy friendly voice there to show how nice you could be when you owned a ranch.

"A small group of radicals and extremists has assumed control of the National Democratic party, taking its name but repudiating its principles. The sudden storm of McGovern has devastated the house of Jackson, Wilson, Roosevelt and Kennedy, and millions of Democrats now stand homeless in its wake.

"We say to you millions of Democrats deserted by McGovern and his extremists, 'We are the party of the open door. That door is open to everyone. . . . Come in and join us.' "

On the Republican party would move, with its new friends, "up the broad middle road to progress," she said, and one had an image suddenly of all the pokey finicky nervous little women and old men who crawled their automobiles in panic down narrow roads, all the drivers who should have had their licenses revoked a decade ago, and Anne Armstrong was calling to them.

10

There were calls to many a corner of the land before the first Nixon Spectacular had finished its first day. If the three elements of the production had been Business, Representation of American groups (via the Jeannette Weiss Principle) and Entertainment, it was part of the aesthetic wealth of such a spectacular to convert the high business of major political speakers into entertainment as well. In the afternoon, William Rogers, the Secretary of State, had offered a tender memoir of his recollections of Dwight D. Eisenhower and a movie followed of Mamie Eisenhower sitting in her widowed living room at Gettysburg and reminiscing about Ike.

"I want to tell you a little story about the night at Walter Reed before Mr. Nixon was inaugurated. Ike called him up to wish him good luck and, at the end of the conversation, I could see the tears in his eyes and he said, 'This is the last time I can ever call you 'Dick,' tomorrow it will be 'Mr. President.' He was very proud of Mr. Nixon and if ever Ike had a disciple, certainly it was Mr. Nixon."

Since Republicans could only play in the Key of C, be certain they played Beethoven wherever they could.

In the evening, Hugh Scott, the Senate Minority Leader, introduced Alf Landon who looked incongruously like an old labor leader. Speaking in the bland and colorless voice which had lost him every state in the union but Maine and Vermont when he ran against Roosevelt in 1936, Landon said of Nixon, "One good term deserves another," thus suggesting the symbolic value of his appearance—as FDR had done to Landon, so would Nixon do to McGovern, and the delegates gave him a standing ovation. Over and over at this convention would the delegates be like the crowd at a football game when the score for the team goes higher and higher—as it does, so rises their greed for more points. It is records they wish to set, as if only a high-scoring record can cauterize the last of their inferiority complex, and Republicans had a huge if private inferiority complex —it was that America really did not want them, not that melting-pot majority of America they had once been so foolish as to let in.

Hugh Scott being given the opportunity of introducing a man so old as Alf Landon then extracted full value from the spirit of veneration. It is but a step from veneration to awe and worship—Scott stepped from all the eighty-plus years of Landon's life into a roll call:

". . . we wish to take a moment this evening to commemorate those great Americans who gave so much to this country, and have passed from us within those same four years.

"Their past dedication will help to inspire this nation's future. Out of the temporarity of life on this planet, they have become permanent. A tribute to all of those who have left us since last we gathered is symbolized tonight by the names we call. I ask this convention for a moment of silent prayer in the memory of: Dwight David Eisenhower, John L. Lewis, Everett McKinley Dirksen, Francis Cardinal Spellman, John Steinbeck, Vincent T. Lombardi, Richard Cardinal Cushing, Richard B. Russell, Whitney M. Young, Jr., Thomas E. Dewey, Louis Armstrong, Dorothy Elston Kabis, David Sarnoff, Winston L. Prouty, Hugo L. Black, Dean Acheson, Spessard Holland, Ralph Bunche, John M. Harlan, Cary Hayden, Mahalia Jackson, Marianne Moore, Llewellyn Thompson, James F. Byrnes, J. Edgar Hoover, Allen J. Ellender."

One did not expect Hugh Scott to mention Janis Joplin, Jimi Hendrix or Jim Morrison of the Doors but where was Lenny Bruce and Edmund Wilson and Brian Piccolo? Or Sharon Tate? It was possible she was worth as much in the cosmic hall of names as Allen Ellender.

Scott's appearance and the tribute to Alf Landon had been planned originally to precede a tribute to Pat Nixon. From the dead to the aged to the living had been the implicit progression, but Barry Goldwater was the only actor in this three-day spectacular to show temperament. Sched-

uled for ten minutes—he had written a speech to go half
an hour. Since he had also been scheduled early, much
too early, scheduled before the Keynote and the Nixon film,
before the tribute to Landon and the appearance of Pat
Nixon—he would be buried by the number of speakers
scheduled to follow him. And he would not cut his speech.
He had not run for President of the United States eight
years ago in order to be cut down now to ten minutes,
he was not willing to live with the possibility that one of
Richard Nixon's favorite old Italian sayings might be "Re-
venge is a dish which people of taste eat cold." (Barry
riding high in '64 had said of Nixon, "He's getting more
like Harold Stassen every day.") Goldwater was not often
right, but he had principles, and one of them was that a
former candidate for the presidency was entitled to more
than ten minutes of America's time at an hour when people
were still at dinner. So he objected to the order of the
program, and before negotiations were over, Hugh Scott
and Alf Landon had been brought in to fill his place and
Barry was on toward the end of the evening, and with
more than ten minutes if he still had to cut down from
thirty. Nonetheless, his speech had all the Goldwater virtues.
While Barry had a political screw-tight at the corner of
his mouth (a manly tension which comes from the civilized
inability to grind on the bones of one's dead foes and bite
the hams of the living), still it did not disfigure him as
it would a woman, perhaps it even added to his particular
charisma, for if at his worst he was a prejudice-panderer
and bias-monger, the sour emotional butt of the great
American heart, he had at least an air of primeval ferocity
(which arose from the low-slung profile of his brain long
dislocated into his jaw). Barry was there!—you could see
him at the end, glasses broken, hair matted, but on that
field of nuclear desolation he was wielding a club, swinging
at the buzzards. What a sweet speech he gave:
"I would like to call attention to what happened last
month when the shattered remnants of a once great party
met in this city and what I listened to and saw on my television set made me question whether I was sitting in the
United States or someplace else. I was reminded when I
listened to their constant complaints of the coyotes who live
on my hill with me in the desert of Arizona. These coyotes,

particularly on a moonlit night, just sit and bay and moan and cry over everything that exists but never suggest anything new, anything better or anything constructive to replace them. They just wait, like the coyote, until they can tear something down or destroy a part of America.

"I'm tired of hearing about what is wrong with America. I'd like for all Americans to think about what is right with America tonight and in the days ahead."

Right on. Barry had to stop more than once for the cheers. They were coming hard from the gallery where most of the three thousand Young Voters for the President were sitting tonight. "By golly," said Goldwater as they brought him to silence with their cheers. Earlier, during Mayor Lugar's speech, the children had yelled whenever Pistol Dick uttered the word "youth." The YVPers had not spent their adolescence going to live TV shows for no purpose—they knew when a sign said, "Applause." By golly —this was the answer to the coyotes.

All night, Ronald Reagan as temporary chairman of these spectacular ceremonies had been sticking it into the soft belly of the Democrats, flicking their eyes with forensic jabs while introducing other speakers and giving his own speech. Rap, tap, rap, rap, tap, tap, he would go with his good lines and his good timing, and his easy voice, full of the chuckles of good corporate living.

"A few days ago McGovern announced that his economists would be presenting a program very shortly to which he would be committed. Now, if that means he'll stand behind it 1,000 percent, we will have at least a week to look it over before he dumps it.

"McGovern has promised hand-outs of such lavishness that even *he* had to offer the reassurance that if his proposals proved dangerously extravagant, we could count on Congress to restrain him."

Reagan would never beef up to a political heavyweight but he was one of the better lightweights around and gave every evidence of being managed by Bob Hope who might just as well have written Reagan's speech tonight.

"Our traditional two-party system has become a three-party system—Republican, McGovern, and Democrat. And, only the first two parties have a presidential candidate.

"The rhetoric was the high-sounding phraseology of the 'new politics.' But, their tactics were the old politics of bossism and the smoke-filled rooms—although in some of the rooms it was reported that the smoke smelled a little funny.

"They didn't complete the ticket until a few weeks later when they had time to run through the yellow pages and call central casting.

"You could imagine the high drama of that moment of decision there in Hyannis Port—surrounded by their families, two men watching the flip of a coin. Sargent Shriver lost.

"A man of the common people. Shriver understands their language. He learned it from talking to his butler."

After a while souls even so simple as Aquarius began to recognize that Republicans had not been owning and managing the biggest advertising agencies on Madison Avenue for half a century without being able to contribute to the genius of the presidency. A film, *Portrait of a President,* was shown. But we can quote a fair description from John Huddy of the *Miami Herald:*

"We do not know whether the brief glimpses of Nixon wielding this power are actual or staged, but in any instance the director and his editor have shrewdly chosen to use dialog in which Nixon scraps for the little guy (in a phone discussion apparently involving a federal funding program) and for children (in another meeting about busing).

" 'Let's keep the children out of the racial fight!' a tough Nixon is heard to say, a moment no doubt intended for the ears of every parent whose child faces busing in the next year.

"The theme in the film is obvious and it is driven home at every turn: Nixon is the president. . . . Never mind the issues; he is the president! Only Nixon can understand what that means. (Not accidentally, the film begins with portraits of a long line of presidential greats: Not illogically, it ends with a freeze-frame of Nixon on the phone and the film begins.)

"*The Nixon Years* may not have a cast of thousands, but

it does have Nixon with Chou in Peking and Nixon with
the Russians in Moscow. And how can any competitor
possibly top that?"

Kissinger follows by saying: "I, like most of my colleagues, had always been opposed to him and had formed
certain images about him and I found that he was really,
was totally different from the image the intellectuals have
of him. He's very analytical but quite gentle in his manner,
and I always had a quite different view."

Then Pat Buchanan offers a recollection: "When I joined
him back in 1965, I was an editorial writer for a conservative paper in the Midwest and I went over to Bellevue,
Illinois, to meet him and if he had told me that day that a
few years hence that I would be sitting in a great hall of
people in Peking, China, clinking glasses with Chou En-lai
when the People's Liberation Army Band played "Home
on the Range," I would have said you're out of your ever-
loving mind."

Buchanan gave the good-drinking head-shaking grin that
young executives of the middle lands of America give when
they are talking of the wonders of their boss. Never had
the right wing of America been taught so easily to take ten
steps to the left and smile at the center.

Then Kissinger was back with a cultivated verdict:
"There's a certain, you know it's a big word, but it's a
certain heroic quality about how he conducts his business
because he does it all in a very understated way. Of course,
I can only judge foreign policy and I believe that his impact
on foreign policy will be historic no matter what happens.
He has—provided one of the big watersheds in American
international history."

There was a last shot of Nixon wearing a sport jacket
and strolling along the beach with Pat. It is a deserted
beach and evening is near. The voice of the narrator says,
"This is a man who calls out to America to have faith in
itself, to go forward without fear, to build on the founda-
tions he has laid down. . . . America will hear him."

The evening ended with a film about Pat Nixon. She
was shown as Mrs. Ambassador. Then Jimmy Stewart
brought her forward to take a bow. She came up in all the
happiness of a movie star receiving an Academy Award,

and the convention broke loose. They were scoring again
and again, but if they had been the Minnesota Vikings
scrimmaging a high-school team, still they would have
screamed to keep on scoring. They were ready to lift the
roof for a good few minutes.

For a good few minutes. But the demonstration in the
gallery went on and on. It was the YVPers. They kept
yelling. After a while the smile of happiness on Pat Nixon's
face began to look like the freeze-frame in the film. Her
sense of TV timing must have suggested that this demonstration was going on too long for its purpose. She was only
up there to receive her tribute and say hello. The yaws
which accompany a fall from maximum attention were
hovering in the TV ears of every antenna—she would lose
her national audience if those idiots in the gallery didn't
stop cheering. A successful TV show is built on the TV
viewers' past experience with television. Perhaps an ovation
for a speaker had three good built-in minutes, not much
more. Pat Nixon grinned. She waved her arms aloft with
love to the delegates and to America, she lofted the heavy
gavel and made a female face, a gesture of "oh, how heavy
it is even for a wiry girl like me," she used every resource
available for situations such as this and she like her husband
had studied every lesson of her professional life, but the
YVPers were in hysteria. They, too, were on television now!
So they kept screaming for ten minutes. They were screaming like a crowd of kids who pour through the school gate
on the last school day before Christmas vacation, and now
can yell their hatred of the teachers. The YVPers were
screaming with all the pent-up energy of having paid their
own way here to be shunted from function to function, they
were screaming with all the hysteria of the obedient. If it
went on too long, they would no longer be showing their
love for the charm of Pat Nixon as the President's wife,
they would be revealing the heart of their own therapy
which was to yell on TV. So, subtly, the hint of an indrawn
critical look came back into the mellowed political screw-
tight of the jaw of Pat Nixon, and she began to show the
faintest trace of the high-powered displeasure of a wife
who is going to tell her husband later, "You boob, you've
overdone it again."

The evening ended with Rabbi Herschel Schacter of Mosholu Center of the Bronx giving the benediction.

From Nixon's Maxims: The virtue of the triple Keynote speech is that having three legs, it is an ideological stool. Brooke, Lugar and Armstrong offer sturdy legs for such a stool, since crudely speaking these three names present an image of a tranquil brook, a World War II Luger, and a fine body, which in turn will symbolize Peace, Military Might, and a Healthy Economy.

11A

It is back to the La Ronde Room of the Fontainebleau in the morning, same room where so many press conferences have taken place, same tables and cloths are there, wrinkled even more, but there is a new turnout Tuesday morning because Paul McCloskey is using the facilities to present Daniel Ellsberg, who has a communication to divulge, and the Press have responded in the hope of some disclosure which will crack into the facial expressions of the Republicans who are running this convention.

McCloskey stands at the microphone making the opening remarks. There are strains of premature gray in his dark hair which is worn in a pompadour reminiscent of J.F.K. but he is still young enough to look like an officer in the Marine Corps who has earned a Navy Cross, in fact, McCloskey is the only Republican militantly against the war in Vietnam who has the look of a real conservative. By every standard of neatness, he belongs more in the FBI than on a podium introducing Dan Ellsberg, yes, a personality like an Irish hero sandwich—Black Irish severity on gloom! His persona speaks of that bull-headed Irish propensity to drink which can be found in jocks who are debating whether to take priestly vows. Still there is God's own integrity in the frown on his brow. He is an impressive man as he says in his soft-spoken voice that he would have liked to bring a debate to the floor of the convention but it had not been possible, "So unfortunately we're forced to have it here."

He has had his tribulations and frustrations. Possessor of one delegate, he will still not be nominated because of a decision of the Rules Committee that one must have representation on three delegations and a certified minimum of delegates. He will not even have his own delegate, merely one Nixon man on the New Mexican slate of fourteen who will mutter his name when the time comes. Nor has the Platform Committee given him time. He has been closed out. So, now, having invited Ellsberg to fly in from California, McCloskey contents himself with saying, "We are a rich country bombarding and destroying the people and economy of a poor country," which is the true, fundamental and legitimate conservative objection, for any war which pits rich against poor is an ugly combat which must erode the moral substance of a nation. This subject, McCloskey now says quietly, is not even going to be debated on the floor of the convention. "We are creating wholesale destruction in a war we are not even willing to die in." Gloom upon him (his wife will file suit for *divorce* over "irreconcilable differences" in just a few days, after twenty-three years of marriage), McCloskey now introduces Ellsberg and turns the conference over to him.

Ellsberg is handsome and slender in build with a large well-shaped nose and large expressive eyes light in color. They stare at the Press with a look which could partake of childhood woe if it were not so grave, for his eyes seem to say, "I know you will believe me, but will you believe me enough?" So he has the manner of someone who suspects he is ready to lose, and lose seriously. On trial now for divulging the Pentagon Papers, he can spend the rest of his life in jail if found guilty; the turn in public sentiment over the last few months from disapproval of the war to a grudging pleasure in the way our airplanes have stopped the North Vietnamese spring offensive is equivalent to some future echo of a penitentiary door closing behind him. While he is a man considerably more favored in features than Eddie Albert or Eddie Bracken, that same unhappy note is struck of a modest man pitting himself against giants, and so suggesting pathos with every move. Even a touch of the tenderest comedy clings to his seriousness. Ellsberg is so serious. The Press study him with curiosity. Can he possibly be as solemn as he seems?

He is trying to advance a complex argument. It is that when Richard Nixon came to office in 1968, he asked

Henry Kissinger to prepare a Vietnam Options Paper which would outline every alternative he had, and having discarded only one of the seven alternatives (which was of course complete and unilateral withdrawal of the U.S. from Vietnam), Nixon had laid out a grand plan which included invasions of Cambodia and Laos as well as a resumption of the bombing of North Vietnam and a mining of the harbor of Haiphong, all of which would be accompanied by a phased withdrawal of ground forces. So, Ellsberg suggests to the Press, it is not that the North Vietnamese have refused our peace terms so much as it is that Richard Nixon has pursued a war plan which no one would have believed credible in 1968 or 1969, and in the course of fulfilling this war plan, has carried out the heaviest aerial bombardment in the history of the world. "That is his prerogative," says Ellsberg, "and it is possible the American people would have supported such a plan, but we will never know because they were never told about it in advance."

The Press asks him questions, and he answers, but the story while large in its implications is not conclusively proved by the Vietnam Options Paper Ellsberg is releasing. There is not the shock nor bite of a big news story—there are no remarks in these new papers which sit in a journalist's mind and give him his lead, just more of the same depressing sense that yes, Nixon has planned these acts in advance, but only as possibilities—there is no way to prove he was determined to pursue the war from the beginning of his administration—and no way to believe any longer that the majority of American people are concerned about the immorality of the war.

Afterward, Irving Wallace, the novelist, offers his suite for reporters and Media men to talk with Ellsberg. Eager to communicate the living incalculable horror of the war, Aquarius and he talk of statistics. It is the only way to begin to appraise such incomprehensibility. Because by every measure, but American casualties, the war has increased in scope during Nixon's administration. 1,489,240 combatants on all sides have been killed or wounded under Nixon as opposed to 1,333,215 under Johnson. 4,789,000 civilians have been killed, wounded, or become refugees under Nixon. The number was 4,146,000 under Johnson. And these figures are from the *Congressional Record* and the Senate Subcommittee on Refugees. While we have had only a little more than half as many American casualties under Nixon as under Johnson, the South Vietnamese have suffered more casualties, one and a half times as many, and the North Vietnamese have also had higher casualties. We have dropped 3,633,022 tons of bombs between January, 1969, and June 30, 1972, as compared to 3,191,417 tons for Johnson. Out in the Pacific and the China Sea, we now have the greatest air and naval armada in the history of war.

In South Vietnam we have even accepted the Phoenix program which has executed 40,994 civilians since January, 1969.

"That is to say forty thousand civilians," Ellsberg says, "who've been executed without trial. Under Johnson, the comparable figure is a little over two thousand. Still, we talk of the blood bath when the Communists come in. Can they do any worse?"

No, they cannot, Aquarius says. It is possible that nobody can do any worse than we have done. He is thinking that once bombing has achieved its strategic objective which is to obliterate military sites and production sites, all further bombing lands right in the essence of the superficial which is to say against the surface of the earth and the surface of human flesh.

"Look," says Ellsberg, "Cambodia is a country with a little more than six and a half million people. It's now two years since we've gone in, and there are two million refugees. That's the fastest destruction of any country I know."

And Ellsberg, his eyes burning into the incomprehensible night of these dark statistics, has the look of a lawyer who is losing the most heartrending case of his life. "I'd like to send Martha Mitchell to North Vietnam," he says. "I think she'd tell the truth."

> *From Nixon's Maxims:* The Silent Majority, while often accused of being non-political, actually prefer to have a definite idea and will often drift at surprising speed from one position to its opposite. May I point to the shift of opinion on the war in Vietnam. The American public once ready to get out is now ready to stay in and win provided no American blood is shed.

11B

And yet the world planner responsible for these figures of population increase in Eternity ("out of the temporarity of life they have become permanent!") is such a nice man as he steps off his United States of America plane, The Spirit of '76, and descends the gangplank to embrace his family. The YVPers are waiting for him to arrive in Miami, and they give a lusty cheer as he walks across the tarmac to talk to all several thousand of them sitting in temporary stands erected by an airplane hangar. Perhaps it is because they have been waiting for considerably more than an hour and in the rain!—like troops they are transported about in a great hurry in order that they may wait—or it may be the quality of his presence, but there is, considering it is the YVPers, almost no hysteria; rather, they cheer him as if he is the most popular high-school principal they have ever had. Still a principal does not excite hysteria. Or have their section leaders warned them to avoid the excesses of the night before? A sign stands out. "I'm not a Daley 6th Ward sewer worker." During one of their demonstrations from the gallery, John Chancellor of NBC had said, "At Democratic conventions we have seen Mayor Daley pack the hall with members of the 6th Ward sewer workers. What we have seen tonight seems to be the Republican equivalent," a remark for which Chancellor will yet have to apologize, but the epithet together with the benign presence of the President seems to have quieted the crowd.

The cast of the celebrity press conference is also on hand, John Wayne and Ethel Merman and Ruta Lee. Stan Livingston of *My Three Sons* is there and Mary Ann Mobley and Kathy Garver. Johnny Grant has done his best to entertain the crowd with his patter in the rain. Speaking of Agnew, he says, "I love that guy. Know why? He really knows how to give 'em oral karate."

There is an image! Swimming just out of reach we see the head of a liberal politician stuck onto some sort of pus-filled penile shaft (black presumably) and wham! go Agnew's teeth. What a karate chop! The head of the liberal has just been clipped off its Black backing.

Well, such an image is not near to Nixon. At the foot of the plane he embraces his wife and kisses his daughters but with appropriate reserve—they are being watched after all. The embrace is suggestive of five million similar such greetings each evening as commuters get off at a suburban stop and go through the revelation, and the guard they throw up against revelation, of their carnal nitty-gritty. A good game for a face-watcher, and Nixon's is not different from many another man who pecks a kiss in public. But as he walks toward the Young Voters for the President and salutes and smiles and grins, preparing to stop before them and raise both his arms (for they are now no longer just cheering him as the principal, but are off on all the autoerotics of thrusting their own arms in the air four fingers up while screaming "Four more years, four more years"), so Nixon promenading toward them exhibits again that characteristic gait which is his alone and might have provided thought for analysis in even so profound a student of body movements as Wilhelm Reich, for Nixon has character-armor, hordes of it! Several schemes of armor are stacked all on top of one another, but none complete. It is as if he is wearing two breastplates and yet you can still get peeks of his midriff. He walks like a puppet more curious than most human beings, for all the strings are pulled by a hand within his own head, an inquiring hand which never pulls the same string in quite the same way as the previous time—it is always trying something out—and so the movements of his arms and legs while superficially conventional, even highly restrained, are all impregnated with attempts, still timid—after all these years!—to express attitudes and emotions with his body. But he handles his body like an adolescent suffering excruciations of self-consciousness with every move. After all these years! It is as if his incredible facility of brain which manages to capture every contradiction in every question put to him, and never fails to reply with the maximum of advantage for himself in a language which is resolutely without experiment, is, facile and incredible brain, off on a journey of inquiry into the stubborn refusal of the body to obey it. He must be obsessed with the powers he could employ if his body could also function intimately as an instrument of his will, as intimate perhaps as his intelligence (which has become so free of the *distortions* of serious moral motivation), but his body refuses. Like a recalcitrant hound, it refuses. So he is still trying out a half dozen separate gestures with each step, a turn of his neck to say one thing, a folding of his wrist to show another, a sprightly step up with one leg, a hint of a drag with the other, and all the movements are immediately restrained, pulled back to zero revelation as quickly as possible by a brain which is more afraid of what the body will reveal than of what it can discover by just once making an authentic move which gets authentic audience response. Yet he remains divided on the utility of this project. Stubborn as an animal, the body does not give up and keeps making its disjunctive moves while the will almost as quickly snaps them back.

Yet when he begins to talk to the crowd, this muted rebellion of his activities comes to a halt. Like an undertaker's assistant who fixes you with his stare and thereby gives promise that no matter the provocation, he will not giggle, Nixon has made a compact with his body. When the brain stops experimenting with its limbs, and takes over a cerebral function (like manipulating an audience), then the body becomes obedient to the speaker's posture installed on it.

Now, hands clasped behind him, Nixon begins. "I was under some illusion that the convention was downtown," he says.

It takes a while for the kids to get it. YVPers are not the sort of hogs who grab the high I.Q.'s. But when they realize he is not only complimenting them for the size of their numbers but on their importance, they come back with all the fervor of that arm in the air and the four fingers up in the double V. Nixon has appropriated the old V for Victory sign; better! he has cuckolded all the old sentimental meanings—V for Victory means liberalism united and the people in compact against tyranny. Et cetera. It is his now, and doubled. Up go the double horns of the kids. "Four more years."

One thing can be said for the presidency—it gives every sign of curing incurable malaise. Nixon is genial! Now, he jokes with the crowd. "I think I'm going to be nominated tonight. I *think* so," he says charmingly. It is the first time he has ever spoken with italics in public. "And so is Vice-President Agnew," he adds. "He's going to be nominated too." They cheer. Ever since they arrived on Saturday, the YVPers have been cheering, on the street, at receptions in the gallery, in the lobby of each hotel they visit, and here at the airport they exhibit all the inner confidence of a Fail-Safe. When in doubt, cheer.

Once again Aquarius is depressed at the sight of their faces. It is not only that all those kids seem to exist at the same level of intelligence—which is probably not quite high enough to become Army officers—but they also seem to thrive on the same level of expression. They have the feverish look of children who are up playing beyond the hour of going to sleep; their eyes are determined, disoriented, happy and bewildered. So they shriek. With hysteria. The gleam in their eye speaks of no desire to go beyond the spirit they have already been given. Rather, they want more of what they've got. It is unhappy but true. They are young pigs for the President. He thinks of all the half-nude sclerotic pirates of Flamingo Park, over whom America (which is to say Republicans) are so worried. Perhaps America has been worrying about the wrong kids.

"I've been watching the convention on television," Nixon says through the microphone. "I want to thank you for the tribute you paid my wife." Now for the first time he puffs his chest up, which—given the mating dance he performs whenever addressing a crowd—has to signify that a remark of portent is on its way. "Based on what I've seen on television, and based on what I have seen here today,"—Four more years!—"those who predict the other side is going to win the young voters are simply wrong." Deep breath. Solemn stare. Now comes the low voice which backs the personality with the presidential bond of integrity: "We're going to win the young voters." Shrieks. Squeals. Cheers. Four more years! They are the respectable youth and they are going to triumph over fucked-up youth.

Back at the convention, the delegates are watching this arrival on the three huge screens above the podium—it is being televised live both to the convention and to America. Only the galleries are empty this afternoon, but that is because the YVPers are not present to fill their seats—they are here!

Nixon takes them into his confidence. He knows they are interested in politics, or they would not be in Miami, he says. And maybe one of them someday will be President, "Maybe one of your faces that I now am looking at will be President. It is possible. One thing I want you to know. That is that we want to work with the trust and faith and idealism of young people. You want to participate in government and you're going to." Cheers. He smiles genially. "However, let me give you a bit of advice. To succeed in politics, the first thing you want to do, is to marry above yourself."

They do not begin to comprehend the seismographic profundity of this advice. They only yell, "We want Pat. We want Pat."

"Well, you can't have her," Nixon says. "I want to keep her."

Yes, he had wanted her and he had wanted to keep her. Back in Whittier, before they were married, he would drive her to Los Angeles when she had a date with another man. Then he would pick her up and drive her back to Whittier when the date was done. That is not an ordinary masochism. It is the near to bottomless bowl in which the fortitude of a future political genius is being compounded. It had made him the loser who did not lose.

But how many years and decades it must have taken before he recognized that in a face-off with another man, he would be the second most attractive. Once he had made the mistake of fighting Kennedy man to man, and wife to wife. Jack had beaten Dick, and Jackie had certainly taken Pat—Nixon cried out with no ordinary bitterness over what America could not stand. But now he had learned that the movies were wrong and the second most attractive man was the one to pick up the marbles, since losers (by the laws of existential economy) had to be more numerous than winners.

"Some public men," he had said in an interview, "are destined to be loved, and other public men are destined to be disliked, but the most important thing about a public man is not whether he's loved or disliked, but whether he's respected. So I hope to restore respect to the presidency at all levels of my conduct.

"My strong point, if I have a strong point, is performance. I always do more than I say. I always produce more than 1 promise."

It was as true for Vietnam as for China. And now here was this nice man talking to children. Aquarius stood in that stricken zone of oscillating dots which comes upon the mind when one tries to comprehend the dichotomies of the century. Here is this nice man who has the reputation of being considerate about small things to the people who work for him, this family man married so many years to the same wife, possessor of two daughters who are almost beautiful and very obedient. He is a genius. Who would know?

Yes, the loser stands talking to all of his gang of adolescent losers who are so proud to have chosen stupidity as a way of life, and they are going to win. The smog of the wad lies over the heart. Freud is obsolete. To explain Nixon, nothing less than a new theory of personality can now suffice.

11C

Convention Center is a compound of buildings and parking areas which runs for several city blocks on every side, and is surrounded by a wire fence. On Tuesday night, in one of the deserted side lobbies of the main convention hall, a company of Miami Beach police are dinging their riot clubs in rhythm on the composition floor of the lobby. It is a peculiar operation. They stand in ranks, swaying and chanting and about every fourth beat they bounce the end of their long riot clubs off the floor. Then as the tempo increases, they begin to bounce the club faster and faster, chanting all the way. Soon they are bouncing the club on every beat. It is the war dance of the Miami Beach police and one hardly knows if they do it to get ready for battle, or to cool off after the frustration of early evening. Street

tempo has picked up all day. Between the afternoon session
and the evening, delegates had gone to eat in restaurants
near the Convention Center. On their way back, there was
trouble. Delegates were harassed by demonstrators, and
called "war criminals." Windows were smashed and some
red-white-and-blue bunting outside Convention Hall was set
on fire by a bare-breasted girl who shimmied up a light
pole. The cars of some delegates were stopped and protesters had pounded on their roofs, or jumped on the hood.
One Continental panicked and jerked forward. A girl on the
hood fell off; the limousine ran over her leg. In another
place fifteen demonstrators were picked up by police when
they tried to disconnect distributor caps from automobiles
which were waiting at traffic lights. A brick was thrown
through the window of the Pan American Bank, a display
case at the Gaiety Burlesque was smashed. The police had
finally made over two hundred arrests, and Rocky Pomerance, the Chief of Police, was in gloom. He had been trying
through two conventions to keep from making busts. He
had had consciousness-raising sessions with his cops on the
psychology of dissent, and colloquys all these summer weeks
with spokesmen for the contingents at Flamingo Park. It
was said that he was even in walkie-talkie communication
with some of the street leaders. He must have seen *Man of
La Mancha* for he has been embarked on the impossible
dream of trying to take Miami Beach through its convention days without any violence. During all of the Democratic Convention and until this night, he has been able
to keep incidents at a minimum. He has not even made
any arrests until Monday. Now, on Tuesday, there are two
hundred. Tomorrow is going to be worse. For Nixon will
give his acceptance speech and the demonstrators have
announced they will try to create havoc so that delegates
will be delayed and the convention not start on time.

Aquarius has wondered about the police chief. He could
conceive of a cop who desired to show that some police
could handle difficult situations with subtlety, but how had
this police chief been able to control his troops? These
troops who are moaning now in the rhythms of their war
chant as they wait in the deserted lobby. But the answer
proves simple once he meets Pomerance. Rocky is a tribute
to the Jews. He has blue eyes, a friendly face, and is immense enough to be a Sumi wrestler. He has to be the

strongest man on the force. The answer is very simple. All
the other cops in Miami Beach are afraid of him. It opens
a perspective on the way to achieve good police forces.
One has only to find police chiefs who are strong, inspired,
and benevolent. "The police can't win," Pomerance says.
"They just can lose as gracefully as possible." Back of him
in the lobby, the cops are still dinging their riot clubs.

11D

Calculating that a three-day spectacular was going to be
in need of a basic set which should be impressive yet responsive to changes in mood, and symbolic of the epic it
presented, the Republicans had designed a formidable podium. It was built high up over the deck the Democrats
had used and it was painted white instead of blue, an
immense podium—sixty-four feet wide and ninety-two feet
deep. It looked like the bastions of a castle and the battlements of a medieval fort, it looked like some huge white
ship in the sky. Speakers at the altar of that high and
immense podium spoke as if from the heights of the white
knights of Christendom. Blue curtains rose to the heavens
of the ceiling, red-and-blue carpet lined the aisle, and
American flags were hung in a row along the full length
of a wall. The country was the religion. Once again America
was readying for a crusade which no one was ready to
name, but the heads were tiny upon that podium, and the
faces were huge on the three white screens. After a while
it became part of the viewer's logic to look from the tiny
head to the huge face.

It was Rockefeller who put Nixon in nomination, ". . .
brought us to the threshold of a generation of peace . . .
skilled management and leadership . . . *we need this man.*
We need this man of action, this man of courage. We need
this man of faith in America. It is my great honor. . . ."

He gave the speech almost perfunctorily. There was no
drama in his symbolic relinquishment of the role of Nixon's
oldest party competitor, nor any drama to the fall of liberal
Republicanism. Nixon had gone farther to the left than

Rockefeller might ever have dared, Nixon had gone farther to the right. Rockefeller had come to politics almost by accident—what else could a man of his wealth, ambition, and lack of specific talent do with his life? Nixon had lived with politics as Michelangelo had lived with pigments. So even if he did not know how to move his body, Nixon knew how to move to his right and to his left. Nixon knew how to occupy the center. Kings, presidents of corporation, and *don capos* of the Mafia look to be installed by the man they deposed. So Nixon was nominated by Rockefeller.

The nomination was seconded by eleven speakers. It is a happy number in craps and full of good connotation for football. Since the number of nominating speeches in all, however, counting Rockefeller's, was twelve, it could also be said that Nelson was the first of the twelve apostles and Nixon was the twelve hours of the clock. It is precisely the kind of symbolic hyperbole which will do no harm to the unconscious of the electorate and might even convert one voter in a hundred while it sways another five.

One of the seconding speeches was given by Walter J. Hickel—two years ago, he had been dismissed from the President's Cabinet after talking out against the war. But the Republican Godfather was good and he was gracious. The guilty could return. Manuel Lujan, Jr., who had had the disgrace of fielding the only delegation to cast a vote for Paul McCloskey, stood up to second the President. So did Senator Buckley the Conservative and John McCarrell, a Democrat and president of Local 1544 of the UAW. The Conservative Irish and the labor union Irish were in for Nixon; so too was a Vietnam war veteran, John O'Neill of the Texas Irish. There was Representative Edward Derwinski, a Polish-American Republican, and Anne Smith Bedsole, a housewife from Mobile, an Alabama delegate for the Wallace folk; and there was Frank Borman. An hour after he gave the seconding speech his face was still shining with happiness on the floor. Mrs. Henry Maier, the wife of the Democratic Mayor of Milwaukee, was the Co-Chairman of Democrats for Nixon, and she said, "I am here because I am more nervous and frightened for America than for myself." They cheered her with delight. The Democrats were making better speeches for the Republicans these days than the Republicans. That was living, politically speaking, off the real fat of the land. The people sitting on the floor of the convention were sophisticated enough to know. Two-thirds of the Republican governors of America were here as delegates, and half of the Republican senators, a good quarter of their congressmen, and many Republican mayors. Only 19 percent of McGovern's delegates had ever held elective office. In contrast the figure was 84 percent for Republicans. So they could show their appreciation for the boss, they knew how good he was. Of course only 3 percent of the delegates were black where the Democrats had had almost 15, but that merely expressed the real quota of politics since the Democrats could count on four-fifths of the Negro vote. No more than 7 percent of the delegates were under thirty years of age, and the Democrats had had 27 percent, but maybe that was why the average income of the convention Republicans was so much higher than the Democrats!

Aquarius was hardly however in need of such statistics. A walk down these wide and comfortable aisles was all anyone needed to comprehend the divisions of the nation. For there was probably as much difference between Democratic and Republican faces as between the French and English, or the athletic and the intellectual—there is no need for a list of opposites. The point is that Democrats and Republicans belong on such a list, they are different, more different certainly than New Yorkers and Californians and if one would look for the center of that difference it has been expressed probably on the night before when Reagan said, "This nation will do whatever has to be done so long as one American remains in enemy hands." It was the fetishism of American blood. Conservative Aquarius, left-conservative Aquarius, could know at that moment he was wholly a Democrat, for in the midst of the roar of the deepest sentiments rising up in one animal growl from the happy Republican throng, he felt only the cold observation that Ronald Reagan was a moral fathead. It was not that Aquarius could never comprehend how the country was the secret of one's strength if only one believed in it. Then the blood of a countryman was different in kind, more valuable in the existence of the cosmos than a foreigner, especially if you insisted on it. (Indeed the cosmos might only comprehend the unities of human endeavor— and compromise, therefore, quota, and the absence of dis-

tinction, all fell away like mud.) The clearest and the most
powerful emotions might even travel the farthest through
space. No, Aquarius was not one to believe that a modern
interfaith prefabricated meeting hall had more to offer
one's survival than a quick view of Notre Dame from across
the Seine. Nor did he think that order was to be debased
before the virtues of the slovenly. He had had enough of
the slovenly forever, including its swamp-like effusions in
his own mind. And indeed he had regard for many a
Republican face. There were distinguished faces on that
floor. He saw faces which were models of discipline, or
of elegance, or orderly style, faces which spoke of fire and
pride and the idea that character was the only ceramic to
hold human fire and pride; there were dry Republican faces
which proved models of crystallized wit, and kindly urbane
gentlemen whose minds were rich with concept when they
thought of the commonweal. One could even say that if
there was a drop of common but immortal belief in every
Republican, it might be over that drop of American blood.
It was where they would have their sacrament. Not in the
numbers, no, never in the numbers game (although they
played it too) but in the idea that the life of nations lay
like a clear view across the horizon from past to future,
and one drop of American blood also contained the rights
of assembly for three centuries and fifty years, and so was
linked to all the other blood which had been shed, a tran-
substantiation of the nation's blood which would believe
that no, not all blood was equal, and American blood was
worth more. It was a passion he might even appreciate,
although he never felt it, and he could see that passion in
the common denominator of Republican faces. They were
practical to the last muttering of the last clause, but only
because they also believed that the spark of every Christian
light was concealed in each good clause. So the best of the
Republicans had fine faces, a few had faces which were
even splendid, for they knew that flesh was never so noble
as with its hint of such a light, and a few of the Republican
ladies looked wise or passionate or bold or pleased with
the private knowledge that beauty and style were part of
a life which did not have to cease.

There was even Nixon's daughters. They had had the
most impossible assignments for starlets—they were obliged

to be smiling, pleasant, happy with the team and radiant; no starlet in the memory of any living moviegoer had ever come close to performing that slavish assignment well through an entire role. It could be said the Nixon girls came as close as any starlets he had seen.

But once that was said, how much worse was the rest. "So long as one American remains in enemy hands" the power to avoid all responsibility is also at hand, including the failure to recognize that total faith in one's country might be as dangerous as total faith in one's own moral worth, even worse, for with total patriotism, one's own soul was no longer there to be lost; rather, America could be lost. So as he worked the measure of his comprehension along the rows of faces, all Republican here, there came to him after a time some large detestation of their average. The average Republican face was as selfish or stingy as it was ingrown, and often it was squeezed together with the ferocity of the timid. Worse. So many of these faces were dead to experience they did not already comprehend. They were closed to any face which was not near to their own, or any style of dress. Many lived in the dread of the unde-serving rich, that thick-throated dread which always awaits some disaster from the side (since they have confronted nothing directly in years). So, yes, there was something unformed in these Republican faces, half at least, some refusal to face into the pressure of living in a world where moral questions do not by the end of ten seconds provide an answer. There was a glisten of stupidity in the gleam of the eye—all too many of them had been called pigs and not for nothing. They were kin to the worst expression of a cop—that particular stupidity which reflects all of moral damage, as if the sneaks of childhood are covered now in twenty layers of emotional lard, laid in by the living choice to be mediocre. Bad enough. The Republican women were worse. Did they have a mouth and jaw like the claw of a lobster?—so, too, did they have bodies suggestive of the backs and limbs of old stuffed chairs, Republican woman! Until the years of the Liberation, they had been called frigid—now they were freed of the need to search for v*g*n*l org*sm; the Liberation had declared them free. One look at their faces and, truth, they had not searched hard! The totalitarian will of the Democratic Liberator was easily equaled by the frigidity of the Republican lady. So their faces brought to mind a picture of the patients in the sex clinics of Masters and Johnson—those hard-bitten unforgiving women who never had one at all until their guide at Masters and Johnson could show them how and then the lady let go a machine gun of belted sex—fifty rounds of clitoral fire.

Now the nominations droned on. "Florida," said a voice thick with the emotion of its offering, "casts its votes for the greatest President since Abraham Lincoln."

There was a fear in these frozen Republican faces which could be equal only to the woe of their inability to comprehend the size of our acts in Vietnam.

And now Nixon was over and nominated and the giant screens above the podium burst out, "Nixon is nominated, Nixon is nominated," said a display of signs as they blinked on and off; the scoreboard in a new kind of stadium was celebrating a score. And in that hall like a temple where thousands of lights in every variety of metal reflector and cylinder high overhead blazed down out of a heaven of girders and spotlights, crates of balloons began to open, thousands of red-white-and-blue balloons came cascading out of great crates overhead and descended toward the floor. And as the balloons tumbled down, a band of middle-aged musicians came marching out to play "As the Saints Come Marching In," and Young Voters for the President were storming center stage from the wings carrying large plastic bags which they opened to release more red-white-and-blue balloons which ascended up to the girdered heavens, the Young Voters in with such a rush of stampede that older delegates were in a horror to get out of their way for the YVPers might trample them. Anything to reach those balloons which were coming down! Young Voters were there to devour balloons, burst them like bits of meat thrown into a pond of piranhas, balloons exploded in a cacophony of small arms' fire. And the Young Voters waved American flags they carried on small sticks, waved them violently. The fins of piranhas were in on a new kill. It was as of a celebration of all the murder you could shake loose in America. "Four more years," they screamed, and the sticks vibrated in the air, and the red of the flags was like a foaming of the froth.

11E

Nixon had been on his way to a Youth Rally in Marine Stadium of Miami. Since his limousine had the newest and best of radio equipment, he timed his arrival to enter just as he was being nominated back in Miami Beach. We are about to witness the record application of the Jeannette Weiss Principle. Nixon is embraced by a Black Jew who sings for the young, does imitations for the old and has turned from Democrat to Republican. The scene is shown on the great screens above the podium, and excites the war dance of the Young Voters to vibrate even faster. "Four more years."

11F

From Nixon's Maxims: Phineas T. Barnum was a sucker.

12A

"Welcome to Flamingo Park." It said, "The liberated zone of revolutionary living, organizing and non-violent direct action. Here we shall work to expose, confront and defeat the oppressive Nixon Administration."

Thus enlightened the elderly couple moved through the gates, turned left on the Ho Chi Minh Trail and walked past:

The women's tent

The Free Berkeley Booth

The Neo-American Church

The Free Gays

The Jesus Freaks

The Society for the Advancement of Non-Verbal Communication

The Yippie Headquarters, arriving finally with no little sense of wonderment at

The People's Pot Park.

New York Times, August 22

Sunday, 20th. Dishonor Amerika Day . . . The Zippies present . . . THE SECOND COMING. Jesus in a Zippie T-shirt will descend and lead a march to Convention Hall bearing a cross with Billy Graham on it. At the hall, there will be a piss-in on objects of honkie culture, we'll destroy a welfare Cadillac (to be burned previously but impounded), apple pies will be fed to running dogs, eggs tossed at a huge picture of Martha Raye (America's mom), flags burned, and a compulsory o.d. program for delegates, followed by an Om-out at which Jell-O will be served. . . .

Youth International Party

The kid . . . sat on his yellow blanket beneath the banyan tree, snorting defiantly from a clear plastic baggie. The small cloth inside the baggie was soaked with paint thinner. . . . "Man," said one of several self-appointed Flamingo Park peacekeepers, "take your death trip somewhere else. You don't understand that a lot of us don't dig what you're into. Go off the park, man." . . . "yeah," said someone else . . . die somewhere else, man. If you die on this park, man, you're putting a bad number on all of us."

Miami Herald, August 19

Six Yippies resorted to a "puke-in" and vomited on the sidewalk outside the Fontainebleau to show that "Nixon makes us sick." A network TV producer was there but ordered no film, turning away in disgust.

Miami Herald, August 21

The name of the operation is The Last Patrol. Pat Pappas, 22, an Army medic at Chulai during 1970, explained why he was heading for Miami Beach.
"It's just a moral obligation, simply, and that doesn't help the cause very much. I don't expect to change anything much, I just want people to remember us."

Washington Post, August 19

The Flamingo Park campsite was gassed several times during the night—once, reportedly, from a helicopter.

New York Times, August 25

A committee of "religious observers" from local churches and synagogues watched the campsite and the demonstrators and issued detailed daily reports.

New York Times, August 25

Four girls in Vietnamese costumes stood outside the hall today holding disemboweled dolls and moaning funeral chants.

New York Times, August 23

This afternoon, the Rev. Carl McIntire, the Fundamentalist preacher, visited the park and was met with hoots, jeers, and shouts of "to the lions with him." He left, trailed by a band of youths chanting "kill for Christ."

New York Times, August 19

Members of the Vietnam Vets Against the War destroyed two fused Molotov cocktails, three wrist rockets, two lead-weighted arrows, 200 marbles and 100 sharpened bolts Sunday after surrendering a man they said had them in his possession to Miami Beach police.

. . . Det. Sgt. Richard Procyk, liaison officer between the non-delegates . . . and police said police permitted the weapons to be destroyed in an act of "good faith" and symbolic non-violence by six regional coordinators of the VVAW.

. . . VVAW members . . . destroyed the weapons with knives and sledge hammers.

Miami Herald, August 21

"We have a lot of sore throats here," said a VVAW medic who would be identified only as "Bill" because of possible repercussions when he returned to his full-time job as a member of a fire department rescue team somewhere in Florida. . . . Bill said he could use at least a thousand more pills to treat the sore throats. Dr. David Spiegel, Massachusetts Mental Health Center, blames the passing around of canteens, cups and eating utensils for the spread of throat infections. . . .

Miami Herald, August 22

Bill Wyman, 21 . . . stepped on a land mine while on patrol in Phy Bai . . . has been as active as anyone . . . despite loss of both his legs. Monday he was back in a wheelchair, victim of the next most common complaint among non-delegates—blisters. Bill had been wearing artificial legs . . . because of heat or too much walking the stumps of his legs became chafed and swollen.

Miami Herald, August 22

Mayor Chuck Hall ordered Matt Koehl, American Nazi Party Leader, arrested for displaying the swastika. . . . Koehl met with Hall to protest treatment of the American Nazi party members by Republican Convention protesters at Flamingo Park, and refused to remove the arm band. . . . It's against the law to display the swastika in Miami Beach. . . .

New York Times, August 24

"Oh, can I see my picture?" Tina Hill, 20, of Los Angeles begged as she was put into a van. A trooper obliged. . . .
Once inside the yellow vans, though, the protesters seemed to come back to life, pounding gleefully the sides, singing "God Bless America," and, perhaps appropriately, "We All Live in a Yellow Submarine."
The five rental Deatrick vans carrying male prisoners drove to the east side of Dade County Jail.
Steam came out of the hot unventilated van when the first doors were opened. A few youths had fainted and lay on the floor. The others stood.

At Flamingo Park, Zippies began taking up a collection to post bond for other protesters.

Miami Herald, August 23

"We like to sleep on the ground, because 'The Land' (the protesters' name for their encampment) belongs to the people."

New York Times, August 23

MIAMI NONVIOLENCE PROJECT PROPOSAL

"THAT THE PARTY GO ON RECOND AND SO INSTRUCT THE SARGENT OF ARMS TO KEEP ALL MURDERS, WAR CRIMINALS, AND INTERNATIONAL OUTLAWS FROM ENTERING THE CONVENTION HALL. . . ."

Richard M. Nixon happens to be a straight white man. A recent study shows that San Francisco is governed by a group who represent but 8½ % of the population—married white men. This is no coincidence! Need we say more?

Unconventional News

The oppression of sexism makes it hard for us to survive—and we don't want to just survive—we want to create. We struggle against the death dreams of Nixon and other men's power in the government and also against the male attitudes we find among leftist movement people and others who want to live in alternative ways to American society. We try to support all women in the effort to end male supremacy. The vision we have of a revolutionary society is not one where men continue to dominate. We urge men to *come out* into revolutionary consciousness. We think that men should become effeminate to learn to live and work collectively and to leave space free of male influence, for sisters.

Unconventional News

PLACENTA RECIPE

1 placenta from self or friend
1 onion (2 if placenta is large)
½ cup of melted butter or ghee

Steam the placenta until it can be ground in a meat grinder without drippings. Sauté the onion until light brown. Grind fine together and pour in butter or ghee. From this mixture form one or more attractive mounds and garnish with whatever you have around. Serve with crackers, tortillas, chapati.

PEOPLE'S ALMANAC

Men who are asked to leave the women's tent or women's meetings should be no more offended than they would be if they were asked to leave a Black caucus. . . .

Miami Women's Coalition

. . . At Flamingo Park . . . we organized a Women's Anti-Rape Squad (WARS)—groups of 3 to 5 women who patrolled the campsite from 9 P.M. to 5 A.M. to deal with the harassment of women.

Many of the women in MWC want to make sure that the group continues after the conventions. Sisters, please send us your ideas, comments, photographs, poems, money, support, strength, creativity, and love. A fresh wind is blowing against the empire.

Miami Women's Coalition

The YIP gathers for resistance and change. We are the direct descendants of a freedom and justice seeking people

which links us with every century, with every decent cause,
with every plant and mammal that ever lived.
We stand at the barricades of decency and beauty.

We want change!
We want to change the environment!
We want to change the economy!

Change the government!
Change the culture! Change your spirit!
Change your diet! Change your sex!
Ex-change everything!

Youth International Party

From Nixon's Maxims: Franklin Delano Roosevelt
spoke of the four freedoms. There is only one freedom
looked for by the American voter who votes for Nixon
—it is freedom from dread.

12B

Compared to the demonstrations of Berkeley and Oak-
land, the March on the Pentagon, or May Day, the week
in Flamingo Park has been a failure. The number of protesters has never increased to more than a few thousand,
and they are divided by every idea but one: that Richard
Nixon is a war criminal. It is not enough. Other divisions
are too numerous. They quarrel about sexism and revolution, about the merits of violent demonstration as opposed
to peaceful sit-ins; before they are done, every old argument
about revolutionary tactics from the paving stones of the
Paris Commune to the grass of Flamingo Park has been
recapitulated, and brother is hung up with brother, and
sister hoots them out both because they are too doctrinaire
or too ego trip, too heavy, too sexist, too liberated, too ir-
responsible or too fucking chicken to get their shit together.
They even argue whether there should be a single loud-

speaker system or many. Their common enemy, the pigs, are no longer common, for the pigs are not acting like pigs. So still another ideological dispute is laid on the babel—they divide whether to trash or cooperate. Since the police are not vicious, the threat of brutal arrests no longer draws them together nor gives the dignity of combating large fear. Since the danger is less than they have anticipated, they cannot even know after a time if they are serious or have become video-swingers who do the dance of the seven veils for Media men—it is possible they have become no more than actors—just so much as the politicians they despise. Television pollutes identity, and television cameras are about them all the time. So the most serious cannot even finally know if they protest the war or contribute to the entertainment of Nixon's Epic—across the screens of the nation they flurry, cawing like gulls in adenoidal complaints, a medieval people's band of lepers and jesters who put a whiff of demonology on the screen, or lay an entertaining shiver along the incantations of their witches. Did that hint of a gay demented air now serve only to dignify the battlements of the white knights of Christendom up on Nixon Heights?

Even their true show of revolutionary strength for the Media—Vietnamese Veterans Against the War—is a strength now sliced, for the Viet Veterans have six of their members on trial in Gainesville for conspiracy to cause disorder and rioting in Miami Beach during the Republican Convention—what jurisprudential coincidence!—and so must keep their deportment proper while in Miami: trashing by the Vets would hurt the men on trial. Yet they have to wonder if real fear of the war might be inspired more by the Vets of Vietnam getting violent in the streets—that might dig deeper into the nature of national distress than the wilder fringes of suburbia screaming up the tube.

Of course, it is possible that nothing would have worked. It was even likely. For the greater their numbers, and the more complete their disruption, greater was the likelihood that they would merely contribute to Nixon's consensus. So the troops of the Miami Convention Coalition and the People's Coalition for Peace and Justice, the Miami Women's Coalition, and the Vietnam Veterans Against the War, the People's Pot Party, the Coalition of Gay Organizations and the SDS, the Yippies and the Zippies, have all possibly headed into the worst trap of them all which is to attack the Godfather in a Media war. Benefactor of the American corporation, spiritual leader of the military industrial complex, and only *don capo* ever to have survived the tortures of the Media, he is learned in the wisdom of wise leaders, and knows how to put a foot in front of your ankle as you go forward and a knee in your seat as you back up, a ring in your nostrils to lead you and a hook in your ear for sit down! The art of Media war is to benefit whether your adversary does well or fails. In a strategy session at the Doral, it has already been decided that if the demonstrators ever succeed on Wednesday night in getting things out of control, then the Republicans will issue a call to McGovern and ask him to call off the kids.

So the protesters cannot win. They are doomed to be the most ineffectual of all the major demonstrations against the war in Vietnam. Yet, they are probably the most interesting, for their ideas are pioneer, and they have led a private demonstration beneath the public exhibition to show that they can live in the field like an army, house every private war, police themselves, feed themselves, drug themselves, and even with a variety of vigilante justice (which stops well short of anybody hanging—merely confiscates weapons and ejects Nazis) they govern themselves. They keep the park in some relation to order, and the tourists and sightseers who come through are sometimes welcome and never molested. They entertain themselves and share their goods and sleep on the ground. They are an area of liberty free to some great extent of civic law—they function as a community of consent—separate from the city about them. There will be others to follow. For the atmosphere is different in the park, different from the air of other communities, just as there are regions of the skin where the flesh is not like other flesh. In Flamingo Park the mood does not speak precisely of a bruise which has begun to heal nor of the pleasure beneath a piece of one's sexual skin; it is more, he supposes, like something of the air of a rain forest. He has never been in such a forest but has been told that deep in the jungle, the shade is cool and has the tenderness of any atmosphere which is never free of danger. Senses come alive. One steps out of the pressure of habit, lays down one's habits like a back pack—there is a limit to how long some live without their load. The tourists enjoy Flamingo Park but leave before too long. So does he. It is too separate from everything in the Republican Convention, too sweet, contentious, hassled, frayed, tawdry, boring, comic, comfortable, menacing, and the faces are always in opposition, so direct and so spaced out, so handsome, so full of acne, so innocent, so open, so depraved, so freaky, so violent, so gentle that first one's senses are alive as one is alive before the sight of a painting and then are fatigued, as in a museum where there is too much great painting and too much stale air. The air is also stale in Flamingo Park, stale with the butt end of dead souls all over the grass, washed out, leached out, processed-out, souls dead with the consumptions of their own drug-fired awareness, and the vision is always at hand of the American Left disappearing in the vortex of the great cosmic hole of the drug while Nixon speaks from the Heights of the White Knights and says, "I will destroy 200,000,000 Asians before I let American youth go over to drugs." Audiences will cheer because nothing is worse than American Youth on drugs (and they are right!) (even if the South Vietnamese with the sanction of the CIA are sending their smack on that Bob Hope road which leads from Saigon to Miami). What a world and what knots! The devil has tied them with fingers of steel.

So Aquarius never remains in Flamingo Park too long at a time, or he might be tempted to stay and do a book about communities of consent. He is not ready for that. He is in Miami of his own desire to study Republicans—such opportunities do not come much more often than every four years. He does his duty, therefore, and breathes that other air of listening to Republican concepts which have never been illumined by any drug, or indeed any breeze which does not pass through the vaults of a bank. He does not care to state which is worse. Left meets Right at the end of ideology, and the smell of dead drugs is like the smell of old green bills. Fungus in the cellar is growth in the damp.

12C

By Wednesday afternoon, however, he could bear the Republicans no longer and so went out to the streets around Convention Center to watch the demonstrations but they were divided and disorganized and he never found the major confrontation for which he looked, and indeed only found out in the following days and by reading the papers (which is the true humiliation for a journalist!) that plans to block traffic and delay the convention had been shifted at the last minute. The police had brought in a number of old buses and parked them bumper to bumper across certain intersections but so tightly pressed against one another, and so touching the buildings on either side of the street that they made a wall, and the police had set these walls at strategic positions to create the sides of a funnel through city streets down which the buses of the delegates could pass and enter convention gates protected all the way by police on the inside. The sight of these buses divided the demonstrators into three camps (which as Napoleon has been known to remark is the first military error of them all.) A majority now decided that Security had been changed to the *highest level* around the hall, and too many demonstrators would be hurt; so Miami Coalition leaders Rennie Davis and Jeff Nightbyrd urged protesters who were nonviolent to accompany them up Collins Avenue to the Fontainebleau, a march of two miles which was joined by five hundred people, some of whom later broke up to trash, while others went on to sit down before the Doral, there to be arrested for blocking the street. It was a peaceful demonstration. Of those who were left in Flamingo Park, perhaps so many as another five hundred stayed in their tents and never went out at all, and two hundred of the VVAW left at 5:30 in the afternoon for Gainesville where their six members were scheduled for arraignment on Thursday. Some hundreds more went down to the Convention Center and milled about on a street or two held open for them until a sufficient number of scat-

tered episodes finally brought attacks of tear gas by the
police which increased in intensity until even the air conditioning of Convention Hall began to suck it in and the
cooling system had to be turned off. Scattered groups
trashed where they could on Collins Avenue and buses of
the Mississippi and South Carolina delegation were halted
by protesters who yanked wires off the engine and flattened
their tires, forcing the delegates to walk six or eight blocks
to the hall. The Illinois bus had its windshield sprayed with
black paint right after it was forced to come to a stop
because a platoon of demonstrators lay down before it.
Then the tires were slashed and an American flag was put
on fire and thrown into the engine. When the delegates
rushed out, some protesters pushed them while others
worked to protect them; policemen finally brought the
delegates through. Delegate LeRoy Stocks of Whiteville,
North Carolina, was quoted as saying, "If they want to
act like dogs, they should be treated like dogs. I think next
time they should issue every delegate and alternate a
submachine gun." A delegate from Mississippi caught a
blob of red paint on his new green-striped suit. He was in
a group of twenty-five Mississippians who were taken in
convoy by police after their bus was stopped; then ran a
"gauntlet of curses, spit, tear gas and flying eggs." Delegate
Sharon Kelly from South Carolina, reported to be an
"attractice blonde," said, "Twenty hippie girls surrounded
me. They bounced me around like a ping-pong ball. One
of them screamed, 'You sure smell pretty, you blond
bitch!' It was disgusting." Perhaps the number was less
than twenty. Southern belles are notorious for the ability
not to do arithmetic under pressure.

So it went, and there were other scattered incidents.
Later in the night protesters would march through hotels,
and light trashing took place in the streets; arrests continued; but the demonstrators were defeated, although
Aquarius hardly knew it for he spent two hours promenading the streets around the convention, waiting in his
ignorance like the others for the possible arrival of delegates, and since the main promenade was on a closed-off
block of Washington Avenue, the same wide street which
ran by the front of the Convention Center, there was every
intimation of action to come, and hundreds of kids prowled
back and forth, stalking like adolescents on a boardwalk,

waiting for the encounters which will forge the character that carries them into the future, back and forth they prowled, a panoply of protesters' faces, the girls almost without exception exhibiting bodies more beautiful than their heads, which were fierce in expression, female pirates, bandanas about their hair, bandanas about their breast, wearing hip-hugger pants with their navels out for all the police to see, as if the eye of the revolution to come was here in the navels of the women. And the boys had beards, or long hair, or both, and many wore glasses. Many were students and many were bright—it was in the complacent rest of their head on their neck, as if the head had been told from childhood it was the center of value, and these were the boys who were usually nonviolent, out of ideology more than fear, since some had the smug fearlessness of the unblooded, and other were ready to bleed if it came to it (they saw themselves as blood of atonement) and indeed their fear was in their responsibility: there were protesters and provokers, and they were fearful of the second—one incident which was ugly enough and Nixon would win the headlines again. So they did their best to placate and to serve as police, and those college voices, just a little thin with the tremor of exercising an authority they did not wholly possess, would cry out in a whine of exasperation, "Come on, we're here to protest the war, not to trash the police," and some listened, some did not. Some of the non-delegates were handsome and in for the action, athletes, off a surf board, hip and with an edge, they carried themselves the way Robert Redford might if playing a protester, floated on the edge of the action, assessing it and moving on, and there were kids no gang of bikers would ever accept, hyena eyes and the odor of yesterday's dead drug came off them on the reopening of yesterday's old sweat now riding on the perspiration of their new charge. With the jolt, their attention went up like a column boring into the electric core of space, out in space were their heads (and still the look of the hyena to rip off some little prey), and others, mired down on downers but still mugged in the skull with all the low lowering pressures of violence that shoved them forward, fear which pulled them back. They were holding rocks in their fists, and now one of them, half in stupor, throws it over the wire fence which borders Washington Avenue, over into the loose-spaced ranks of the cops on the other side of the fence and a girl in a bandana shouts, fearless of his wad of congested violence, "Hey, you asshole —don't throw rocks. You bring a bust on all of us." But the rocks go on. They are being thrown from time to time. Every five minutes a rock goes over the fence, and once or twice a cop throws one back. Protesters pass near the fence and give the cops a finger. "Eat the rich," they cry, and the cops lift squirt cans and give them Mace. A dwarf stands in the crowd. He has powerful forearms near to normal in length and they are held behind him. He is concealing a weapon. A couple of steel balls are wrapped in a red rag and slung from his wrist—his bare forearm looks like a phallus with two maroon testicles attached. He merely stands there waiting, a grin on his dwarf's mouth.

"One, Two, Three, Four," the kids shout at the cops. "We don't want your fucking war." Signs are walked back and forth, one shows a host of skulls. "The Silent Minority," it says. Another displays a Vietnamese child with a scandalous wound of open flesh across her face. "Our Gross National Product" says the sign. Yes, it is a fair exchange. We are bombing Vietnam, and the drugs of Indochina are bombing our young.

After a while he tries to circle around to other sides of the Convention Center, but the walls of buses make him detour. The odor of tear gas is beginning to collect in pockets on the side streets, and the old who are sitting on the balconies and patios of their cheap apartments in the cheap white stucco buildings of this part of Miami Beach are beginning to suffer, here and there. Only in Miami Beach would old people go out on their second-story porch to watch a war. Like the Orange Bowl parade, it is full of interest for them. A long-haired boy who lingers near a stoop finally antagonizes the old lady who occupies it, and seeing a cop across the street she is bold. "Stop staring at me," she says, "or I'll pour some water on you," her voice cracked with the violence that her life has almost been lived and justice has not necessarily been done. On one corner, a kid, aimlessly, hardly knowing why, sets fire to a heap of newspapers. A cop yells, "Hey," moves in, kicks out the fire, but does not arrest the boy. Another fire is burning in a wire basket at a street corner, and a fire truck comes tolling and pealing its bell, cream-green police cars with their blue lights turning and their sirens wailing, come up, crawl by, and now cruise Washington Street in front of Convention Center. He sees the buses of delegates go by, and a lost patrol of six delegates being guided by two cops, passes along the porch of a hotel; the ladies are helped over the balcony when they have to jump down in order to go around a bus. The demonstrators ignore them, and the delegates are silent and proper. They have the We-are-here-to-make-no-trouble look of white tourists in Harlem.

Then, for reasons he never learns, there comes a point when the cops start clearing Washington Street and Seventeenth Street, and a battle starts, very one-sided, with the crowd advancing down Seventeenth Street, Aquarius among them, moving they don't know quite why nor for which reason in this direction only to be halted by a line of cops and then before long to be dispersed with the firing of canisters of tear gas. The crowd slips back and away at the edge of the gas, and retreating to another corner, he finds an intersection held by an impromptu guerrilla patrol of protesters who have removed a police barricade from one street and put it on another. Now—perhaps there is some last notion of disruption in all of this—they signal the occasional car which comes up to go by another route, and obligingly open the barrier to let an ambulance through; they stand stony-faced as two cops come up in a patrol car, and do not change expression as one cop gets out, removes the barricade, waits for the other to drive through, restores the barricade, says, "Thanks fellows"—sarcastically—"for helping me," gets back in the patrol car, and the police drive on. The guerrillas laugh shamefacedly. They were frightened when the cops first came.

It is the lightest kind of war, easier than maneuvers in basic training, part of the correspondent's good life— Aquarius is almost nostalgic that he has missed the good wars of other eras, and now knows why Hemingway loved to cover a war with even the thought of liquor to taste so good, he even loves this evening in Miami and the softness of the approaching tropical night, the pop of tear-gas canisters around the corner, the wail of an ambulance, all the sounds of action in a city, but now intensified, as if part of the sorrow of his lost adolescence is tied up in the memory of games played in the hurry to finish before it got

too dark on the city streets: the action which is going on
is sad and absurd and pointless and lost and will not save
a life in Vietnam, and yet he loves it, loves Miami Beach
to his amazement, this crazy city of permissions and symbolic wars, and now watching the action from the vast
roof of a vast parking garage, sees the rising full moon
look misty as if obscured by tear gas. Is the day actually
coming when there will be real battles in the cities and
true smoke over the moon? Americans play many games
and enjoy them well; they cannot really understand how
airplanes lay death in strings of defecation on the earth.
But he hates the sound of the helicopters surveying the
scene from above, the noise of the blade-like chops of
instruction to the back of the ear. And the wind is shifting
and more canisters falling. He is trapped in tear gas at last,
more now than the smarting of his eyes and the souring of
his nose and throat like a catarrh upon him, this is more, and
now is abruptly the end of two hours of promenading, for he
can no longer see, the gas has come all around him, he has
finally had enough, and good obliging war with an exit visa
stamped and ready to leave, he has finally and most certainly
had enough of the tear gas, and eyes screwed into the searing
sorrow of bereavements he has not suffered, goes blinded
with weeping like any other victim into the Convention
Center for refuge, and there honored by his Press card is
given a healing solution by a fireman on duty to take care
precisely of all the delegates and Press who come through,
the fireman saying to each of the stumbling victims as they
approach, "This won't hurt you, I promise. Will you accept
it? Please open your eyes." And considerate as a saint he
laves gouts of solution into the fiery stream of the tears—
eyes relieved, Aquarius goes on into the convention and
hears a security guard in the men's room (where he has
gone to wash his eyes again) say that it was the hippies
who were throwing the gas. That was great. It was good
to know cops were still liars—a security was left in your
knowledge of the world—and Aquarius went in to the
temple of politics and listened to Agnew and Nixon give
acceptance speeches, and was struck with Agnew's use of
metaphor. "A President lives in the spotlight, but a Vice-
President lives in the flickering strobe lights that alternately
illuminate or shadow his unwritten duties. It is sometimes
uncomfortable. It is sometimes ego-diminishing. But it is

also . . ." and even if Agnew said, "rewarding," still it
was the first time in twelve years of listening to Republican
Presidents and Vice-Presidents that he had heard a metaphor and a good one, and perhaps it was no more than
the relief and merriment of having had his light touch of
combat, but he was in a good mood as he listened to Nixon
and was struck again with the knowledge that the Godfather could manipulate much in politics and do even more
as a sculptor (to the fecal emotions of the American electorate) but he could not give a good speech—God had at
least denied him that—and so after three days of the most
consummate spectacular in the history of television (considering how modest in content was the original material)
the climax was Nixon whose voice dependably lay like
Bromo Seltzer upon the pumping of the heart.

"Speaking on behalf of the American people, I was proud
to be able to say in my television address to the Russian
people in May, we covet no one else's territory, we seek
no dominion over any other nation, we seek peace, not
only for ourselves, but for all the people of the world.

"This dedication to idealism runs through America's history. During the tragic war between the states, Abraham
Lincoln was asked whether God was on his side. He replied,
"My concern is not whether God is on our side but whether
we are on God's side.

"May that always be our prayer for America.

"We hold the future of peace in the world and our own
future in our hands.

"Let us reject, therefore, the policies of those who whine
and whimper about our frustrations and call on us to turn
inward. Let us not turn away from greatness.

"The chance America now has to lead the way to a last-
ing peace in the world may never come again.

"With faith in God and faith in ourselves and faith in
our country, let us have the vision and the courage to seize
the moment and meet the challenge before it slips away.

"On your television screens last night, you saw the cemetery in Leningrad I visited on my trip to the Soviet Union
where 300,000 people died in the siege of that city during
World War II. At the cemetery, I saw the picture of a
twelve-year-old girl. She was a beautiful child. Her name
was Tanya. I read her diary. It tells the terrible story of
war. In the simple words of a child, she wrote of the deaths

of the members of her family—Zhenya in December, Grannie in January, then Leka, then Uncle Vasta, then Uncle Lyosha, then Mama in May.

"And finally these were the last words in her diary: 'All are dead, only Tanya is left.'

"Let us think of Tanya and of the other Tanyas and their brothers and sisters everywhere in Russia and in China and in America as we proudly meet our responsibilities for leadership in the world in a way worthy of a great people.

"I ask you, my fellow Americans, to join our new majority not just in the cause of winning an election but in achieving a hope that mankind has had since the beginning of civilization.

"Let us build a peace that our children and all the children of the world can enjoy for generations to come."

12D

From the Diary of T'Nayen en Dhieu:

For the last five weeks the airplanes have been coming over.

On the first day Uncle Nguyen was killed. Three days later, my brother Nang Da.

Last week Aunt Vinh Tan was killed together with my baby sister Minou.

Yesterday Papa bled to death.

Today Mama burned to death.

All are dead. Only T'Nayen writes this.

12E

From Nixon's Maxims: Politics is effrontery.

12F

Nixon has a wife who gives every evidence she is fond of him. Her arm goes around her husband now that his speech is done, and with their free arms they wave to the audience who is near. Aquarius is part of that near audience down on the floor, and can see the dimensions of a diamond in the sparkle of a ring on her finger. Encouraged thereby to experiment, Aquarius looks hard at the diamond as her hand goes around her husband's back. Pat Nixon may feel his eyes on the diamond. She removes her hand. Diamonds! Basic life material is carbon, and diamonds are their hardest form. Is that why they receive our thoughts?

The Spectacular ends. The band plays "God Bless America." Nixon stands at one end of the Convention Hall and shakes hands with each of the delegates as they walk by in file. Aquarius wonders if he should try to stand in line himself, and fulfill the last duty of this week's long job by going all the way up to the man so that he will be able to bear witness to the historic feel of his skin, but Aquarius is not a delegate and they will probably not let him make the line, and besides he does not want to shake hands with the nice man. Even in politics, some hands are not yours to shake.